And The Meek Shall Inherit...

By John Lars Shoberg

Dedication:
To my wife.

© 2021 by John Lars Shoberg

Print 1 - December 2021

MoonPhaze LLC, 613 del Pilar Dr., Groveland FL, 34736
MoonPhaze.com

Cover Art and Layout by Mitchell Davidson Bentley, MA

Contents

The Landing

Lankmere, as it was called by its inhabitants—at least, according to the television broadcasts the Earth First Contact armada watched—was a peaceful world. None of those programs even hinted at the existence of firearms. None of their plots centered on theft or major crimes. Oh, there was the occasional small item pilfered or lie told, but those stories always ended in a moral lesson. Most of the shows were educational in nature, as though the viewers were college students catching up on a missed lecture. This, of course, was perfect for the Earth linguists trying to learn the Lankmeran language.

They weren't a backward people; they had satellites in orbit that the *Nyumbani* and her accompaning ships under General Adam Chi's command had to avoid. It was easy enough to do as they were in geosynchronous orbit; the Earth fleet just had to maintain an orbit a thousand miles higher. Since none of those satellites were surveillance-equipped, the humans didn't have to worry about detection. Every satellite fed their signals, the ones relayed up to them, back to the planet to keep the television and communications systems working.

The humans had been sitting in orbit for two weeks. Two weeks that the linguists had been working on the language. But two weeks was long enough to try General Chi's patience. Either they knew the language by now, or they didn't. It was now time for them to prove their worth. The General ordered three reconnaissance teams to go planetside and make contact with the more rural communities. It was his only concession to their pleas to give them more time to study the language.

Captain Randolph (Rowdy) Palmer led the northern-most of these expeditions. His small town was on the edge of one of the larger lakes high in the mountains on the larger of the two continents.

"The order is to not spook these people by landing in their midst. Put her down in the first available clearing about a mile north of the town," he told Lieutenant Jason (Jarhead) Simmons, the pilot of his landing shuttle. They found a clearing beside a small stream that fed into the lake with a sandy enough bank to keep the trees from closing in. Large enough to put all three shuttles in.

"Sir?" the shuttle pilot asked.

"Looks good to me." Palmer turned and called into the Surveillance section of the shuttle. "Solski, radio the other ships to put down in this location." He turned back around, leaning on the back of the pilot's chair as the pilot made his final approach. Then he leaned forward and pressed the activation button for the shuttle's intercom. "Lieutenant Mason, have your men ready to move out as soon as we touch down."

There was less room on the southern side of the stream that fed the lake, so Jason choose to put his craft down there. It would give the others a larger landing area to work with.

As the forty soldiers in the back of the shuttle ran down the lowered ramp and began separating needed supplies from future supplies, the pilot powered his craft down. Troops in each of the four squads began burying those extra supplies and preparing to march down to the native village. They, and the platoon's pair of linguists, followed Captain Palmer across the stream to coordinate with the other two platoons.

"You guys are ready for this, right?" Palmer asked the linguists as they waded through the ankle-deep water.

"*Acklum*," one of them answered, before the other replied, "That's Lankmeran for yes."

"The natives speak this language; I expect to be addressed in English. I understand one of you specialized in reading their language?"

"That would be me, sir," Gus Grimwald said.

"I saw they had a library in some of those shows. Find it and see what's worth copying. You've got your scanner, right?"

"It's in my pack, Sir."

"Then let's move out. 'Cause I'm betting the other two platoons are itching to get a move on." He stepped out of the water back onto dry land and walked over to the other landed shuttles. Lieutenants Angelov and Dae-Jung had their troops ready to go.

Seeing the shuttle pilots waiting at the bottom of their crafts' ramps, Randy turned to Lieutenants Williams and Chen. "Everything locked down?"

"There's no EM signatures coming off our crafts," Lieutenant Chen said. "Even if this culture did have a way to detect them."

"No point in getting sloppy," Palmer replied. "Stay with your craft. I'll let you know when we're heading back." He turned from them to look over his troops. "Okay, let's get ready to move out," he called out to the soldiers already lined up. "'Headhunter platoon will take point. Followed by Listener platoon. Finally, Coverfire platoon protecting our rear."

"What about us linguists?" asked Gus Grimwald.

"You're with me behind the Headhunters. Now shoulder that pack." Palmer was staring at the backpacks piled by the feet of the six linguists. "And get ready to move out. Lag behind, and Deke here will be carrying you. Head first, over his shoulder." The Captain thumbed over to the biggest brute of a soldier in his squad, in case any of the newer linguists didn't know who he referred to.

As the linguists quickly moved to strap on their packs, Headhunter platoon began moving to the south along the beach between the lake and the forest. Only one of the linguists was struggling with his pack as their part of the line moved out.

Palmer chafed at the almost half hour it took his company to make the march from their landing crafts to the first village, but the linguists weren't trained to keep up forced marching the way his troops had been.

The first thing they saw, as they approached, were the docks and small boats moored to them. Most of the boats looked like they could've been Earth-based fishing trawlers, wider than a normal Earthen pleasure craft, with net-like rigging hanging off the back. It was a mild weather but there was nobody working on the boats this late in the Lankmeran afternoon.

As they cleared the final stand of trees, they were able to see the buildings that made up this small town. Most of them single story, with several two-story, and a couple of three-story units. Nothing higher. The people that had been walking in the village came to a stop as they saw the Earthmen approach.

Lankmeran physiology had many similarity with Humans. They were bipedal, walked upright, two arms and single head appendage but the Lankmeran had to have evolved from a cat-like ancestor rather than the ape line humans had evolved from. They had a wide variety of fur patterns all over the parts of their bodies that weren't clothed. And from a review of their television shows, the Earthmen didn't know if they had the feline claws or not.

"Okay, guys," Randy turned to the linguists. "It's time to start earning your pay. Find out who runs this place so we can introduce ourselves."

They spread out, with each linguist taking a different member of the growing curious crowd. Randy called for his platoon to come to a halt and allow the other two to assume flanking positions on it. They stood there, waiting for the linguists to return.

A few minutes later, Grimwald returned to his Captain and reported, "The purvitorian of this town, I'm having the translator set to translate their word into mayor, is in the large building on the other side of the open field in the center of town there." He pointed to an open grassy area. "These guys are willing to take you there to meet with her." There were five of the town's people standing behind Grimwald and moving closer to the Captain.

"Okay. Let's go," he replied.

Gus turned to the Lankmerans and said a few words, then they all moved in the direction of the town central building. "We seem to be a new experience for them," Gus said as they walked. "And that fact seems to intrigue them. Even now, we are attracting more of them to follow us."

"I'm counting on them being peaceful. Otherwise they're getting too close to us, if we have to fight our way out."

The number of Lankmerans had grown to the point where both of the large ten foot doors to the city's central building had to be held open to let them enter. Palmer instructed his men to wait outside while they met with the mayor.

Inside, a central desk had a single Lankmeran female behind it. When Gus asked to see the mayor, she directed them to the office behind her desk. There had been a couple of offices on either side of that one, making five in total on this floor of the two-story building.

"She said the top floor is for town hall meetings. It's the entire floor, and just large enough to get everybody in. The mayor's through here," Gus walked ahead and opened the office door.

"How many of these guys are coming with us?" Palmer asked. But as he turned to look over the crowd, they had apparently stopped at the receptionist's desk.

"None, sir. They'll be waiting out here."

As they entered the twenty-by-twenty-foot space with a desk in the center near the back wall, one of the Lankmerans was returning with what had to be a coffee, or the local equivalent, urn. She said something as she returned to her desk, set the cup down and offered her hand to the arriving guests.

"She wants to know if you'd like a *tonglee*," Gus said to Captain Palmer. "I'm not sure what it is, but from the steam coming off her cup, it must be hot."

"Tell her, 'No Thanks, but we'd like a sample of it when we leave, to see if it's compatible with our systems'," Lieutenant Lattimer, the field medic, responded before Palmer could think of an answer.

Palmer turned his head to look at his responding officer. "We don't know what will affect us nor how," the medic said. "It's best we test everything before we consume it."

Palmer looked back at the mayor, who was still holding her paw out. He was having a little trouble thinking of that furry thing pointed his way as a hand, it was something he had to work on. He offered his to meet hers.

She reached past his palm and stroked the inside of his forearm. He recoiled slightly at the unexpected invasion of his personal space. Her eyebrows dipped slightly at his response. There had been no pressure exerted against his skin, he was just unprepared for this greeting.

"She's asking if there is a problem," Gus relayed what the mayor was saying.

"No. Tell her she just caught me by surprise. I thought she was offering me her hand to shake. Can you demonstrate it to her?"

Gus said a few things in Lankmeran before offering his hand to the mayor. As she offered hers back, he took hold of it and pressed it against his hand, curled his fingers and raise and lowered his to demonstrate the human greeting of shaking hands. Then he reached to the inside of her forearm and did the same maneuver she had tried with the Captain.

As she began smiling with understanding, she offered her guests log benches to sit on. "Or she says you can use the cushions, if you prefer," Gus translated.

"Tell her the benches will do just fine," Palmer said as the four officers sat two to a bench.

The mayor jumped up on her desk and sat in the open area with her two front limbs propping her up. This brought her eye level with everyone else.

"What brings you to Anora?" Gus translated again.

"Anora?" Palmer said. "I thought this place was Lankmere?"

"Anora is the name of this town, Captain. Lankmere, the name of the world." The mayor began speaking again. Gus translated, "Why are you here? We have explored the entirety of Lankmere and have never encountered people who are as bald as you people are. Where do you come from?"

"Tell her," Palmer began. "We are not from her planet, but from one of the stars she sees at night. We are from a planet called Earth; many, many miles from here. We began receiving signals from here a few years back. It took us most of the intervening time to understand what those signals were. Once we did, we knew we needed to come and visit your people. This expedition took almost two years of planning and travel, but we finally made it. We want to understand you and become your friends."

After Gus ran through his translation to the mayor, her response was "Why?"

Palmer sensed this was the time to go into the Terran sales pitch, so he stood back up and began. "Your broadcasts intrigued us. You are a society without the violence that plagues all civilizations we have encountered to date. And that includes our own. How you have been able to do this is of great interest to us."

"How long do you wish to study us?" was Gus's next translation.

"We came prepared to stay for a long time; years, if necessary. We just need to find a clearing and we can set up our own community. We've brought everything we'll need for a two-year stay." He turned and looked over the room. Feeling a little bit self-conscious, he sat back down. The mayor relaxed from trying to keep Palmer at eye level once eye level got lowered again.

"If it is your intention to study us," Gus began translating the mayor again. "It might make more sense for you to stay in our community. But we do not have the room here in Anora. Yet if you are willing to help, we were about to begin a civic enhancement project. We need more homes and apartments. Would you and your people be willing to help us build those?"

Lieutenant Lattimer nudged Palmer in his side and nodded his head when the captain looked over at him. "That is a very good idea. My people could learn a lot about your culture from working side-by-side with you. In the meantime, is there somewhere that we can set up a temporary camp?"

The mayor laid on her stomach to reach one of the buttons on the far side of her desk. She pressed it and said something. "I think she's getting help," was Gus's reply. A moment later, another Lankmeran walked into her office. He and the mayor had a quick conversation before the mayor nodded to Captain Palmer and turned to Gus.

"There is a clearing just south of Anora that should suit your, er, our, needs. Loton will lead our men there. I can remain, if you'd like to stay and talk with her Honor."

"Let me give the troops their orders, and I'll be right back." Palmer got off his bench and followed this male Lankmeran out of the office and back to where his company was still lined up waiting in the main Anora plaza, albeit sitting and laying around instead of standing.

Native Construction

It had taken Sergeant Gary Adams and his squad less than half a day to get the temporary canvas housing erected for his men and women, along with the troops of the third and fourth squads of Listener platoon. At least he didn't have the latrine duty they'd had. Once fourth squad of Headhunters had gotten the mess hall constructed, he told his troops to get some lunch. A lunch of standard MREs, as the field kitchen hadn't been set up yet. A mac and cheese MRE may be quite tasteless, but was not as bad as some of the other possibilities. Captain Palmer had said something about fraternization with the locals in the future. Gary just hoped their food stuffs were compatible with human metabolisms before he had to suffer another cream chipped beef on toast MRE.

They spent the rest of that first day after contact listening to lectures from the Captain, the linguists, and their Lieutenants about what had been established about Lankmeran culture and how not to violate any of its customs. The last thing they were told was their duty assignments for the next several days. Adam's squad was assigned to house construction duty. His boys mostly came from the construction boom area of Orlando back on Earth; at least they knew how to swing a hammer.

Getting themselves time synced with the Lankmerans was another problem. Six AM on this part of the planet was different than ship's time. About five hours different. Yet by the third day, Gary was getting everyone up and moving in time to meet the dawn for the day's work shift. After breakfast—rehydrated eggs had not gotten better in the four hundred years humans had worked on the process—they donned a lightened field pack, shouldered their rifles and headed for Anora.

Most of the squads headed directly into town to work on the infrastructure to expand the city. They worked on water lines, filtration systems and environmental control systems. Two squads were simply digging deep holes to insert large pipes for geothermal heat pumps. Another squad was assigned to switch out the fuel cell electrical converters on several of the older buildings. There were no power lines marring the vertical view in the village.

While a few other squads were working on raising new apartment complexes, Gary's troops had finished constructing the molds for laying concrete for about fifteen new single family dwellings the day before. Today the concrete was to be brought in so the homes' foundations could be poured. The Lankemerans had a person to watch over the pour at each of the dwellings, Gary assigned one of his own to as many as he could. There were a handful of homes he had to have his people double up on.

Trucks approached the sites. They were not what Gary thought of as concrete trucks. They looked more like elongated liquid transport vehicles. They weren't rotating as they approached.

He turned to his Lankmeran supervisor to ask, then realized he still didn't speak the language. He had to call a linguist over to help him out.

"What's up?" Robert Bykov asked as the first of the large trucks rolled past Gary to the last house in this section.

"I just wanted to ask, Georow here, what kind of trucks he's got rolling in here."

After a brief exchange, Robert turned to Gary. "They're carrying the slab material. Once it's poured, they'll bring in the ranto gas to cure the seminate. It's like concrete, once cured."

"Guess I missed those details in the briefing."

"I'm in the dark as well. I'm using their words for the stuff as I don't know how to translate into English."

"Well, I guess we'll see what it is in a minute. Here comes the last truck."

Gary and Robert had to move aside with Georow as the last of the trucks pulled in closer to the home they were working on. It parked, the driver left his cab and came to the middle of the rig and pulled a six-inch-diameter hose out of a box mounted on the center. He handed one end to Georow, who motioned that Gary should help him pull that end away from the truck, as the truck driver checked his connections on the other end. Gary looked up long enough to see the same thing happening with the other four trucks.

As they got to the furthest point of the mold box from the truck, Georow hollered something back to the driver. The driver hollered back and waved at Georow. A moment later, Gary could feel something flowing through the tube he was helping Georow keep pointed into the mold box.

Soon a grayish liquid came pouring out of the tube. It had a lot less viscosity than the concrete Gary had watched his father pour into job sites. It was so thin it flowed from their corner of the mold to the other in seconds and by the time Georow called back to the driver to have the flow shut off, it had leveled itself into a smooth finish.

The Lankmeran passed the hose from where they were standing over to the team at the next house. Then he turned to Gary and motioned him to follow. He lifted the corner of a clear, plastic-like material and pulled it over to the far side of the mold. He motioned Gary should do the same when the next corner was exposed, but over to the other side of the back of the slab. Georow hooked his end to one of the poles Gary hadn't understood why it was there. Gary did the same and continued to pull the sheet out to attach it to the next pole, the way Georow had done.

Within minutes, they had covered the entire foundation of the house with a tarp about four feet above the freshly poured concrete material. They waited at the front of the house until the last of the slabs had been poured and the trucks had moved away. Then another truck pulled up to their location and Georow began taking a hose out of the back of it. Another six-inch hose. He connected it up to the valve mounted into the side of the plastic tarp before turning to see the driver had gotten out and was waiting at the back of the truck. He called and waved. The driver opened a valve on the truck and a reddish gas began flowing into the tent they had made with the plastic material.

When the tent expanded slightly, the driver shut the gas off and the next house's worker took the tube over to his. Georow turned to Gary and made the hand gesture they had established for asking for a translator. Gary radioed for Robert to come back, and after he had a brief conversation with the Lankmeran, spoke to Gary.

"The seminate needs about an hour to set up. So you might as well go to lunch. When you get back, it'll be time to repack the tents and start actual construction."

"This stuff'll set in an hour?"

"Actually, he said a half hour, but if you're going to lunch, I wanted you guys to have some time off."

Instead of spending the afternoon pulling apart the tents surrounding the house slabs, Sergeant Adams's crew was sent to the Anora citizen's chamber. There they were given instructions on what to do when they arrived at the job site the next day to apply the structural support and insulation to the body of the homes that were being grown over night.

Native Nightlife

The majority of Listener platoon had decided to go to the dance the city was staging in City Hall. They had to arrive early and help the citizens move the log benches out of the way to make up the dance floor. The mayor's table had been converted to a stage, while Gary Adams and his troops were pulling apart the benches and storing them away in the large closets off to the side of the hall. Despite the fact that it was a wooden floor and they were wooden benches, there were no scuff marks marring the surface. Gary was looking forward to some fun this evening.

"What the hell was that weird paneling they were having us glue onto the internal structure?" Peter Collins asked as he carried the legs of the bench Gary had the seat for.

"Really?" Gary replied. "They somehow grow their entire home's structure overnight, and that's what you find interesting?"

"It's silvered on both sides with less than an inch of corrugated material between them, I can't think that's enough for insulation. They don't have the structural strength to keep the house in shape. Yet, here we are, gluing them to the outside of the shell over the power lines and plumbing pipes."

"Well, I wouldn't worry about them. I understand a couple of the homes were finished enough today that the Lankmerans were planning on growing the outer shell of the home overnight." Gary closed the closet door after a couple of other members of his squad filled it up with bench pieces.

"I'm just glad we didn't have to wear our coats," said Bai Myers from the fifth squad. "Otherwise we couldn't use their coat room to store our weapons.

"I'm glad the Lankmerans don't know what they are," added his friend, Haun Chin, from the same squad. "They're willing to leave them alone wherever we store them."

"I'm glad we didn't have to post a guard on those job sites," Gary added. Though he'd had his squad stack them right next to the house he was working on so he could keep an eye on them. But Captain Palmer had wanted everyone's rifle at hand in case they were needed.

"I thought they said there was a band for this thing," said one of the members of the first squad. Gary had been surprised that Clint had decided his squad could attend the event unsupervised. He had gone off to participate in some game the Lankmerans had invited him to.

They watched as a couple of natives were setting up a computer system on the reinforced table. After about five minutes, a green light shot out of the center of the boxes installed. It was just over head height for a Lankmeran, but eye-level for the humans. Gary and his people jumped to the floor in the direction of the coat closet as several more lights, in varying colors, burst from the central box.

"Guys, it's okay," Gary called out. He stood up and ran his hand through one of the beams. "It's just a lighting effect. Everyone stand up. Let one of the beams bounce off you. I think they need to adjust them."

He scanned the room, looking for one of the human linguists that were here tonight. When he found one, he took him up to the Lankmerans setting up the system. After a brief discussion with them, Gary found out the lights were supposed to be over the heads of the dancers. They measured the crowd density through the dance, giving feedback to the Music Master about how he was doing. He could then alter the selections to fit the mood of the crowd. He thanked Gary for his input, and asked if the humans could bring a couple of the bench seats out for them to raise the lighting rack up higher.

As the dance progressed that evening, Sergeant Patel Singh and a few other members of first squad were attending a Dot Chase event at the Eliahwich Bar half-way across town. "The idea behind this game," the linguist he'd brought translated, "is to jump at each of the dots as they appear in the field in front of you. But only if they match or compliment the color of the square they appear in.

When you touch the dot, the light will go out and another dot will appear elsewhere."

"That shouldn't be so hard," said one of the privates Singh had brought.

"Ah, but if you don't cover the dot completely in your jump, it will move until you do. Also, there is a time limit on how long you can chase the dots. And each turn, the number of dots you're striving to catch will be increased by one."

"Unless you boys are itching to try," Singh said. "I suggest we watch how they do it for a while." He turned to the linguist and gestured for him to translate their intentions to their hosts.

The first group of Lankmerans ran through the batches of dots up to a five-dot run, in the two minute allotted time, before eliminating one of its members. Another two were eliminated during the seven-dot sequence, leaving the last two competing on the ten-dot sequence before one of them won the game.

As the next set of contestants were organizing themselves, the winner of the first session came up to the human standing in the corner and asked them if they would like to try.

When the linguist translated for them, and Sergeant Singh began to hem haw, his troops encouraged him to give it a try. "Do it for the company," one of his privates said.

He agreed, and began removing his combat boots, since he would be jumping around on all fours across a twelve-foot-by-twelve-foot mat spread across the floor. Six squares across and six down, and he was going to have to hit the dot inside their two by two foot interior.

Singh got the single dot easily enough, but had trouble with the second dot in the next sequence. He found it and qualified to go onto the third sequence. In the fourth one, he couldn't find the red dot in the red square in time and was eliminated from the session.

"It gets harder to see the dots the closer you get to the floor. The further you can keep your eyes away from the mat, the better your view. So who's next?"

"What do you Earth people do for fun?" asked one of the Lankmerans through the linguist.

Not waiting for a reply from the soldiers he was escorting, he drew his comm device out of his pocket. It was a rectangle three inches by five inches and a quarter-inch thick. He set it on the table they were sitting around watching the next round. "This little guy has about four thousand individual games stored in its memory." He pressed a couple of buttons and brought up one of the hundreds of card games available. He scooted his chair closer to the Lankmeran and showed him how it was played. Singh pulled his comm out of his pocket and motioned to a couple of his friends to do likewise.

"And putting them together opens up the files on larger board games," Singh said as the linguist translated. "And there are more extensive ones back at our barracks. We just don't bring them into the field with us."

"Yeah," said one of his men. "We didn't know what to expect when we landed on your planet."

"So you play games also," the Lankmeran said.

"As often as we can. It breaks up the monotony of being a soldier."

"What is a soldier?" the Lankmeran asked.

"We have to go out and defend the rights and lives of people who are working for a living. We protect them so they can focus on what they need to do."

"Protect them from what?"

"From people who mean them harm. Not every planet we visit is as peaceful as yours. This is paradise compared to a lot of the ones we've visited," Singh said.

One of his squad members standing with his back to the conversation as he watched the finals of the event begin, added, "We carry those guns around with us, but I doubt we're going to need them here."

Alien Incursion

It was early morning on the beginning of the third month of the Earth Force mission to the Lankmeran people, and Captain Palmer was planning on meeting with Mayor L'mere. Almost immediately after breakfast, he'd collected his three platoon lieutenants, along with Gus, and hurried over to the mayor's office. But this was not unusual, in Gus' opinion of the Captain; he found Palmer did everything in a hurry. Walking was no exception.

As they were ushered into the mayor's office, they found her sitting upon her desk going through some papers. She pushed them aside as they entered, swung her legs off the front of it and turned her attention to the entering soldiers. Gus and the platoon leaders took a seat on one of the benches, while Captain Palmer sat down in the folding chair his men had brought in for him weeks ago.

"Good morning, gentlemen," Gus translated for the mayor. "What can I do for you this morning. I hear that you've finished the housing units. Are you looking for new assignments?"

"No. Moving..." Captain Palmer tried out what he had learned of the Lankmeran language before giving up and turning to Gus. "Tell her we've decided it's time we moved on to one of the larger cities. To learn more about her people."

As Gus was midway through his translation, several alarms sounded from the western side of the city, the side where Palmer's troops had been working on the home construction. Then the communicators Captain Palmer and Lieutenant Danika Angelov carried began talking. Angelov got up and went to the far corner of the office to better hear what was being said.

"Sir, we're taking fire," began Squad Two's leader. "I've got all the troops under cover, but one of the villagers is dead, and another four are wounded. We're trying to get them pulled back to medical right now. We've hustled the rest of the Lankmerans back into town for cover. And here's the crazy part, Lieutenant. We're not hearing or seeing any bullets, just an occasional light beam when it goes through a cloud of dust."

Angelov looked over to Palmer. He'd just heard something similar on his radio. Angelov turned back to her radio, "Do you see the aggressors?"

"No, sir."

She looked again at her commanding officer. Palmer ordered, "Tell them to get under cover and take up firing positions, but do not respond until they can see who they're dealing with. Get your other squads in position to offer covering fire, in case the aggressors decide to move into town. Which, hopefully, they'll do if we don't offer any resistance."

Angelov relayed the orders, then added to Captain Palmer, "I'm going down to join my troops, sir. I'll let you know what we have as soon as I know."

"You do that, Lieutenant, and be quick about it." He rose from his chair to address his other troops. "Lieutenant Lee, take your platoon and fortify the city. Turn every road coming in into a kill zone. Mason, divide your platoon into two and send one north and the other south. Let's assume that whoever's firing is doing so from the woods to the west. See if we can surround whoever it is." Both men were standing up and heading for the door. "A little more hustle, gentlemen, civilians are dying out there."

He turned to Gus, "Ask her honor if she knows anything about what is happening. Does anyone on Lankmere have guns?"

After a brief conversation, Gus responded, "She's never heard of projectile weapons. Hunting has always been done by claw."

"Then we'll have to see who these people are after we grab a few of them. Tell her that her people need to get to cover. Somewhere safe. We'll deal with these intruders." He turned and headed for the door, not waiting for Gus' response.

* * *

Palmer checked on the placement of third platoon. Lee had placed his forces to Palmer's liking, every access road leading into the city from the north and south had at least two troopers across from each other, covering it. He walked between the homes as he drew closer to where Listener Platoon was hunkered down, waiting for whoever had attacked those Lankmerans to make their appearance. He cut through backyards and jumped fences when needed. He had no intentions of walking up the main road like a target inviting fire.

When he came to the last row of houses before the open fields that were ready to be planted next month, he opened the back door on the house just north of the main road and entered the kitchen. Moving to the front room, he saw the troops hunkered down below the large windows facing west. "All of you stay down," he said as the first man who saw him began to rise from his crouched position. "Where's Sergeant Adams?" he quietly asked.

Corporal Banachek turned and pointed north, "He's in the next home, sir."

Palmer got on the other side of the window from Banachek and patted him on the shoulder. "Thanks. Keep an eye out and wait for orders to fire. We didn't know they had guns, they may not know we have them also. And all of you, sing out if you see anything." He patted the communicator in his vest pocket to reinforce the method of singing.

Palmer made his way out the back door and over to the next house. Sergeant Adams was standing over a counter in the kitchen, hastily drawing maps of the area on his command PADD, making notes on where he had placed his people. As he heard the door close, he turned, saw Palmer enter and saluted him.

Palmer returned the salute and added, "It looks like you've got your people ready. They know to wait until I give the word?"

"Yes, sir."

"And the rest of the platoon?"

"Fourth squad is hunkered in across the main road in those homes. The snipers from third are on the roof of the apartment building, with the rest of the squad on the lower floors. First and fifth squads are covering the secondary roads into town, in case the enemy bypasses the main road, sir."

"And where is Lieutenant Angelov?"

"She's off inspecting our positions, sir. She should be back shortly."

"Has anyone seen anything?"

"One of the snipers reported some rustling in the woods on the other side of the field, but it quieted down and we've seen nothing since, sir. Those trees are almost a mile away, if they can hit us from that distance..."

"Yeah, it means they have some really long range capacity. Keep your people hidden until they're close enough." He looked over the empty house. Waiting was the worst part. He didn't know who they were up against, what the capacity of the enemy was, or why they were firing on the Lankmeran populace. But waiting was the only plan that offered the fewest casualties for his people, or the people of Anora.

"Lieutenant Angelov," came a message over the radio channel.

She was just walking in the door of the house Palmer had been waiting for her in. "Angelov here, go ahead."

"Sir, this is Marklinov in the crow's nest. Something is coming out of the woods to the west-southwest. They're breaking cover now, still outside optimal firing range, though, sir."

"Describe what you see," said Angelov into the radio.

"They're still a good deal off. Even with my scope. They're a biped race, wearing a large red suit with a glassy dome over their head. I'm going to have to wait until they get closer to give you more details, sir."

"Numbers?" asked Captain Palmer pulled his communicator from his pocket to break into the conversation.

"Over a dozen have emerged so far, Captain. Wait. I hate the tunnel vision you get with these scopes. There's five more rows of them coming out of the woods. Each with what looks like two dozen men, now. They're spreading out as they cross the field, into a long line marching forward, sir."

"Let me know when they get within two hundred yards, or if they're doing anything more than just walking across that field." Palmer clicked the communicator to idle and placed it back into his pocket, then started looking over Angelov's command center. "Lieutenant, you got a pair of binoculars around here somewhere?"

She reached into her lower vest pocket and pulled out one of the micro-miniature models that were currently being issued. "These work?"

"I hate these things, I was hoping for a real pair." He went over to the large picture window in the front room of the house and looked out. "But at least you're able to carry them into combat without them getting in the way." He located the line of newcomers forming on the outer fringe of the untilled field. "We've got to let them get closer before we let them know we can fight back. So we wait."

Five minutes later, Palmer could see them better. They looked to him like the invading army they were. Then they suddenly dropped to the ground. Palmer slid behind the screening of the building's wall and watched the aliens begin to crawl forward. Something had given the human position away.

"All units, open fire. Keep the enemy pinned to the ground and unmoving," Palmer said into his command circuit. He dropped back to the floor and worked his way back into the cover of the kitchen. Lieutenant Angelov was on her communicator coordinating the fire of her squads to where the incoming troops had gone to ground.

"Marklinov, what do you see from your position?" Palmer called over his Company channel.

"A bunch of belly-crawling red suits, sir."

"Stop as many of them as you can." Palmer looked over at Angelov, who nodded that she had this position covered. Palmer went out the back door and looked back at city hall. "Lieutenant Grimwald, we've got a force of over a hundred fighters headed our way. Make sure the mayor has her people safe."

"Will do, sir."

Palmer needed to get a look at what was going on. The best place for him to do that was in the sniper's nest; his people had things under control at the moment. He patted his armored vest pocket. *Yup*, he thought as he realized he had pocketed Lieutenant Angelov's binoculars. Then he darted across the main street and into the newly-constructed apartment complex where his team was waiting.

He took the steps two at a time.. "Harrison, Fitzgibbons, stay where you are. Keep an eye on those beings out there." Palmer dropped under the ledge running the entire expanse of the roof. He pulled out Angelov's binoculars and looked over the field where the invading force had hunkered to the ground.

It looked to him like they were firing their weapons, but he couldn't see any effect from them. And he couldn't hear any report from their rifles. But they were laying there in the dirt of the field too low for the soldiers in the houses to hit.

He grabbed his communicator. "Mr. Angelov, divide your firing teams in half and send some up to the upper floor of each building, where you can. They should be able to hit their targets better from there." He turned to the two men inhabiting the apartment with him.

"Did you see that?" Harrison asked as Palmer finished his radio call. "His helmet just exploded, but he's still moving." Harrison's rifle barked again, and the alien soldier stopped crawling.

"Looks like they don't need a special air mixture to breath," Fitzgibbons said.

As he watched the enemy soldiers inching their way forward, he saw a bush separating the field from the housing development had miniature holes punched in some of its leaves, without removing the leaf from the bush.

"Do what you guys can to stop them. Headhunter Platoon is going to try to surround them." He turned around and sat with his back against the two-foot ledge, returning to his communicator. "Lieutenant Chen, have you been listening?"

"Yes, sir."

"I need you go get word to the Command station and inform them of our situation. See what they want us to do. Let them know I've opened fire on these bozos."

"Right away, Captain."

Palmer turned his attention back to the field and watched the red uniforms crawl across it. His attention was interrupted by a call. "Captain Palmer," it was Angelov. "Private Agarwal's been hit in the arm. But the shot came through the window, right through it, without shattering the glass."

"Increase your rate of fire to suppression fire." He adjusted his comm unit. "All personnel, suppression fire. I repeat, suppression fire on the enemy positions, keep those bastards down." He released the button on his microphone and turned to the men still launching shot after shot down on the field below, racking up a body count. "I'm heading back to talk to command. Good hunting, gentlemen." He crawled over to the roof access door and left.

"Lieutenant Mason, how close is your platoon to beginning your pincer action on the enemy?" Palmer asked over his communicator as he dashed across the street to check on Angelov before heading back uptown.

After a few seconds, Mason responded, "The northern squads are in position, waiting for the southern squads. We should be ready to go in a couple of minutes."

"Don't wait for my signal. As soon as everyone's in position, move. If the opportunity presents itself, a few prisoners would be nice. But don't take any chances. Am I clear?"

"Yes, sir. Protect my men."

Palmer stepped into the kitchen of the house Angelov's people were firing from. Angelov herself was in the main room directing fire and adding her own support. Private Agarwal was sitting on the floor with her back against the far wall rubbing the wound that looked like it had been recently bandaged. "How are you doing, soldier?" Palmer knelt down to address his warrior.

"Fine, sir. The bandage is almost superfluous. Whatever they hit me with cauterized the wound going through. There was no bleeding, it didn't hit a bone, nor is it restricting my arms' movement. I should be good to go after I catch my breath, sir."

He looked at the bandage around the wound on her left arm. "Make sure you're ready. I don't need soldiers dying on me today. Let the Lieutenant know I was here. Not now," he placed his hand on her shoulder as she started to rise. "When you've got that breath back. Your CO has things under control." He made his way out of the building before she could respond.

Specialist Harry Malone

Specialist Malone sat with his back against the outer wall of the home with his Electronics Enhanced rifle leaned up against it as he checked its electronics package. He was still recovering from the night before; Lankmeran beer was stronger than what's brewed on Earth. He tried compensating for his blurry vision by increasing the resolution of his scope monitor before placing the PADD on the floor next to him. It was wired into his assault rifle with the scope set to find its own targets, just point out what you're looking for and the computer can do the rest. The earlier EE-18 had a wireless version of the scope monitor, but the Octogon found that was too easily hacked and went back to having each one wired into the PADD each soldier used.

Now it was time to deploy the tripod to allow the weapon to free stand while he sat safely behind the wall and operated it. Of course it wasn't really a physical tripod but rather miniaturized anti-gravity units that could tilt his rifle in whatever direction he set it in. He set the four feet on the floor, each two feet from each other, set the focal field for three feet and placed his rifle in its center. The rifle floated just where he'd set it. Malone picked up his PADD and raised the rifle up to the level of the window. He reached over to the butt of the rifle and gave it a sharp push, breaking the glass. This setup promised a faster reaction time on target than Malone was able to produce, especially until his head cleared up. *What a day to miss morning chow and the corresponding coffee*, he thought.

"It's kind of eerie to see pieces of the back wall being chipped away without any noise coming from enemy fire," Corporal Buson said from the other side of the window.

"I don't like that they can fire through the glass without breaking it," said Specialist Bykov from just over half way across the room by another window. "It's a little spooky."

"It looks like they've developed the ray guns R & D always says they're twenty years away from developing," Sergeant Adams said as he low-walked into the room from the kitchen, making sure he stayed away from any of the windows. They could see the effects of the light rounds that had to be coming from them, but they hadn't seen any effects of the enemy's weapons coming through the actual walls of the house yet.

"I think it's about time to see where their attacks are coming from." Kozlov, cracked the door and tossed a smoke grenade outside. "Let's see if that lights up the path of their rays." It landed in front of the window Malone was crouched next to.

Smoke spewed from the can and clouded the whole area in front of the window. As it did, dozens of light paths could be seen hitting the house. Some going right through the window, but most just hitting the side of the house and bouncing back.

"It must be the silver insulation we put into these homes," Malone said. "It's reflecting their beams." He patted the wall behind him. "Let's hope they don't intensify their fire to the point where they break through the silver material."

"You guys got your units set up?" Adams asked of the eight men positioned around the room.

"Roger that, sarge," came their response, just slightly out of unison.

"Give me three rounds rapid to poke a hole in your windows and be ready to begin live fire."

All the weapons barked and glass could be heard to shatter, but the holes produced were only slightly larger than the opening each man needed to push his barrel through. They all instructed their tripods to inch forward so the flash suppressor was just outside the glass of the window. Malone already had his extended to where the glass wouldn't obstruct his shots.

Sergeant Adams had walked up behind Malone, who was standing with his back against the wall. "Stop bashing in the windows. One of these days you'll get pieces lodged in your barrel and fowl your rifle."

"I've never found that a problem in a combat situation," Malone responded.

Adams stood away from the wall to address everyone in the room. "Try and pick a target, use single round fire, and let's whittle these attackers down."

"They're too low," Malone said. "They've taken up positions behind the mounds of dirt we left on the far side of the road during construction."

"Malone, get up to the second floor then, and take a position there," Adams commanded. "Kozlov, you go with him. Keep those guys pinned to the ground for another fifteen minutes. The Captain's got something planned for them they ain't gonna like."

"Roger, sarge." They almost made their way back to the stairs when Kozlov got up a little too high and felt something push him back towards the rear wall. He was swatting a spot on his back, when Malone pulled him out of the living room.

"Stay low," Malone began. "Hey, you got a hole in your body armor."

Kozlov set his rifle against the wall, unbuckled his vest and pulled it off. Both men could see there wasn't a hole on the other side of it. "It must have been one of their beams," Kozlov said. "But it couldn't get through the Kevlar. Hey, sarge," he yelled back into the other room. "Them beams can't penetrate our Kevlar."

"Fine, but you ain't got it all over. Keep your head down, got it?"

"Yes, sarge." They made their way up the stairs to a bedroom facing the attacking troops. It had two windows that looked out onto the road bordering the town. Across that road, they could see dozens of red-suited bodies still wearing their tall helmets, laying in the ground, those suits slowly cutting through the earth, lowing them further out of reach. Malone fired off a couple of shots that burst one of their helmets. The only response he got was the alien turning his head and looking for where the shot had come from. But the face that was staring in his direction wasn't a feline one. Whoever these guys were, they weren't Lankmerans. He backed his site a couple of inches, just enough to put that head in his crosshairs and fired again. The alien's head exploded before Malone could get a better look at it.

"Sergeant Adams," Kozlov said as his sergeant walked through their doorway.

"Higgins, get in here and cover the other window. You three," he was pointing outside the room, down the hall, "set up a firing station in the next bedroom. The Captain needs those things securely pinned down."

Malone watched a transparent bubble drift above a mound of dirt and fired off a burst of three at it. The helmet shattered. "They're diggin' in. The Captain got a plan for driving them back above ground?"

"Above our pay grades. Anything exposing itself, take it out." The sergeant left the room, Malone could hear his footsteps heading for the other bedroom to check on his troops.

Malone widened the view finder on his scope to keep an eye on the field. He could hear the triple bursts of gunfire coming from below, their frequency greatly diminished due to how deep the aliens were hiding. He knew his comrades wouldn't waste bullets driving them into the ground.

"You got any idea where these guys came from?" asked Higgins as he fired off a burst of seven rounds. "They don't look like anything we've experienced before."

"You see something, say something, kid," said Kozlov from the other window. "Pick your targets. And keep your round selector set on three No point in wasting ammo." Kozlov had been mentoring Higgins ever since he was assigned right out of boot camp to their unit. This was Higgins' first actual deployment.

"I thought I saw movement, sir," Higgins responded as he reached up and adjusted the settings on his rifle. Malone watched his finger linger over the rocket round switch. While they would be great for space combat, it would be utterly useless now. They had left all those clips up on the station still in orbit, anyway. Higgins' rifle seemed to be the only one in the platoon that had a clip in where those rounds were stored.

Kozlov rolled over on his back and dropped his hand holding his PADD by his side. "Look, I know this is your first mission kid, but we can't waste ammunition up here."

"Yeah," replied Malone from his window next to the kid. "That's the Captain's job. Besides, we don't know how many more of these things are out there. Ten o'clock deep." He dropped two bursts of three rounds each in the area. The first to mark the area for the others and the second better aimed. All six rounds splattered dirt around the field.

"I must have missed it," Kozlov said.

"I think he was just turning."

"Another of their rifles just flew up," Higgins said. "The guys in the crow's nest must have gotten another one."

Sergeant Steven Pak

"We're too far out, sarge," Specialist Hendrics said as the rest of First Squad of the Headhunters got into position.

"Yeah," said Private Jaheem. "My scope is painting a red circle over the target. Too far away."

"We have to wait for second and third squads to get into position or this trap won't work." Sergeant Pak set his binoculars down next to himself as he rolled over to talk with his two men. He had stationed his men in pairs along this berm for about a hundred yards. Enough that they could cover each other and still control enough ground to box the enemy in.

He rolled back onto his stomach and brought his glasses back up when his communicator signaled. "Sergeant Pak, this is Lieutenant Mason. Prepare your squad. We are going in one minute from now."

"First Squad," Pak said after switching to his squad channel. "Rise and march on my orders. Stay on this frequency for the duration."

"Now, sergeant," came over the platoon channel. Only unit commanders had communicators that could multi-channel. Pak could monitor both the squad and platoon channel at the same time, but his troops couldn't hear both messages.

"Move out," Pak said. He could hear similar commands coming from the other two squads south of them.

His men moved out in a quiet but rapid pace across the open field. Crouched over, they ran, kicking up the soil as they did. They got half way to the enemy, well within firing range before the enemy noticed them. They kept running while the enemy troops rose from their holes and took up a kneeling position. Before they were completely set, Pak shouted for everyone to hit the dirt. As he watched his troops drop to the ground, he could hear firing in the distance and saw several of the enemy soldiers drop motionless.

"Open fire!" Pak called to his men. He said it over their communication's circuit but also loud enough for them to hear him without it.

As a couple of the squad members who hadn't dropped to the ground were spun around and fell, the Earth Force fire was causing the enemy troops to go to ground again. They were being hit by fire from the homes, as well as the advancing troops.

Pak dropped back to check on his fallen troops, only to find them getting back up before he got to them.

"Hendricks, you okay?"

"Fine, sarge. Something hit me and knocked me over, but I don't feel wounded anywhere." Hendricks stretched out on the ground as Pak gave him a cursory inspection. He saw a hole in Hendricks' jacket and stuck his finger in it. It went in only through the fabric, the Kevlar in its pockets wasn't damaged. "Well, we'd better catch up with the rest of the squad," Pak said as he realized nothing was wrong with Hendricks. The pair of them began crawling as fast as they could to catch up with their advancing team members.

As Pak approached the grounded enemy forces, he came across other members of his squad who had been hit in places their Kevlar hadn't covered. Some, wounded in the legs, couldn't push forward. Those wounded in their arms had to sling their rifles and draw hand weapons to press on. Pak had always been proud of the members of Headhunters under his command.

As with all split activities that Headhunters did, it became a competition. Second and Third squads racing each other north to see who would get there first. And First squad racing the two of them to claim the bragging rights.

As they got within fifty yards of the enemies' position, the suppression fire from the home stopped. Lieutenant Angelov wasn't going to take any chances of her people accidently hitting a member of the Headhunters. Pak's troops picked up the pace, almost running towards the enemy, but it was members of Second squad that started yanking the rifles out of the enemies' hands first.

As they did, the enemy soldiers began dropping their hands against their sides. Those still holding rifles dropped theirs and did likewise. By the time Third squad finally made it to the enemy position, some of the enemy had already begun having their hands restrained behind their backs.

As the last of the enemy troops were zip-tied, Lieutenant Mason was organizing them into lines that could be marched into town for Captain Palmer or General Chi to decide what to do with them. It took the troops of Listener platoon to come out of the city and help monitor the prisoners. They marched them into town to where Captain Palmer was waiting, standing on the steps of the City Hall.

Captain "Rowdy" Randolph Palmer

Lieutenant Chen raised this troop transport from under the lake and brought it to the docks of Anora. From the steps of the City Hall, Captain Palmer watched it set down before walking the five blocks to the craft. He needed its long range communicator to reach the command post orbiting Lankmere. The sounds of gunfire were trending down and the General was going to want to know what happened.

"Any word from the station?" Palmer asked as he walked into the craft's lower loading ramp. He found Chen sitting at a bench mounted to the port wall of the vessel directly behind the cockpit. Chen was talking to someone over the deep space communication system.

Chen swiveled his chair around as Palmer drew close. "They'd heard about the enemy forces minutes before I tried to contact them. The other two companies that'd been sent down, are also under fire, sir."

"Lieutenant Griswald," Palmer called into his field radio. "Have you got the villagers safe?"

"We're down in the grain storage bins, sir."

"Headhunter platoon, what's your status?"

"We have the enemy rounded up, sir. About 20 of them finally surrendered. The rest forced us to kill them."

"Restrain them and keep them under guard. I'm contacting command for instructions. Angelov, what's your situation?"

"Just moving out into the field to support Lieutenant Mason's platoon, Sir."

"Good. When I know more, you will also. Palmer out."

He motioned for Chen to get out of the radio seat and dropped into it while picking up the microphone. "Captain Palmer of Bravo Company calling General Chi. I have a report, if the General is available." He set the mic on the counter in front of the radio and looked up at Chen while he waited for a response. "So, Lieutenant, what are your opinions of today's action?"

"I could only hear what came over..."

The radio kept Chen from finishing his thought. "Palmer, this is Chi. What happened down there?"

Palmer scooped up the handheld mic and gave the general an account of what'd happened. There was only silence from the radio; Palmer and Chen could feel the general working out what to do next. They waited for the General's response rather than finish their earlier conversation.

"Okay, we have no idea who these invaders are? You're sure they aren't from somewhere else on the planet?"

Palmer was looking at Chen as he keyed the radio. "The Mayor of Anora has never heard of other sentient creatures living on Lankmere. And we were just talking about their explorations of the planet last week."

"Then we need information. Send us some of the bodies and equipment up here so we can analyze them. And send a few of your prisoners as well. Let's see if our linguists are as smart as they think they are."

"Sir?"

"If we can learn their language, then we can interrogate them," the General explained. "We can figure out how to deal with them, once we find out what they want."

"I'll get a pair of the shuttles ready and be up there in the morning."

"No, Captain Palmer, I want you to stay down there. Their first attack failed, do you really think that's going to be enough to discourage them?"

"No, I guess you're right, sir."

"I also need you to send one of your platoons to help Alpha Company out. Captain Nilsson didn't have the luck you and Captain Pangestu had. She got hit harder and is still picking up the pieces."

"That's going to leave me shorthanded if your attack materializes, general."

"Can't be helped, captain. First order of business, stop the bleeding and Nilsson's still bleeding. I'll get the MPs up here to go down and set up a POW camp in the meantime. That should take some of the pressure off you. Chi out!"

Palmer lightly tossed the microphone against the radio console, before letting out a loud sigh and turning his chair to look at the shuttle's pilot. "I swear, once you promote someone to staff, they forget about everything that happens in the field." He raised his cap and ran his hand through his slightly too-long-for-military-regulation hair. Then he reached over and activated the communicator he kept in his vest pocket. "Lieutenants Simmons and Williams, bring your shuttles to the beach." He looked over at Chen, who had moved over to the pilot's seat to sit down. "I'm sending you back up to the Nyumbani, Bao. Prepare this thing to receive prisoners and cargo."

"Yes, sir." Chen turned to the control board for the shuttle and had the back section of the shuttle seal itself off as its programmable wall appeared.

Palmer was back in communication with his subordinates while this was happening. "Lieutenant Simmons, once you've landed, prepare to take Second platoon down to the next village to assist Alpha Company. Lieutenant Angelov, come in."

"Yes, sir," he heard after a few seconds.

"Get your platoon ready to move out. Alpha Company is in trouble and needs your assistance. Lieutenant Simmons will have a shuttle ready here at the docks to take you there. Remember, it's going to be an active situation. Coordinate with Captain Nilsson on your way in. Good luck. Palmer out!" Palmer rose from the chair and made his way over to the shuttle's side door. "Lieutenant Mason."

"Yes, sir," came an immediate reply.

"Round up all the prisoners we took and get them incarcerated in the town's jail. Except for two. Send two of them to the second platoon shuttle along with a couple of troopers to help Mr. Chen get them to orbit."

"Roger that, sir."

He stepped off the ramp coming from the shuttle and turned to look up the main street of Anora. "Lieutenant Lee."

"Lee here, sir."

He walked up the main road, he wanted to catch the mayor and see what help they could give his men. "I need you to have your men move as many of the dead enemy bodies as you can back to your platoon's shuttle. Collect all their gear also. The General wants to do some research on them."

"Right away, sir. The Lankmerans have started piling them up for what I think was going to be a bonfire."

"Well, don't let them. General Chi wants to cut those bodies open to see what makes them tick. I'll check with the mayor and put a stop to it. No less than twelve of them, understood?"

"Yes, sir."

He double-timed up the dozen steps to the municipal building and pulled open the door. He didn't slow down as he approached the Mayor's office. "Grimwald," he called into his communicator, "I need you in the mayor's office five minutes ago."

"I'm going to assume you want to talk to the mayor," came back as Palmer reached the door to the mayor's office. "I'm with her now. Your problem is that she's not in her office." Palmer opened the door to find the mayor's office empty.

"So where are you?" Palmer leaned against the office threshold and let his breathing catch up with him. Then he turned and headed back out of City Hall.

"We're at the bonfire site."

"Don't let them light that fire. I need to talk to the mayor. General Chi wants the bodies." He was at a dead run when he finally realized he didn't know where they were planning the burning.

Communication went dead for a couple minutes. Palmer couldn't take it any longer and by the time he reached the main road he was reaching for his device again. Gus came back on before he could key it. "The mayor's addressing the crowd now, but you'd better get here quick. I'm hearing some hissing coming from it. I think they really want to burn these bodies."

Palmer stopped for a second to get his direction. "Where are you?"

"Just north of the city. Once you clear the houses, you can't miss us."

"I'll get there as quick as I can." Palmer took off running again, cursing under his breath for not including some form of transportation in his landing equipment. Even a powered skateboard would be welcomed right now.

With the additions they had made to the town, it took him about ten minutes to run to the edge of town, just over a mile away. He then had to find the right field they were piling the corpses in, so it took him another five minutes to find Mr. Grimwald and the mayor. He slowed his pace down to a double-time to give himself a chance to breath slower and talk normally.

"Ms. Mayor, please. Don't burn those bodies. We need those to learn what you and we are facing down here. Like you, we Earthmen have never encountered these beings before."

"They are totally new to us," was her reply he got through Grimwald. "As are you. And what is this killing at a distance the two of you do?"

Palmer took one final deep breath before continuing. "They have laser rifles and we have projectile rifles. We call them guns. They equalize the soldiers' abilities on the battlefield. I understand the personal nature of a kill when your people go hunting, a one-on-one experience. But in war, many people are assembled on each side, and another means had to be developed for one group to enforce their will on the other. Or in this case, we needed something to keep these invaders from killing all of you."

It took Grimwald a few minutes to translate that speech to her. Palmer could hear him stopping occasionally, then use the English word; he assumed Gus didn't have any Lankmeran word to use. After he finished, the mayor reached down and picked up one of the invader's rifles. Holding it across her chest the way she had seen Palmer's men hold their rifles. She continued. "You will take them all away? You will take these all away?" She shoved the rifles into Palmer's chest.

He had a blank look on his face until Grimwald translated for him. "Yes, we need them to understand who they are and what they are capable of. The more we know, the better we can protect you."

"Then take them. We never wish to see them again." She turned back to her people around the burning circle and addressed them as Grimwald translated.

Palmer keyed his communicator again. "Mr. Chen, bring the shuttle to the field north of town. Land near bodies you see stacked in a mound out there. Lieutenant Lee, get a squad out there and start loading the enemy bodies in the shuttle. And their equipment, everything you can find. High Command wants to learn everything it's able to about these guys." He turned to Grimwald, "This is the kind of day that wrecks all the benefits we've gained over the last two months."

Bergland

"Captain Nilsson, this is Lieutenant Angelov." The shuttle had gotten airborne and was almost half way to the next village in under fifteen minutes.

"Go ahead, Lieutenant," came over the shuttle's radio.

"Sir, we're ten minutes from your location. Where do you want me to bring my platoon in?"

"The enemy has gotten a foot hold here in Bergland. It's going to be a house-by-house search to root them out. Bring your men in on the north-east corner of the town and begin sweeps there. We'll try to get them out of the apartment complexes and municipal buildings."

"Roger that, sir. Just get the Lankmerans to safety and we'll deal with these thugs."

"Good hunting, Lieutenant. Nilsson out."

Simmons swung the shuttle to the left and headed for an open field where he could land Angelov's platoon. "Once you're down, I'm heading back to Anora, Angelov . The Captain is going to be needing this shuttle more than you guys until this town is pacified."

"I concur, Jarhead." She was looking out the window as the town gave way to an unplowed field. "How does that spot look?"

"I can set down there easily enough."

"Good, it's in close proximity to those homes," Angelov pointed out the window at the rows of houses marking the edge of the town.

Simmons drew closer to the field while descending to bring the shuttle to the ground. Within five minutes, he touched down on the loose soil. Having landed his shuttle with the ramp away from the buildings, he lowered it so the soldiers could safely disembark. Had they been occupied by the enemy, the troops would have been an easy target for the enemy fighters.

"Okay, everybody hit the ground and form into your respective squads," Angelov commanded over the platoon circuit. "Be ready to move into the first row of houses. One squad to each house. Search and secure before moving southward. Lieutenant Simmons will give us cover until we've secured a foothold and are moving forward." The green light indicating the ramp was secured to the ground came on. "Now go!"

Her troops having disengaged their seat harnesses and prepared their equipment while the shuttle was lowering the ramp, stood ready at the door for her signal. When it came, they double-timed down the ramp and broke up into their respective squads, waiting for Angleov to descend from the shuttle.

The Lieutenant rose from her seat, grabbed her backpack from behind it and pressed the button to open the cockpit door. "Good luck, Jason. I'll let you know when you can come get us."

"Roger that, lieutenant. Now get your ass off my bird, so I can get her airborne and ready to provide covering fire."

She slapped the button on the other side and pivoted right to go down the ramp. "I'm down," she said into her communicator as she made two steps away from the ramp. The ramp rose up and locked itself into place. The shuttle lifted away from the ground using its gravitational field to avoid kicking up dust. It ascended to twenty feet and pivoted to bring its anti-spacecraft cannons to bear on the Lankmeran houses.

The First through Third squads ran across the hundred yards of field and the paved streets of the Lankmeran city to arrive at their assigned houses. Each team prepared to bust down the front door, until one man in first squad had the idea to check. The door was unlocked and they could easily open it to enter.

The first three men ran into the room with weapons pointed in differing directions. They cleared the adjoining main room and kitchen. The next three charged up the stairs, followed by three more of their comrades. The bathroom and single bedroom on the first floor were quickly secured before the units that went up stairs could report back.

Lieutenant Angelov walked through the front door of the first home on the block. Specialist Malone was just walking back from the kitchen, gnawing on a bird-leg he's recovered from the refrigerator. Upon seeing his lieutenant approaching, he dropped the leg and snapped a salute. "Building secured, sir."

"Thank you, Malone. Pick up the leg and get rid of it. We're under battle conditions." She strode through the room and back out the door. She stood on the front porch and keyed her communicator, "All squads, repeat all squads, move on to your second target." Independently, her three sergeants acknowledged her orders. Hearing the commotion coming from inside the house she was in front of, she moved to the side of the door to allow her troops to exit and make their way to the next house.

Later, as her troops were clearing the buildings two blocks down from where they'd begun, Lieutenant Angelov tried to contact Captain Nilssen to report on their progress and see how the operation was going.

"They're still holding the buildings they've captured and pinning us down wherever they find us. Keep moving, but when you get to the main street, start making your way west to our position. I'll start combining Sword and Switchblade platoons on the south side for a push up that side of the street."

"Roger that, sir. We'll push in three blocks and I'll get back with you. Angelov, out."

Angelov looked over the troops in the main room of the building and spotted Sergeant Singh. She walked over to where he was standing. "Sergeant take your men two houses to the west, then prepare them to push east. We should be running into resistance shortly."

"Roger that, lieutenant." He turned away from her and began yelling orders that even the guys upstairs could hear.

"Sergeant Adams, take your men back one building, then westward. Get ready for a push towards the center of town. Sergeant Wilcox, take your troops two buildings north and get them ready to move out. We will be experiencing enemy resistance from here on out."

She walked out into the main street to look down at what was to come. The rest of the buildings on this block were single family units. But across the street, she saw apartment buildings. They looked to have five floors for her troops to clear out. And across the street was another complex of apartment units that the enemy could be dug into and ready to fire on her troops. According to her talk with Captain Nilsson, the enemy had overcome the problem with their lasers not penetrating Kevlar. She knew her sergeants, they were good men, she'd warned them of this development and was going to trust them to take care of her troops.

"All squads. Move out."

* * *

Malone was in the squad about to clear the apartment complexes that had their primary entrances facing the main street. They were going to have to expose themselves to fire from across the main drag to get into the building. Sergeant Adams took the binoculars off Lieutenant Angelov's neck and scanned the windows of the hotel across the main street. "I don't see anyone in the adjacent hotel up the block." He handed the glass back to his superior. "We should be able to get into the building across the street." He turned to the men waiting behind him. "Malone, Higgins, Roberts; secure the entryway. The rest of you follow them in."

Higgins was out the side door of the house they'd just secured, followed by Malone and Roberts. They raced across the street and got to the apartment's front door. The automatic activators on the glass doors parted to let them in. Each of them ran in covering different corners of the room. Since it was clear, Malone stuck his head back out the door and waved the rest of his squad in.

Using hand signs, he started breaking the arrivals into parties to scour the ground floor and the one above it. As he was about to assign troopers to the third floor, Adams put his hand on Malone's. Then he signed to Malone to only go two floors at a time. Malone nodded, realizing that the Sergeant didn't want the squad broken up too thinly.

Malone, Higgins and Roberts found a couple of Lankmeran bodies when they investigated the communal cooking facility. Keeping the door with Lankmeran lettering on it open was another body.

"They must have..." Higgins started to say. Malone brought his finger to his lips to silence him.

41

Malone signed, "We don't know if anyone's here. We're in stealth mode."

Higgins fingered back, "It looks like they caught these guys before they had a chance to evacuate."

They cleared the office and moved back to the central stairs. The two other teams working the ground floor were also coming back. Adams was still in the complex's lobby and signed them to cover the third floor. He followed them to the second floor to wait on the team working it.

It took Malone's team about twenty minutes to clear their share of rooms on the third floor and report back. Adams was waiting for them when they arrived. "Move to the fifth floor and when you've finished it, check out the roof. If the enemy left any snipers up there, I want them eliminated. Their laser rifles have a longer range than our slug-throwers do," he signed.

The roof was clear when Malone and his team made it through the door at the head of the stairs. Staring down the fire escape ladder, they found a couple more bodies. But the rooms they had cleared didn't have any in them, at least those Lankmerans had managed to get away. Malone kept his men below the edge of the roof perimeter as he pulled his mini-binoculars out of his vest pocket and checked out the nearby roofs.

There was no one on them for a couple of blocks. He looked over to the office building in the middle of the city, the tallest in the city, a good four blocks from their position; six of the red-suited aliens were keeping the human troops off the streets.

Malone rolled over onto his back, "They're too far away for us to get a good shot at them. And if we miss, they'll just move to someplace on that roof where we can't hit them." He grabbed his communicator, "Sarge, this building is cleared. It looks like resistance is going to happen about four blocks further in. And they have a sniper's nest on the tall building across the street."

"You guys get back down here. I'm going to check with Angelov and see what she wants to do."

They crawled over to the still open door and made their way back down to the lobby. Adams motioned them over to where everyone else had already congregated. The couches and chairs were already taken.

"According to Malone here, we should have smooth sailing for the next couple of blocks. The Lieutenant doesn't believe the enemy even knows we're here. And if we can keep it that way until we are across from that tall office building, I think we can move up and take that sniper nest. But we have to do it by the book and make sure no one is behind us. That means we keep clearing these buildings, one by one. So let's get ready to move out. Kozlov, Banachek, Hamidi; you guys take point this time."

Without any resistance, they cleared the buildings in half the time of the first apartment complex, finding only three dead Lankmerans in each. The last home they secured was across the street from a shopping complex. Outside the mall and littering their way across the street were a series of merchandise bins and overturned desks being used as makeshift barricades. Adams could see enemy troops lined up behind them in positions that looked like they were firing on something.

Adams called Angelov and reported what they'd found. Her instructions were for him to bring his squad to the third home down this street. The entire platoon would go into the shopping center from there and work their way up to the barricades. Adams took his men out the back of the house and moved north until they reached the rest of the waiting platoon.

Malone and Higgins pulled open the back doors of the shopping center. Two sets of three troopers rushed in, each set training their weapons in different directions to cover the entire food center. When the "Clear" announcement came, the rest of the platoon rushed into the center, with Higgins and Malone bringing up the rear after Lieutenant Angelov.

"As we planned," Angelov said. "First squad up stairs, go shop by shop. Second squad up stairs also, cover the main floor from the balcony. And Third squad, main floor, shop by shop. Go!"

First squad ran around what looked to be a kid's area, it was a playground with actual climbing posts going to the second floor as well as a lot of rope obstacles for the junior Lankmerans to work their claws into. Second squad ran right through the sand covered area, tracking sand over to the stairs they were about to climb.

By the time Malone got to the second floor, he heard a couple of quick bursts from the rifles of Third squad on the main floor. He looked over the stair's banister and thought he placed them in a sit-down eatery next to the food center. By the time he got to the second floor, Michelsen and Morley were pulling the bodies of the enemy invaders out of the establishment.

Malone pointed Higgins and Roberts to the first shop. It's doors were open and he assumed the proprietor left in a hurry, not taking time to secure them. The clothing store they secured had several Lankmeran-looking manikins throughout the shop. Some were knocked over, but every one had a hole burned through their forehead, some had an extra hole in their torso, also.

"Check the changing rooms," Malone said. "I'm going back to the office. We've got lots more shops to clear, so we need to keep moving." He didn't watch his friends move to the left of the shop, he went straight to the back office. They knew the drill.

He pushed the door open with his left hand while holding his EE-19 against his shoulder in case he needed it. The room was empty at first glance, but when Malone looked under the desk, a shivering Lankmeran was kneeing under it.

He dropped his rifle down to his side, he slung it so it could stay there while he offered his hand to the scared native. When the man pressed himself against the back of the desk, Malone tried one of the few words he'd learned in Lankmeran. "*Bisneu*", he pointed at himself as he repeated the word he'd been told meant friend. After several unsuccessful attempts, he reached into one of his pants pockets and pulled out one of the Lankmeran snack bars he'd been given in Anora and tried offering it to the man.

The man stared at the bar for a minute, then reached out and grabbed Malone by the wrist. Malone quickly pulled him out from under the desk as Higgins and Roberts opened the office door and entered. "I thought we were in a hurry," Higgins said before seeing the Lankmeran standing next to Malone.

"This complicates things," Roberts said. "How are we going to get him safely out of here?"

"We could have him go back to the shuttle. If any of us spoke his language," Malone summed up. He let the alien have the food bar, which he promptly put in his pocket saying something none of them could understand.

"Lieutenant Angelov, we have a situation here. Sir, we've found a survivor hiding in one of the stores. What do you advise?" Malone sat on the desk and waited for instructions.

"Just a second," she replied. Then the radio went quiet for a couple of minutes. "Take him downstairs to the food area and find a restaurant back room where we can hide him. As long as we keep going forward, whoever's shooting at these guys isn't likely to find him. We can come back for him after we've cleared the town."

"Roger that, sir."

"Once he's settled, meet us at the front door. Okay, everyone listen up. First squad, I need you to get across Main street as quickly as possible, then find a position where you can lay down covering fire for everyone else. Second squad, you go straight in the front door over there and neutralize those guards in the lobby. Third squad, find a side door and begin moving up the floors of the building. Sergeant Wilcox, use your own judgment. It's time we crossed the street, people. Let's move."

The first two men of First squad ran into the street, about half way across, they stopped and began firing at the buildings east of them. The rest of the squad was laying down a covering fire. The next two members of the squad took off and stopped on the sidewalk across the street, found a couple of benches to hide behind and began laying down fire. The men who were in the center of the street took off towards the benches when their buddies began covering them. Finally, the rest of the squad ran into the building across the way, overturned several tables against the glass walls of the building to hide behind, and began laying down fire of their own.

In that time, Second squad ran across the street and through the front double doors of the building, firing as they entered. The two guards at the reception desk dropped. Another two were by the elevators and missed the barrage. One fired at the incoming troopers while the other ran for the stairs. Banachek felt a searing pain in his shoulder and slapped his hand over the spot. Single handedly, he fired his rifle in the direction the shot had come from. They heard the alien's plastic rifle hit the tiled floor as his footsteps said he was running away.

"Banachek, stay here," Malone called to the man. "Higgins, Kozlov, Hamidi, Roberts, follow me." He ran around the front of the desk to the hall where the elevators waited. Malone kicked the enemy rifle out of the way and saw the door to the stairs close. He motioned everyone over to it and pushed the metal door inward quickly. He jumped across the landing for the floor and looked up the tower that held a set of four stair stringers between each floor. He heard the door a few floors up closing.

"They got away. We'll find them in the floor-by-floor search." He came back into the lobby, propping the door open behind him. He led the squad over to where Sergeant Adams was talking to Angelov.

"Just the men we need," Lieutenant Angelov said as she saw Malone and company approach. "I need the four of you to go straight up to the roof and take out those snipers. Secure the roof until the rest of the platoon gets there. Understood?"

"Yes, Ma'am," he replied. "Any preferences on how we get up there?"

"Take the stairs. I don't think the elevator goes all the way to the roof. And that was your once. Captain Nilssen lets her troops get away with 'Ma'am', I don't. I've earned my 'Sir', capeesh corporal?"

"Yes, sir." Malone turned and motioned for the others to head back to the stairs. "We've got a several-story climb coming, boys."

"I hope those two we ran into aren't waiting somewhere to ambush us."

"I think Banachek hit one. The one who dropped their gun. We should be alright, besides, Angelov ordered the rest of the platoon to commence a floor-by-floor search. Let's get moving."

"Yeah, I heard those snipers are wrecking havoc on Alpha Company."

Malone lead the way up the stairs, taking them two at a time as they went from first to sixth floor. When they got to the seventh floor, he began to take them more slowly and quietly. He got up to the rooftop door and turned to face Higgins. He spun his finger to get the kid to turn around, then pulled a smoke grenade out of his field pack. He tapped him twice on his left shoulder and he turned back around. Malone held the grenade up for them all to see and motioned he was going to toss it out on the roof to give them some cover to take up firing positions. After everyone nodded their heads, he turned back to the door, turned the handle and gave it an inch push to see that it could move.

Malone held up his free hand, showing three fingers. He dropped them one at a time until none were left. At that point, he pushed the door outward as hard as he could and tossed the grenade, already smoking, out onto the roof. He ran across the roof, opposite to where the door now lay up against the wall and shoved one of the dining tables over to hide behind. He was able to make out three aliens turning towards the sound of the door crashing before the smoke got so thick it obscured everything.

He fired off three triple-round bursts to try and get the aliens' attention while his comrades piled in across the roof to find their own hiding places. As he dropped behind his barricade after his triple bursts, he saw a spark hit the wall behind him. He looked at the table and a hole had been drilled through it. It wasn't one large enough to get his rifle barrel through, it was the same size as the holes he'd seen the aliens cut into the houses back in Anora. The snipers were using a higher setting than the aliens they encountered earlier. They could punch through an inch of wood. Just to make sure, he lifted his rifle over the table and swung the barrel from side to side while firing off a twenty round burst.

He knocked on his table three times and waited for a returning signal. He got all three of his friends. Then using Morse code, he tapped out they should move their barricades forward ten feet before the smoke cleared. After he got the third response, he began pushing his table forward. He got nine feet before he ran into something that stopped his progress.

There was no hint of a breeze that day, so Malone was going to have to wait for diffusion to clear out the smoke. He was worrying about where the enemy might have moved to as the white smoke cleared.

Two of the aliens were still against the wall of the roof, while the other had moved to try to get off the roof. "Higgins, the door," he shouted, hoping his comrade would know what he meant. He heard a rapid fire response telling him Higgins had. "First clean shot, take it," he yelled to the others. Seconds later, he heard both of his companions firing on the aliens before the smoke had cleared enough for him to see.

When it finally did, two of the aliens were laying by the roof wall and the third blocking the entrance to the stairs but not moving.

"Sergeant Adams," Malone called into his communicator. "The roof is secured, sir."

The POW Camp

Chen flew the shuttle through the large hanger doors in the large oval section of the Nyumbani, one of the larger space fortresses the Earth sends to planets when it projects its space forces. Above and below the hundred foot tall oval were two cylinders around five hundred feet in either direction. The top half had all the office space needed to run whatever campaign the Earth Government had sent it to oversee. The lower half was the barracks area for the troops needed in that operation. Two levels of landing bays were packed into that oval, Chen was flying his shuttle into one of the upper bays.

As his posterior sensor passed through the magnetic screen, the large metal doors began sliding together to close off the landing area. Most of the shuttles were on the planet below somewhere, so most of the bay doors were open, protected from space by magnetic screens. Curtains of force fields protected the interior of each bay where shuttles could nestle into their allotted areas when aboard. While instruments indicated to his onboard display the flight path he was to take to his landing site, Chen was instead watching the men through his forward window directing him to where he was to set down for refueling and drop off his cargo. When the sensor for his fourth landing foot went green he cut the power to the engines and began switching the shuttle to grounded mode.

"Time to wake our guests up," He was on the PA to the two troopers in the personnel section of the shuttle. They had come along to keep an eye on the prisoners Captain Palmer had sent up.

"Roger, lieutenant." Chen switched his monitor over to view the prisoner removal. The view of the hanger disappeared from his side window and became that of the shuttle's personnel section where two soldiers crossed over from where they were sitting and undid the harnesses of their captives. One by one, they began nudging the prisoners up towards the shuttle's hatch. Chen could hear them giving instructions to their prisoners, but could see it was doing no good.

At least until the last prisoner undid his own harness and began standing up before either of the guards got to him. When the trooper saw this, he quickly stepped in front of the prisoner and commanded, "Get back in your seat." And before he had time to push the prisoner back into his seat, the prisoner was sitting back down.

After they all exited the shuttle, Chen found the department heads, who planned to investigate what he'd brought up, waiting for them. Cargo handlers opened the storage section doors and waited for the cold to wash over them as they adjusted to the refrigeration currently being used in the section. They rubbed their gloved hands together and began pulling out the stretchers with the dead aliens strapped to them. The aliens' equipment was stored in several duffel bags strapped into the personnel section where troops would have strapped their equipment, had they been aboard. They carried the bags into another room to be sorted.

While it wasn't the General that met the group, Chen knew what his aide looked like. He saluted before offering the man his hand. "Colonel Vermillan, I have the merchandise you ordered."

"Thank you, lieutenant." Then he turned to the half dozen MPs behind him. "You men help these soldiers take these prisoners to interrogation. I know Petersen and his boys are waiting to take a crack at their language."

As the MPs moved around the line of five men, the lead MP motioned the direction they should be going with her pistol. The aliens looked at the pistols and remembered what they could do. They offered no resistance to being lead further into the station. Vermillan turned back to Chen. "Are you heading back right away?"

"Captain Palmer asked me to stick around to see what you guys learn. If that meets with the Colonel's approval," Chen responded.

"Everybody's got to pull their weight around here, pilot." The Colonel drummed his fingers against the side of the shuttle Chen had just brought up. "I can't just have you waiting around for test results to come in. But I've got a mission for you that will allow you to be back up here early tomorrow and you can see what we've got by then. I know I'd be shitting my pants not knowing what these guys can do, if I were Palmer."

* * *

An hour later, Chen hovered over the cleared plot of land north of the village his company had been ordered to inspect. Captain Garzia was sitting in the co-pilot seat of the cargo shuttle looking for a good place for Chen to set down so his men could unload. "There, by the edge of the woods. The men can move the supplies and set up the camp a good hundred yards from them."

"I could park closer, sir."

"No, I want to control the open area outside our fenced perimeter. My boys can move this stuff." He reached over and patted Chen once on his right shoulder. "We might even find you some exercise, flyboy."

"Sir, I have to get back up to Command."

"Son, we're going to need your engines to inflate our habitats and harden them. So if you're in a hurry to get back upstairs, I suggest you help us get things set up. Grab one of the fence posts while I go take a look at the land."

Chen opened the hatch and the two of them left the cockpit while the other dozen MPs opened the back ramp and began moving crates out using forklift exo-suits. Garzia walked out into the middle of the mile-by-two-mile field. He stared at the landscape for a few minutes, then walked over to a spot about two hundred yards from any of the trees. He pulled a can out of his tool belt and sprayed a red X on the ground. He walked about six feet towards the lake and sprayed another X. He kept doing this as Chen finally got to the front of the line of MPs grabbing stuff from the back of his shuttle.

"Take this post over to where the captain marked its location," the MP directing the unloading said. He added, "Sir," upon seeing the bar on Chen's shoulder.

"Then what?" Chen asked.

"Set it in position and let it drill itself secure, sir."

51

Chen looked at the six foot of electronic equipment that had a six foot auger mounted on its base. "How?"

"Hank," said the MP behind Chen. "Give me one of those. Lieutenant, follow me. I'll show you how the thing works." The man lifted the twelve foot device onto his shoulder and made his way to where Garzia had marked locations.

"Put the tip of the auger where you want to secure the post, like this." He placed the point of the device on the middle of the X Garzia had made. He gave it a little push to imbed it in the soil. "Once you have it where you want it. Flip this switch and hold it in position until it's buried about a foot in the ground. Then let go and stand back. The auger will keep digging until it hits the point between the digging section and the fence post. Then it'll shut itself off and inject a foam around the auger blades to cement itself into the soil. Once it's in place, make sure you take the key out of the unit. We don't want the prisoners removing the posts making up the fence."

"Huh?"

"Once we're done with this camp, we flip the switch the other way, and the auger reverses itself and digs out of the foam. We can't have the fence dropping after we've filled the yard with POWs. Think you're up to trying?"

"It looks simple enough." Chen got another auger and started walking over to the next unattended X. He planted the auger and was about to flip the switch.

"Make sure you hang on." He jumped a bit but caught the post before it fell to the ground. He hadn't noticed the sergeant following him. "Sorry. The thing does have a mind of its own until it's a foot down. And flip the switch to the right, you won't get anywhere if you have the auger spinning backwards."

"Thanks. You gave me a fright there." He pushed the auger into the soil again and flipped the switch to the right. The post kicked, tried to swing from side to side, but settled down after it had drilled into the ground about a foot. Chen stepped back and watched the device drill its way into position. When it stopped, he reached over and pulled the key from its slot.

"One thing you don't have to worry about once you get these things going," said the sergeant. "Is it upright? There's a couple of gyros in each to keep them straight up and down. And the electric current that will be flowing between them is designed for bridging a twelve foot gap. We space them six foot apart to give ourselves a safety margin. Now let's go get some more and get this fence up."

They made their way back to the shuttle and were handed a couple more posts. The stack of them onboard was still eye level with the man handing them out and covered about half the floor of the back.

On his next trip for a post, Chen had to dodge one of the MPs carrying a ten-by-ten-foot box out of the hold. The box was a good twenty feet tall, so the MP couldn't see Chen coming. "What's in the box?" Chen asked as he was handed his next post.

"I didn't catch the marking," said the MP. "Could be a prisoner barracks, mess hall, or guard habitat. I sure hope they packed ones with mattresses this time. Metal sheeting is hard to fall asleep on." He handed Chen his post and went to pull one down for the woman behind Chen.

After about an hour, they had the perimeter defined. Chen took the opportunity to find out what was going on with the boxes. He walked up to the first one that had the sides of the crate it was in removed and set end to end on the ground. three men and two women were spreading the pliable material out over the wood from the crate.

Unfortunately, Garzia caught him watching. Chen felt the Captain's hand descend on his shoulder. "I see we've got the perimeter established. Good job. But now we have to get the habitats built. Grab an end of that hose and take it over to the shuttle. Attach it to the air supply on the port side. Then get back here and attach the other end to the habitat once they got it rolled out."

"Yes, sir." Chen walked over to the hose and looked for an end. It was a two inch diameter hose and he had to drape it over his shoulder to pull it towards the shuttle. It took him over five minutes to get it there, attached, and begin his return. By then the MPs had the building unrolled. They moved on to the box about twelve feet away and began unpacking it.

Garzia watched Chen make the hose connection to the building, after showing him the valve it had to hook into. Then he called to the MP in the shuttle to start the flow of air. The building began to do its final unfolding and took shape. In less than five minutes, it was standing up straight, like every other barracks Chen had seen. He couldn't resist the urge and had to push on the side of the building. "Sir, are you going to house them in a bouncy house?" he asked.

"No," Garzia answered. "See that electrical cord over there?" He took Chen over to the cord lying about five feet from the edge of the barracks. He reached down and pulled one end of it up. "Unlike the hose, there's a male and female end to this cable. Take this end back to the shuttle and plug it in on the same side you connected the hose to. I'll wait for you to get back so you can see how we harden these buildings."

This cable wasn't nearly as heavy as the hose he'd lugged earlier. He got to the shuttle and back in half the time. There he found Garzia had already plugged the other end into the side of the structure.

"Now watch this," he said to Chen as he again called to the MP inside manning the shuttle controls to engage the circuit. The grey of the rubbery building began to turn to a silvery color, as Chen watched the flexibility of it harden into something that might withstand a minor hurricane on Barratis 5, the windiest planet man had ever colonized. Chen reached over to touch it.

"Don't!" Garzia barked. When Chen froze, he explained. "There's enough current running through that building right now that somebody would have to be flying you back to Command for treatment rather than you flying back on your own." He looked into Chen's scared face and smiled. "I need all my men here. I couldn't waste one ferrying you. It'll be safe to touch once it's fully converted and we've removed the power."

It took under five minutes to fully convert the building.

Garzia ordered the power cut off and pulled the plug from the side of the building. "Now it's safe to touch." As Chen did, he added, "In fact, why don't you have a look inside? This is one of the barracks for the prisoners you guys captured."

Chen had just opened the door and was about to enter when he heard the loud thuds of the anchors being driven into the ground to hold the barracks in place. There were no steps, the barracks was kept off the soil by the packing crate it had come in. Inside, Chen found two rows of double bunk beds against the outer walls with enough space between the rows for the prisoners to walk to and from their bunks. The last three bunks on the left side of the barracks didn't exist. There was a space for a heating unit, if needed, or a small common area.

Remembering what the one MP had said, he touched one of the mattresses on the bunks. It was nice and soft. He lifted it up and the underside was composed of the same metal that the walls were made out of. "They've found a way to interrupt the conversion process," he said to no one. "Soft on one side and hard on the other."

He'd seen enough. He left the barracks and closed the door behind him. As he left the building, Garzia ordered him to disconnect the air line from the inflated barracks and connect the line to the building next to it. After it was inflated, he connected it up to the next building ready to be set up. Another MP was already stringing the electrical line. They had five more buildings to do before he could head back to the Nyumbani.

Mayor Krisson L'mere

Captain Palmer was becoming adept at paying attention to Mayor L'mere while listening to his translator. Some of the Lankmeran language was beginning to seep into his brain.

"Let me get this straight," he began his response. "You've never had a period in your history where your people attacked and killed each other? You've never had any wars?" Even Gus had a hard time translating the question, the Lankmerans had no word for war.

"Why would we?" She sat in her desk's chair today. Palmer could see agitated twitches all over her body, strong enough that her fur couldn't hide them. "Why would anyone want to kill their own kind? You don't eat each other, do you?"

"No. Humans do not eat each other, but they have had dozens of reasons to go to war. To force their will on one another; be it religious beliefs, desire for your neighbor's land, perceived insults to a state, to stop illegal actions against one another. We didn't need a really strong reason to go to war until we all came together in our desire to explore the stars and have space to live. Once petty nationalism stopped being a driving force in our lives, wars became a thing of the past.

"And war is what we are talking about here. I don't know what the enemy has against either of us. Hell, we don't even know who they are or where they're from. The only thing we're sure of is that they'll try again. We need to find a place where your people can stay protected from their laser weapons."

"I think the concert hall was built large enough to hold the entire town's population."

"Does Lankmere have a central governing body somewhere, someone that we can talk to and arrange protection for everyone?"

"There is no need. Each city takes care of the needs of its population. Larger institutions that come together to tackle a larger problem do so by contract, by working towards solving a single goal. Then they dissolve once the goal has been achieved. When the Kaltonian Research Organization was formed to research Lungtitus, Mucasballs, and Humpkins, it did so until cures were found and vaccines were discovered, then they disbanded. No, I'm afraid we have no, what you call, planetary government."

"Okay, we can worry about that later. Right now we have to get ready, in case the enemy comes back here again. Can you get enough supplies into that concert hall for your people to live in there for a few weeks? Not that I'm expecting them to have to, but in case whoever is trying to kill everyone decides to make a siege of it." Palmer got up from his chair and walked over to the window and looked down on the town, trying to make out which building was the concert hall.

"What is a siege?"

Research

"This is an interesting suit," began the technician. Chen had been taken to the mess hall for a quick supper before his tour through the lab to show him what the techs had discovered.

"It is not practical as an environmental suit. While it can hold air, the material will rupture if that air bubble is under a vacuum." Chen reached down to the red suit that was laying on the bench in front of him. There were a few more spread out along the bench and a pile of them down at the end opposite the one he was on. The fabric didn't have a natural feel to it. It felt like a plastic of some kind.

"Then why wear them?

"They'll protect the user in an atmosphere. Not a highly toxic atmosphere, they still allow some of the native air through the fabric, it's just that they can't stand the pressure if inflated in a vacuum. They do have other useful features. There are fibers throughout the suit which can act as electrical circuits to move things out of the way of the user. Given enough time, this suit should be able to dig a foxhole for its wearer. We haven't been able to test it, but we believe those fibers somehow act as a communication circuit for the wearer. Don't ask me why we believe that, it's just an idea we get if we hold the material long enough."

"Okay, they've got a super suit. What about their weapons?" the colonel asked as Chen turned the suit over and pushed his finger through the bullet hole in the chest area.

He felt a pocket just above the hole and stuck his hand in it. There was nothing in the pocket but as Chen looked over the suit he saw dozens of such pockets. "Did they have anything in these pockets?"

"There was something in every one of them," the technician said. "Follow me over here and we can discuss their tech." He turned and walked over to another bench a few feet away, but still in the middle of the cavernous cargo hold of the Nyumbani.

On the bench was laid out over a hundred sealed packets. Many had pills in them, some a clear liquid, others a different colored liquid; in fact, there were six different-colored liquids in plastic packages. There were spools of wire packaged up, along with several packages of small tools, not all of them the same. There were many other packets with things Chen couldn't identify.

"We've tested some of the pills," began the technician. "The ones with the white band on the top appear to be food capsules. The rest aren't. The red-striped ones appear to contain a gas inside them. When we opened one of them, it ate the oxygen in the surrounding air for approximately a minute. We had a couple of our technicians pass out when we opened it, but they recovered minutes later. Going for the oxygen says these guys have dealt with other alien species. Species of oxygen breathers, but a species they didn't have enough foreknowledge to know what knockout gas to use."

The technician reached over the pouches and grabbed one of the several different knives on the bench. He aimed it at the backboard on the bench and press the largest button on the hilt. The blade shot out of the knife and embedded in the backboard, two inches deep. "We haven't taken it apart yet. But if that's spring driven, it's one strong spring." He reached across the bench and worked the blade out of the steel back of the backboard. He pushed the blade back into place in the hilt. "And just like that, it's ready to go again. And if I press the button on the other side of the hilt," as he pressed it, a blue glow appeared around the blade, "it gets this color. Now the knife is as sharp as any monofilament blade we've tried to create."

"What can you tell me about their rifles," Chen asked again. "That's what the Captain is going to be most interested in."

"Oh, the rifles are the gems. We're going to have a field day when we get this technology back to Earth and deconstruct these babies. They have a range greater than our eyesight allows. Though when you get too far out, the power starts to drop off. The men you left here mentioned that reflective insulation in the

Lankmeran homes kept the beams from penetrating the houses. At the lowest setting its beams can be easily reflected, but as we ratcheted up the laser's power, it took thicker and thicker mirrors to reflect the beam. We tested Kevlar also. When set on half power the beams will cut through those plates. I wouldn't count on those defenses protecting you the next time you run into these guys."

"Any special sighting mechanisms?"

"No, but then we used to use lasers for sighting mechanisms. I don't think they need any. Another thing; at full power, these babies have the ability to sweep a target. It's a one-second sweep, but you can do a lot of damage in that second."

Chen turned to look up at Vermillan. "Have we gotten anything from the prisoners? I mean, why are they attacking us?"

"As of a half hour ago, the linguists reported that the prisoners haven't said anything." The Colonel held up his hand. "And until they do, the linguists have nothing to work with. We have to find a way to get these guys to talk."

"If they can talk." Chen looked over the items on the bench. "Do you have any idea what's in the black packets?"

"They seemed to have the same outer coating that the food capsules had, but we haven't had a chance to test them yet."

Chen picked a couple of them up. "Why do some of them have five pills, and others only four? Colonel, could they have gotten into those packets while your men lead them in?"

"Suicide pills?" The Colonel was across the hold in under two seconds and activating the room's monitor. "Brig. Brig. This is Colonel Vermillan. Come in."

"Colonel, could you hold on for a minute? We have an emergency down here right now. We're transferring the prisoners to the infirmary. They appear to have died."

Specialist Harry Malone

Sergeant Adams and Specialist Malone were standing next to the First Platoon's commander as the shuttle with the dozen prisoners they'd captured lifted off for the POW camp. Captain Garzia had reported to Captain Nilssen earlier that it was completed and ready to receive prisoners. The shuttle stayed low over the tree line and quickly disappeared from view.

Captain Nilssen turned to the borrowed second squad leader. "Have all the enemies' weapons and equipment been secured?"

"They're in the vault of the Second City Bank, sir," Adams replied. Both men had their own rifles slung, as they watched Lieutenant Angelov approaching. Malone was hoping they would be released so they could go back to their own platoon. To his way of thinking, Anova was not secured when they had left.

"Good. Command says they have enough up there. Who knows, maybe we can arm the populace down here and move on. Lt. Angelov, have your teams finished the emplacements for the second attack Surveillance says is coming?"

"I have two sniper nests set up on the office building's roof. The homes along the unplowed field have been reinforced; they're not bunkers, but they should slow these guys down. Houses on either side of the village have been fortified, just not all of them. Every third home has a two man team in it. You lost twelve men in that first assault, your First platoon barely had enough men to cover that many buildings. I had to grab spotters from Second platoon to help with the snipers. And Third platoon is dispersed throughout the woods, scouting for the enemy, sir."

"Sounds like you and my Lieutenants have everything well in hand. You might as well load your platoon up and head back to Captain Palmer." Just then, several loud whining noises could be heard from the east. "What was that?"

"Captain Nilssen," the communicator in his pocket said. "Captain Nilssen, this is Sergeant Okoro. We're under fire. Lieutenant Danvers has been hit and her troops are carrying her back to a secured position. No other casualties at the moment, but we can see a medium body of enemy troops assuming a kneeling firing position, just out of rifle range. Please advise, sir"

"Hold your position," the Captain looked over to the two shuttles still sitting by city's fishing docks. "I'm sending you some air support."

She released the switch on the side of her communicator, then tapped it twice to cycle through the frequencies to the shuttle pilots' channel. "Walters, Michaelsen. Get your birds in the air. Ground forces east of town are harassing our people. Give them a break."

"Roger, sir," came separate responses from the two pilots.

As the shuttles blew air onto Malone and moved to engage the enemy, Captain Nilssen turned to Angelov. "You have any mortars or long range weaponry in that shuttle of yours?"

"Yes, Ma'am." She turned to Sergeant Adams. "Break out the artillery and missile launchers and get them out to those men."

"Yes, Sir," the sergeant responded, then turned to Malone.

Malone was already running to the shuttle. "I know the drill, sarge." Their shuttle was the last one at the docks, but he was up the ramp in under a minute. He went back to the munitions locker and began pulling the four mortar launchers and the single rocket grenade launcher they had in it. As he was turning to the second bin, the rest of his squad started arriving. "Higgins, Hamidi, get these mortars out to the houses by the field. Roberts, Kozlov, and Banachek, grab the cases of shells and follow them. Tersoo, you grab the rockets and follow me." Malone stepped back to the first locker and extracted the six-by-six-foot rack to hold the rockets in position for launching.

He was halfway to the hatch when he glanced back and saw Tersoo dragging the two boxes. He set the rack against the door and walked back over to the new recruit. "Don't they teach you guys anything in basic these days?" he said as he worked his fingers under the edge of the lowest boxes' lid and found the switch he was searching for. He flipped it and the box rose a foot off the floor, carrying the other box with it. "Use the anti-grav." He hurried back over to the rack and down the ramp.

As he emerged from the shuttle, Higgins was on the ground holding his knee. The whining he had heard earlier was coming from the houses bordering the waterfront. "Tersoo, stay in the shuttle," he hollered back, as he dropped the rack he'd been carrying and swung his rifle around to answer the incoming fire. He dropped low, shot off three separate bursts, grabbed Higgins by his backpack and pulled him behind the closest building.

"Where the hell did they come from?" Malone asked Higgins, who was rolling off his back, trying to take up a prone firing position while shoving his pain med dispenser back in his lower leg pocket.

"They just appeared from nowhere," he replied as he crawled up to the side door and shoved it into its wall pocket. He had a clear view of the red lights appearing in the windows of the adjacent building. "I think everyone else got under cover. But no one got down the street to deliver our goods."

"Which we could use right about now, except both of us were carrying the launchers not the missiles. How many rounds you got in your grenade launcher?"

"I got a full load of three."

"Get your targeting computer to work out a firing solution to put one in that window over there." Malone pointed to one not quite in the middle but it had the most red lights in it.

"I'd never be able to do this without that pain shot," his voice sounded clearer. "Those things work wonders."

"Just make sure you drop one in that window before you're overcome by bliss."

"Don't be such a party poop. I feel great and the computer's on target." He fired off the round that broke through the glass of the upper of the window pair. Seconds later, the grenade detonated, blowing out part of the wall with it. Five enemy troopers fell onto the fragments of the blown wall. Malone saw a couple more dead through the hole and the lights in the other windows close by dying off.

"Nice shot," Malone said. When he didn't get a reply, he looked over to Higgins. He had rolled away from the door and was fast asleep. Malone reached into the pocket, his friend had slipped the injection tube into. Of the two tubes in it, the seal was broken on the Morphsidenal. It was the maximum pain medication the troops carried, to only be used in the direst of circumstances. Unfortunately, it and Acedocordine pain reliever came in similar vials, you couldn't distinguish by touch. Higgins had forgotten to look at the labels in his rush for pain relief. "Well, he's out for the rest of the day," Malone said as he replaced the injector.

Malone triggered Higgin's medic signal and grabbed the man's rifle. He was still waiting for the day they'd issue him a grenade-equipped unit. He took aim at the window two over from where Higgins had cleared and launched another grenade. It had the same results, except only two bodies fell out this time.

Malone drug Higgin's body away from the door and took inventory. He had two trooper rifles, one an EE-19 and the other an EE-19G with a single grenade round. He didn't have time to go through Higgins pack to see if he had any more explosive clips. He had a rocket launcher and a mortar, but not the rounds for either. Unless he could think up a way for Tersoo to get over here.

Malone looked around at what building he was in. Fishing supplies, both personal and trawler. Even a few spears. He did find a selection of spear guns, but they couldn't do much against the lasers he found himself facing.

Wait, maybe the spears, Malone thought to himself. *Tersoo has the boxes in anti-grav mode. She could shove them across the street, and if they get close enough, I could harpoon them.*

He yelled across the street to Tersoo and told her what he wanted her to do. The next thing Malone saw was the boxes emerging from the shuttle and lining up on the building he was in. Then they came rushing in his direction. Due to the direction the ramp was pointed, they came over the side of the ramp about half way down. The anti-grav field lowered them to within a foot of the ground and the parcels made it about half way across the street before their momentum gave out.

"Damn," Malone exclaimed. "I can't reach them."

"I'll get them," he heard Tersoo call over.

"You just stay where you are, missie," Malone yelled back.

He shucked his pack and called over. "Give me continuous covering fire. See if you can't dismantle that building across from me." As soon as he heard Tersoo's rifle go full auto, Malone raised the spear gun he had already prepared. He took aim at the center of the crate and fired his first round. It fell short of the box by three feet. Malone pulled the rubber tube of the gun back and locked it into place. Then he took aim over the top of the box and fired again. This time the spear lodged into the center of the boxes' side. He pulled the crate over to him in under a minute.

Rockets give off a distinctive sound as they are launched, and as they connect with whatever they are fired at. After Malone leveled the homes with a lake front view in the city and he, along with Tersoo, were walking the rubble of his achievement, looking for alien survivors, Captain Nilssen was on the company circuit. "Whoever's on the waterfront, what's going on over there?"

"Specialist Malone here, sir. Several enemy combatants came out of the lake and were attacking from our rear. Specialist Higgins has been injured. Corporal Tersoo and myself have contained the incursion, but we had to expend the entire rocket rack to do so. We think one of the enemy combatants may have gotten away, back into the lake. All the rest have been terminated."

"Malone, stay where you are. I'm heading your way."

"Roger that, captain." Malone looked over to Tersoo, who was skipping a rock across the lake. "You're sure you saw something?"

"I'm sure a glass dome disappeared under water moments after the explosion." She picked up another piece of flat-sided concrete and skipped it across the lake.

Mayoral Briefing

It was about a half hour after Malone had briefed Nilssen about their engagement that the rest of his squad came down Main Street to the Listener platoon shuttle. At least all of them except for Corporal Liu.

"Hey Malone." began Specialist Hanks of third squad. "I see you found a way to sit this one out." He got right up to Malone's ear and whispered, "How'd you do it?"

Malone pushed the trooper away. "We didn't get out of the action. These guys," he pointed over to the bodies he and Tersoo had been piling up for disposal after searching each one for whatever they could find, according to Nilssen's orders, "attacked from the lake. We've had our own little war back here, protecting you guys' behind."

"Use up all the rockets?" Lieutenant Angelov asked, coming down the road.

Malone snapped to attention. "No, sir. We only needed the first box. The buildings came down quite nicely on their heads."

"One did get away, ma'am," Tersoo added.

"Corporal Tersoo, we've gone over this in several briefings. You will address me as Sir, the same as you would were I a man."

"Yes, ma'— sir!"

She turned back to Malone. "I hear Higgins got hit. How bad is he?"

"He got wounded in the leg, but he grabbed the wrong pain med. He'll be out of it for some time, sir."

"The mortars you sent us did the trick. We drove most of the attackers off with minor casualties. But I'm worried now about Bravo Company, especially after what you just told me. Get the rockets back into the shuttle; Sergeant Adams is bringing in the mortars and equipment. Sergeants Singh and Wilcox are rounding up the rest of the platoon. We're heading back to Anora."

"Roger, lieutenant," Malone replied.

"Yes, ma—" Malone hit Tersoo on the back of her head before she could finish. "Ah, sir."

The story was a little better when they got back to their own unit. Headhunter platoon was cleaning up the homes on the west end of the village when the enemy appeared out of the woods again. They got under cover with only Yang taking a hit to his shoulder. As enemy troops were emerging from the lake, Lieutenant Simmons was returning from his prisoner run to the POW camp. He had been providing aerial support as the platoon found whatever cover they could. The water troops were dispatched in minutes, allowing Simmons to bring hell from the sky on the enemy coming out of the woods. As Simmons was racking the enemy in the woods with fire, Headhunter platoon emerged from the houses they were using for cover. The platoon split into squads and covered the field in moments. By the time they'd arrived, the enemy had abandoned their position to head back wherever they came from.

* * *

The Earth commanders set up the Command Conference room in the Mayor's office. Captain Palmer wanted to keep the city officials in the loop as to what the Earth Forces were planning. They'd installed the communications unit on her desk and moved enough chairs into the room to seat all of Palmer's Lieutenants and Sergeants, along with over a dozen Anora city officials in front of the desk. Captain Nilssen's image was the first to be broadcast above the unit, followed shortly after by Colonel Vermillian and Captain Pangestu. Once everyone was present, General Chi logged into the conference.

"Okay, we have a problem," the general began. "We've had six separate engagements with an unknown adversity. Who apparently believes in shoot first, ask questions... Hell, we haven't even determined if they can ask questions. The linguists up here haven't got our prisoners to say anything, nor make any sounds. As far as the autopsies determined, their mouths are just used for eating and breathing. They don't appear to have vocal cords like we do."

"And scenting the air, general," said a man in a lab coat off to the general's left. "They have no noses."

"Okay, fine," he said to the technician before turning back to the screen. "But we haven't found any way to communicate with them. We don't know what they want or why they're killing every person they see. Just sentient life at that, we've seen no traces of animal kills. Have we?"

"No, sir!" They all responded.

"And right now, the animal life is very plentiful in the surrounding woodlands," Mayor L'mere said. "Hunting season is about to begin. I would have thought the Kranslyn would have challenged them for territory as they came here."

"The Kranstons," the General tried to replicate the word. "Oh, never mind. We have to figure out some way to protect the population of Lankmere and drive these enemy off. Can someone find out what these guys are called? I'm tired of referring to them as the enemy."

"Sir," said Captain Palmer. "We're going to have to find somewhere we can move the Lankmerans to, in order to provide a safer environment."

"Move," reacted Mayor L'mere. "This is our home. We ceased being nomads several millennia ago. We need to find a way to stay with the community we have built. Mayor D'thon, do you feel the same way? Mayor Z'coen?"

After they failed to answer. "Where are the mayors of the other lakefront towns?"

"Mayor Z'coen died in the enemies' first assault," responded Captain Pangestu.

"Mayor D'thon is treating the injured with the other doctors of Minor. He felt his time would be better spent there," reported Captain Nilssen.

"Well, if you ask any of the people of Lankmere, they won't want to move away from their homes. No, you must find another way to protect us. Or a way for us to get close enough to strike at our enemy. We have claws and can defend ourselves. I do not like this word, enemy; sentient beings should not be enemies. We should work together for the betterment of everybody. We must find out why this race of beings is trying to kill us."

"We been trying to do that, Your Honor. We still haven't been able to find out how they communicate with each other," General Chi replied. He turned around as a technician tapped him on the shoulder and handed him a note. "Excuse me a second." His image disappeared from above Mayor L'mere's desk.

"It must be something important to interrupt the General," Palmer commented.

"Otherwise, we'll have an opening in the tech section," Pangestu finished for him.

"In the mean time," Colonel Vermillan decided to keep the meeting going. "I'm assuming you're meaning that you don't want to go off planet, Madame Mayor. You do travel around Lankmere, don't you?"

"Yes, we travel freely between our population centers," she answered.

"Good," Nilssen answered. "We weren't sure, since we didn't find any major highways leading out of town, just dirt roads."

"What are roads?" she asked.

"It's how you get from place to place in your automobiles. Usually they're about twice as wide as the streets you have around Anora," Palmer explained to her.

"What is an automobile?"

"For Kilroy's sake," Vermillan exclaimed. "How do you get from town to town?"

Mayor L'mere looked at the projected images and the men sitting around her. "By flyer. How do you get around?"

"They've got bombers," Palmer exclaimed before anyone else could.

"As long as we can reinforce them against the enemies' laser weapons," Pangestu finished. "Colonel, have the tech boys come up with anything to protect us from those lasers? Apparently the enemy has a setting high enough to punch through our Kevlar."

"Not yet," he responded. "We haven't even tried the top setting, fearing it would burn a hole through our hull."

General Chi's image reappeared above the desk. "Linguistics thinks its figured out how these guys communicate, but it won't do us any good. The reason they wear those helmets is to keep a particular chemical near them. As the chemical goes in the right side and out the left it establishes... Hell, you tell them." He handed the papers back to the technician who had brought them in.

"Good afternoon, everyone." The General moved aside and let a white-coated man who was shorter than Chi and wearing a five-day growth on his jaw. The clothing he had on under the coat appeared rumpled, as if he'd been sleeping in it for days. "My name is Hans Schmidt, head of research up here. We've discovered the helmets can only sublimate, that is, add additional gases to the breathing air if it's already at ambient pressure. They are not good in space or at very great depths of water. What they appear to be designed to do is pass along a pheromone through the tongue of the wearer and acts as a link to every other person experiencing that chemical. We believe they have a chemical means of communication. They neither talk, nor do they hear."

"So that means we're not going to find out why they are here from them," the General said. "But our main problem right now is finding a way to keep the Lankmeran population safe while we go out and check on the rest of the planet. You gentlemen are the only combat unit we brought for this mission, and right now, the MP division is holding down a POW camp north of your position. Mayor L'mere, do you have any ideas on how to secure your people?"

"Sir, while you were gone," began Colonel Vermillan, "we began discussing moving the Lankmeran people to a place where we can establish a defensive perimeter that a single platoon can maintain. Leaving the other two free to check out the remaining cities on this planet."

"What will you require to make that happen? Assuming, of course, we can't bring them up here."

"No sir, they won't go for that. But if we equip the armored troop carriers with rapid firing guns and send down some artillery. We can back that up with the flyers the Lankmerans already use, assuming we can harden them against the enemies' laser weapons.

Sir, I think we can build a fortress to protect these cities. Once we get all the people in one place."

"So ordered, colonel. We need to get our men out into the rest of the planet, we have no idea what the enemy has been doing out there."

Making The Kill

The hills to the northeast of Anora were chosen to build the fortress. A stream came down from the mountains further east to supply water. The weather monitoring station the Lankmerans had on the hilltop acted as the construction office. Living units with programmable matter external structure were dropped and placed in a ring around the station. The walls had been hardened to Kevlar strength and were covered with a reflective surface. An entrance was left in the northern-most point where armored vehicles didn't have to drive downhill a great distance, the land slightly dipped into a plateau for several miles before beginning to rise into the mountain range around the area.

"Malone," Captain Palmer called after a member of his platoon. Malone had been assigned, with two others, to train the Lankmerans in how to use the laser rifles. "How are the Lankmerans doing?"

"They're natural shots, sir." He saluted his commanding officer and continued. "They should have no trouble putting down the enemy, if he chooses to storm this encampment."

"Put down?" Mayor D'thon had been coming off the firing range to check on his progress with his instructor. "Do you mean kill?" His translation device had equated 'put down' with 'kill'. He tossed his rifle to the ground at Malone's feet.

"This is war," Captain Palmer said. "It's kill or be killed. You're learning to use those laser rifles to man the outer barracks to repel any enemy attack. And to do that, you will have to kill them. As they want to do to you."

"Killing a creature from a distance is not the way it is meant to be. If you must kill something, it must be up close. You must feel the life they are giving up to your attack. Chase them down, claw and tooth, those are the ways of the kill. Not beams of light over long distances. We thought this was a new sport you were introducing us to. Not a new way, a disgusting way, of killing. No, we will not kill them using these rifles."

Palmer crossed his arms in front of his chest. "Then how do you propose to keep them from killing you?"

"We must find a way to communicate with them."

"They don't talk!" Palmer replied. "They seem to use chemicals to communicate with each other. Even though the science teams upstairs have worked out what the chemicals are, we still don't know how they encode their messages in those chemicals. We can't communicate with them."

"But we will not shoot them," the mayor replied before turning back to the firing range and addressing all the Lankmerans training there. After his speech, they all laid their weapons down and walked back to their assigned barracks.

"This just got a whole lot tougher," Palmer said under his breath.

Malone stood there, thinking for a minute, before saying, "Do they have to kill them?"

"What?"

"I mean, what if they just wounded the oncoming forces? Leg shot, arm shot, burst their helmet. All of those things has to make the enemy soldier useless on the battlefield. And if he has to be removed, it would tie up more of their forces."

"I'm not crazy about the idea. Any wounded soldier could be made well enough to return to the battlefield. But let's see if the Lankmerans will go for it." He turned to go to the barracks where the mayors were housed and Malone along with him. The next group of Lankmeran trainees was approaching, led by Mayor L'mere.

When she was within three feet of the Earth soldiers, she tossed the rifle she was carrying to the ground. Then she pointed to two spots on either side of her and the three dozen Lankmerans following her tossed theirs there.

"We will not distance kill." She turned to go.

"Then don't kill," Malone said as fast as he could. "Stop the enemy without using lethal force. Wound them, hurt them enough that they have to be returned to a health center for treatment.

Somewhere where they can't try and kill you. Just get them off the battlefield."

She thought about it for a moment. Then called down to the western end of the encampment for the other mayors to join her. "This is not an easy decision. The only Deacon we had in the Lake community was killed in the first raids. The other mayors and I will have to deliberate on this idea. It must not violate the initial edict."

"I already told them we won't distance kill a sentient," D'thon said as he approached the gathering.

"They are proposing another strategy. One I am not sure does not violate that precept. We must deliberate on this idea."

"So what do they have in mind?" Mayor D'thon asked as he approached the others.

L'mere explained to the other mayor what Malone had suggested. At first D'thon objected, but he was unsure about the ramifications of strict adherence to the Edicts and Precepts.

"No one has ever suggested this before," D'thon began. "We have never been in a situation like this. We are not killing. And while we are depriving the enemy of freedom of movement, they wish to deprive us of life. The former is a Precept and the latter an Edict. Edicts carry more weight than Precepts. One could argue that we are violating a Precept to keep the enemy from committing a greater violation, that of an Edict. I say we try the Earthmen's idea."

"At least until we can consult a Deacon," L'mere offered an out for D'thon. "We can send to Pantropolis for one. The Earthmen want to go there anyway. I will volunteer to go myself."

"Very well, if you think this will work, Bergland will not object."

They turned back to the waiting Earthmen. "Mr. Malone, we are in agreement to try your suggestion. We will stop the enemy by in-ca-pac-i-tating him. Is that the right word?"

Captain Palmer responded, "Yes. And I'm glad for your decision." He turned to the specialist standing beside him. "Malone, get targets remade. Head and body shots blacked out, no points. And add a dome as a target. I think breaking those might cause a bit of confusion in their ranks."

"Right away, sir." Malone turned to walk over to the weather station turned command complex. It was where they were keeping the printers large enough to generate human-sized targets.

Specialist Harry Malone

Gambler platoon of Charlie Company was considered the party platoon of the entire Earth expeditionary force, so they were given the task of finalizing the training of the Lankmerans and entertaining them while the rest of the battalion went off to check out the other cities on Lankmere. It would have been a smoother ride to have traveled at sixty thousand feet, but here at two hundred, they had better eyes on the ground, in case the enemy made another push against the natives.

"What have these guys got against the Lankmerans, anyway?" Banachek leaned over to ask Malone.

"I don't have the faintest idea," Malone responded from his seat.

Across the open area between the two rows of strapped-in soldiers, Sergeant Adams leaned forward to allow Banacheck to hear him over the low rumble the shuttle was making. "The linguists up in Nyumbani haven't figured out a way to communicate with these guys. They have no vocal cords and seem to talk to each other through chemicals. I understand they are trying to teach them sign language to get some dialog going, but the enemy is resisting their efforts. At least they got their suicide pills away from them this time." Adams leaned back into his seat.

"How long we got to go, sarge?" Higgins, who was sitting two seats down from Malone, asked.

Adams pulled down his helmet monitor to note their ETA. "Okay, everyone," he said into his squad's channel. "Get ready, we're on final approach. This shuttle will set down in ten minutes, which means I want you on the ground in eleven."

Malone made a check of all the zippers on the pockets and packs he was carrying. Made one last check of his seat restraints. He mentally tagged his helmet and rifle for a fast exit off the shuttle and waited for the signal to deploy his friends out of the shuttle.

The minutes it took the landing gear to screech across the city flyer zone stretched longer than the rest of the flight to the city Mayor L'mere had labeled Pantropolis. But they finally quieted down and the green of the disembarkation light came on as the exit ramp began to drop to the ground.

Malone slapped the release button on his restraints with his left hand and reached for his helmet above his head with his right. He tapped the connections for his helmet by slapping the top of it. Then he spun to grab his rifle as he stepped forward to descend the ramp. He was lining up with the rest of his platoon seconds before the deadline Sergeant Adams had imposed.

Lieutenant Angelov was already on the ground using hand signals to direct her troops to their prearranged positions. First squad was to occupy the landing field's tower and set up a sniper loft there. Sergeant Adams and Malone's second squad were to move to the town's main street and begin checking the buildings heading east. Third squad went down the main thoroughfares on the right side of the town and fourth squad took the ones on the left.

Adams broke the squad into two teams, one taking the north side of the street and Malone's group taking the south side. Malone opened the door of a store and let the rest of his team in. It took no time at all to secure the main floor. Nobody was there, at least no one alive. Several Lankmeran bodies were scattered around, mostly in the clothing department, but as before, there were no enemy soldiers present.

They moved up the stairs to the second floor to check out the offices located there. Again they found Lankmeran bodies, but none of the enemy. After they checked out the loft on the third floor, they made their way out of the store and into the bakery just across the alley. Again they found the same scene; Lankmeran bodies, and no aliens.

Banachek, who had never seen this kind of carnage before, was the first to state the obvious. "They're all dead." He placed his hand on the next door to pull it open. "All of them. Why are they all dead?"

"Banachek, get a grip on yourself," Malone said as the junior soldier was about to open the door. "We still have a job to do." He placed his hand on Banachek's before he could pull that door. "And if we don't do it by the book, some of us might be lying there dead with these Lankmerans. Make sure your team's ready before you pull that door."

They found the cashier of the floral shop, laying behind the counter with a hole burned through her skull. No one else was in the shop and nothing was disturbed. Malone and Banachek emerged from the back room to find the rest of their unit waiting to move on.

"What's it all for?" Hamidi asked. He picked up one of flowers held in plastic buckets on counters around the shop. He stared into it like it held the answers he was waiting for. "Why is the enemy doing all this killing? They're not occupying the land. They're not looting. They're not taking anything. They can't be a religious disagreement. They can't even talk to the Lankmerans. Why are they killing all of them?"

Malone took the flower from Hamidi and placed it back into its bucket. "We're not going to get any answers in here. We need to keep moving. If we can find even one Lankmeran still alive, they might be able to tell us what happened here. But we won't if we stand around here whining about not knowing. Now let's move out." He pushed the door open and walked onto the sidewalk, holding the door for the rest of them to emerge from the shop.

They spent the next hour going from building after building, not finding anyone alive until word came over the platoon channel help was needed freeing a Lankmeran trapped under debris in a tanning factory. Squad three had found a survivor.

The location given was about seven blocks from the location Malone's group was in, so he gave the word for his team to hurry over to the animal processing facility and see what they could do to help. As he pulled open the doors to enter, he was glad he had one of the translation apps the linguistics teams had prepared for them.

"Careful, I think my leg is tangled in the wiring and blades of this fur remover," he heard as he walked in the door. "Pull the wrong way and you could cut my leg off."

"Pull those blades out gently," Malone heard Sergeant Wilcox say as he turned into the room where everyone was working. The room was three stories high, with several vats of rank-smelling chemicals. Skins were hanging from a line ready to be placed in the vats. Where the third floor would have been was a catwalk running between the vats. The catwalk was broken close to the wall Malone had come through and there was a break in the line of vats. That walkway and vat were now laying on top of the trapped Lankmeran as Sergeant Wilcox's crew was trying to rescue him.

"Malone, get your men's butts over here." Wilcox had turned his head as daylight from the opening door caught his eye. "We've got to untangle this guy before we can pull him out. Be careful, the vat brought the scraping blades down with it."

"Rifles here," Malone pointed to a bare patch of the wall. "And get busy. we've got a lot of tonnage to move." His men moved alongside those of Wilcox and began pulling wire, after conduit, after sharpened steel blade, after beam off the wounded man. The vat had reached the floor before the Lankmeran had, and he was not completely under it. Though from the movement of the vat, Malone realized that it could easily roll over unto the man if they weren't careful about how they removed things. Then they'd have to send for cutting equipment, unless they could figure out how to work the crane mounted to the roof.

"The crane," Malone exclaimed as the idea struck him. "Sergeant, sergeant. We have to send someone up to the ceiling crane and see if it's still working. This vat is ready to roll over this man. If we can move the vat out of the way, some of this mess might go along with it."

Wilcox looked up at the ceiling where Malone was pointing. "Now, how'd I miss that? Take who you need, get up there and get that hook down here where we can use it."

"Right away, sergeant. I think you've got a great idea."

"Move it, Malone."

Malone grabbed Hamidi and Banachek. The three of them made their way up the stairs mounted against the wall, two steps at a time, until they reached the uppermost catwalk a level above the one that had collapsed.

"Hamidi, check out the junction box over there. Make sure the crane has power. Banachek and I will try to work out how the thing operates.

"Right away, sir."

"Don't call me 'sir'." But Hamidi had already stepped between them and was running down the gantry.

Malone and Banachek picked up their pace also, but they only had half the distance to cover. They climbed over the protective railing and onto the walkway that led to the crane operator's box. Malone pulled open the door as Banachek stepped into the cabin.

"I wish this translation app would work on the printed word," Banachek said as he stared at the gibberish on the crane's control board. "I can't tell which switch does what."

"Look for a joystick or a trackball or some sort of moveable control." Malone worked his way behind the seat Banachek was sitting in. "Like that," he reached over the younger man's shoulder and pointed to a handle standing up from the control board. Does it move?"

"Yes."

"Great, that should control the hook. Now look to the left of it, assuming this thing was built for a right-handed operator. The startup control should be somewhere over there."

"You got power," Hamidi said over the communicator.

A moment later, after they tried a few of the buttons with the crane only making some discordant noises, they heard Wilcox call them. "The green button. The guy down here says the green button starts it. And there should only be one green button."

"Let's give the green button a try," Malone said as he pointed to a button that was green off to the right of the control lever.

Banachek pressed the indicated button, and dials, displays and lights in the cabin came to life. He grabbed hold of the joystick and pushed it forward. The crane moved towards the wall that had the stairs mounted on it. He drove the crane over to where the Lankmeran was pinned, then moved it to the left until he was right over the man.

He stopped and looked over the cabin's controls, then turned around to look at Malone. "Okay, now how do we raise and lower the hook?"

Malone spent another minute looking over the controls until he saw a depressed panel to the right of the joystick. It was about two inches by four inches in size. "Try sliding that open," he pointed to it. Banachek tried sliding the panel up. Nothing happened. Then he tried moving his finger down the panel and the hook began to descend.

"That's it," Malone exclaimed. "Touch pad control. Get that hook down there."

Banachek lowered the hook as fast as he could. But someone had put safety governors into the device, it would only drop about six inches per second no matter how fast he drew his finger down the control panel.

Malone looked, saw the floor of the controller's cabin was clear. He could see that Wilcox had moved away from the debris pile and was motioning with his arms to keep the hook lowering. After a couple of minutes, he crossed his arms to tell Malone to stop his descent.

"Freeze." Malone had to resist the urge to grab Banachek's hand off the controls, though the kid had given him no reason to think he should treat him that way. Banachek stopped all movement of his hand at the command.

Malone watched the men on the ground run a large wide belt around the vat and drop the loops sewn into the ends over the hook of the crane. Wilcox checked the belt, then he looked up to Malone in the crane cabin and motioned to him to raise the vat.

"But keep doing it slowly," he told Banachek. "There. Stop. That's where the Sergeant wants it. Now drop the cover back over the touch pad." As Banachek did, Malone grabbed his right fist with his left hand to signal to Wilcox. "It's locked down, sarge," he said, though Wilcox couldn't hear him. It was the hand gesture that sent the message.

"We'll hold it there until we get him out," Malone heard Wilcox say over their channel. They waited, it took Wilcox's men fifteen minutes to get the Lankmeran pulled out of the entangling debris pile.

The Lankmeran tried to walk once he was free, but Malone saw Wilcox was having his men carry him from the premises. Then he heard the sergeant call him again, "Malone, everyone's clear. Drop the vat and get your men out of here."

"Roger that, sarge. On our way."

Hospital Care

Lieutenant Lattimer, the field doctor for the battalion, walked out of the Lankmeran hospital trying to find where Captain Nilssen or any of the other Captains were hiding. Specialist Lund, Lattimer's assistant, was watching their patient, saw Lattimer emerging. "Did you find anything we could use in there?"

"Nothing." Lattimer continued walking to the center of the town in hopes someone was there that could give him the authorization he needed to work on this patient. "Come along. Malone, keep an eye on our patient."

Lund turned to Malone. "If he begins to regain consciousness or starts thrashing around, contact me immediately. If he starts moving, keep him on the cart until we can get back here." Then he trotted after his boss. "So what are your plans?"

"We need to get that man up to the space station and into a proper medical facility. One where I can read the goddamned labels."

"Do we know enough about their physiology?"

Lattimer turned his head to the right, "There she is." Then he turned and headed in that direction. "Nilssen can have one of the doctors we saved in the other towns sent up to the Nyumbani. With all the crushed bones that man has, I have no idea which of his organs might be damaged." The lieutenant grabbed for his communicator before deciding to run after the captain instead. "Captain Nilssen, Captain Nilssen. Wait up. I need to talk to you." Lattimer picked up the pace and before he knew it, Lund was breathing hard from running to keep up with him.

Lund stopped right behind his lieutanent, bent over to place his hands on his knees while he caught his breath.

Lattimer didn't need to as he was not even breathing hard and so went right into what he had wanted to talk to the captain. "Sir, I cannot do anything for the Lankmeran we found in the rubble. I need to get him up to the facilities on the Nyumbani. I need to work with equipment I know and medications I can read."

Lund stood up, took a couple of deep breaths and added, "And a Lankmeran physician. We also need someone who knows what's going on with Lankmeran physiology."

Nilssen looked from one man to the other and held up her hand as Lieutanent Dee-Jung began to interrupt. She stared at Lattimer in the way Specialist Lund knew the captain was waiting for an action plan.

"Can you get us a shuttle up to the Nyumbani and arrange for someone to send up a Lankmeran doctor to meet us there?" Lattimer requested.

"Get your patient down to the landing area. I'll have Jarhead waiting to take you up." She reached over and pulled her communicator from her pocket. "Williams, get down to Anoca and see if you can locate a Lankmeran doctor to transport up to the Nyumbani. Meet Lieutanent Lattimer there. Inform the doctor, there will be a patient that needs his attention." She turned her head and looked into Lattimer's eyes. "What are the two of you waiting for? Get moving, we need someone to survive from this town. He might give us a clue as to what happened."

Both men saluted their commander, turned and ran back the way they had come.

* * *

Lieutenant "Jarhead" Simmons brought his shuttle down near the building where they were housing the wounded Lankmeran, but kept his engines hot. They were planning on him taking off as soon as the patient was loaded. Malone and Lund scrambled into the back of the shuttle as the rear ramp was being lowered. They released the catches, dropped the center weapons rack onto the shuttle floor and rolled it out on its anti-gravs. With a full six feet of space between the two rows of seats, they began pushing the gravity-less gurney into the back of the shuttle.

Switching off the anti-gravity plating, they lowered the gurney to the floor and engaged the clamps that would hold it in place while they made their way up to the Nyumbani. Lund pressed the intercom button to the cockpit, "Ready back here."

"Strap in," Jarhead replied. "I'm taking her up."

The shuttle had to go vertical for the first hundred feet before it cleared all the undamaged buildings of Pantropolis. From there, Lieutenant Simmons switched from his gravitational lifters to his booster engines, pulled the nose up and lifted his shuttle towards space and the orbiting Command Center.

Doctor Lattimer was glad Lieutenant Dae-Jung had sent another shuttle back to Anoca city to find a Lankmeran doctor to meet them at the space station. Lattimer could easily see where his patient had broken bones. What he didn't see was the internal damage, or where the bones should be, once they were set. There was also a vessel leaking fluids and without the knowledge of Lankmeran anatomy, he could do more harm than good. He knew he would have to rely on the expertise of the native surgeons to treat this poor fellow.

About an hour after leaving the ground, Lattimer's shuttle was setting down in the large hanger bay of the Nyumbani. Malone and Lund waited for Lattimer to check his patient before they moved him from the shuttle and into sick bay. As he made his way around the outside of the shuttle, Lattimer could see another one waiting to land. Unfortunately, Simmons took the first available space due to his critical passenger.

Lattimer pulled his portable scanner out of its pouch and ran it over the areas of the patient he'd been concerned about. Held it up for a closer look, then waved it over the patient once more to be sure. "Get him to Sick Bay," he instructed Lund.

The two men who'd been waiting went to the head and foot of the stretcher. Lund activated the gravity compensaters on the gurney and started moving it off the shuttle. Malone lent his efforts to pushing it from the head, after which, Lund just had to steer it where he wanted it to go.

"Slow down," Lund said as Malone bounced the gurney out of the shuttle. "Okay, let's go," Lund said after they'd cleared the shuttle. The two men picked up the pace as Lund led Malone to the station's medical facilities.

Lattimer was standing beside the shuttle as Simmons raised the ramp. He watched as the waiting shuttle began to enter the hanger and take up the stall to the left of Simmon's shuttle, opposite the side Lattimer had been standing on.

When the gravitional lifters were shut down, the shuttle dropped the inch it had been hovering above the hanger floor. The clank Lattimer heard was loud and made him respect Jarhead more for landing their shuttle without jostling his patient.

He was over to the side door of the landed shuttle as it was opening and a Lankmeran was stepping out. The woman reached back into the shuttle and pulled a bag out of the passenger side of the craft. She turned away from the wall the shuttle had landed in front of and met an out-stretched human hand.

"Hello," Lattimer began. "I'm Rico Lattimer. If you're the physician they were bringing me, please come this way. We've taken the patient to the onboard hospital facility." He turned to head out of the shuttle hanger, then turned back to the native physician. "Oh, I'm sorry. What's your name?"

"I'm laCreata M'lora and if you have time, I would like to get my assistant, Morrn A'braks, out of the back. We might need him." Lattimer could hear the shuttle ramp hitting the hanger floor as she finished. He turned as a tall planetary male native walked down the ramp. "Morrn, how was the ride? This is the human doctor, Rico Lattimer."

"Pleased to meet you, son," Lattimer said as he reached out with his hand.

He pulled his hand back a bit as he saw the Lankmeran hold up his hand, pop out his claws, then retract them. Then the Lankmeran reached down to pick up the case he had let fall to make the gesture. "Pleased to meet you also," he said through the translator mounted on Lattimer's left arm.

"Do not be so shocked, Rico Lattimer, Morrn just gave you our traditional greeting. Shall we go on and see our patient?"

Lattimer wiped his right hand, the one he had offered to Morrn, with his left before turning to the hanger bay main door. "Right this way," he found his composure again as he moved past the landed shuttles and through the dissolving door into the remainder of the ship.

He led them to the three-suite complex that made up the sick bay on Nyumbani Station. There was only a single patient in the large room that had a dozen beds seperated by closable curtains from each other. Only the bed their patient had been transferred to was currently curtained off. Malone was sitting in one of the waiting chairs near the door, while Lund hooked the patient up to the monitors mounted into the bed.

Lattimer guessed that the calliope of sounds was from all the monitors trying to figure out what they were supposed to detect. "Lund, switch that noise off. This is Dr. M'lora and her assistant, A'braks. Once they know what we have, they can tell us what to use and how. " He turned to the incoming Lankmerans. "This man was found under the rubble of a collapsing factory." He walked over to the monitor mounted into the wall, pulled his diagnostic recorder out of his pocket and plugged it into the monitor. He tapped a few virtual buttons as the machine warmed up and said, "This shows the bones he's broken. Those I could mend, what I'm worried about is, has there been any internal injuries that I haven't noticed, causing his blood chemistry to keep changing. It's like something is contaminating his blood. I didn't want to poke around in him until I had an idea where to look."

"You've digitized your internal imaging," M'lora said. "This makes it possible to carry it wherever you go. This rib here," she pointed at the screen to one of the lower snapped ribs that was the most depressed of all of them. "Morrn, does that look like it might have torn the wall of the Familore?"

"It could have." He turned to Lattimer. "Can we see the blood chemistry results?"

"We're not exactly sure what a lot of these numbers mean, but a selection of them seem to be increasing." He handed an electronic tablet over to the man with the results displayed on it.

He showed it to Dr. M'lora. She frowned at what she saw. "He's dumping body toxins into his blood stream." She looked up at Lattimer. "There's a tear in his Familore, its the organ that removes wastes from the blood stream and sends them on to the body's excretion system. We need to open him up and seal up that tear. How quickly can we get him into surgery?"

"Hang on a minute," Lattimer said. "Now that we know what to look for, let's see if we can use a less invasive method than opening him up. Lund, get him into the Diagnostic suite and prep this area," he pointed at the internal scan on the monitor, "for an endoscopy. Let's see how bad that tear is and if we can seal it with microsurgery."

"Right away, doctor." Lund had the bed moving before he finished talking.

* * *

"A little cut and you can slide your scapel into the patient to the point you need to operate?" M'lora asked for the fortieth time.

"Well, it's not a scapel." Lattimer gave his colleague a sample of the device Dr. Aduro was setting up on the operating table. "It's a flexible tube with a camera and laser on its end. We find the tear in this man's familore and cauterize the wound closed. We'll be sending in a second tube to act as a suction device to remove toxins from the working area, making it easier to see what we are doing." He turned from the supply table to walk over to the head of the operating table and checked the gas cylinders set up there. "You're sure these gases will keep him sleeping?"

"Our breathing physiology appears to be very similiar. I believe those are the same gases we use in surgery."

"Then I think we're ready to go. Hank, shall I put him under?"

"The relaxants seem to be doing their job. Yes, now would be the time to get started."

M'lora watched as Lattimer placed a breathing mask over the patient, Chandro R'atan, and counted for him until his breathing dropped into the steady rhythm of sleep. "He's under," Lattimer said to Aduro.

"Now, based on what you told us, Dr. M'lora, if I make an incision here." He pointed at a spot on the patient's side just under his rib cage. "I can slide into an artery that will take me to the damaged organ."

"Unless there's some kind of blockage between there and the familore, it should be less than ten, oh what did you call them, centimeters to your target."

88

They both looked up at the monitor above the operating table and watched as Dr. Aduro pushed the probe deeper into the patient. There was one restriction blocking their path but Dr. Aduro deployed a balloon ahead of the probe and expanded the artery wall enough to allow the probe to pass through.

After he arrived at the site, he ran the suction for a short time to allow himself and Dr. M'lora to examine the wound. "It looks like a fairly straight puncture." He pivoted the camera head and saw the broken rib that had caused it. "Okay, I get this thing sealed, so you think you can get that rib back into place?"

"It shouldn't be a problem. But Mr. R'atan will be on bedrest with that bad a break."

Lattimer said from the head of the table. "Don't worry about that. You get his ribs back where they should be and we'll fuse the bones."

"I'll begin sealing this wound," Aduro said.

"He won't be needing any time for his bones to knit?" M'lora asked Lattimer.

"Nope. Good as new and ready to roll. Of course, I have no idea how long it's going to take the toxins to be removed from his body."

"That should take about two days."

"Lund," said Dr. Aduro, ignoring the other doctors' conversation. "Arterial sealant."

"Here you go, Dr. Aduro." Lund handed the doctor a strip of clear adhesive before the doctor pulled the tubes out of the hole he had cut in the native's abdomen.

He handed the tubes to Lund and pressed hard to keep blood from spurting out of the body, then sealed the wound closed. "Another strip."

Lund had used a single hand to place the tubes on the side table of the operating theater and tore off another strip with his clean glove, so Aduro would have a clean strip to work with.

"Lattimer, get his ribs fixed up and transfer him to recovery. Strict bedrest for at least four hours." Aduro had turned around and was stripping off his gloves to begin cleanup. "I'm off to get a coffee and watch from upstairs." He pointed to the observer gallery overhead.

"Lund, take over monitoring the anesthetics. I'll get the skeletal regenerator while Dr. M'lora adjusts the broken bones." He walked past the Lankmeran physician and patted her on the shoulder. "He's all yours."

Sergeant Harry Malone

Malone tried to get a quiet meal in the Mess Hall while the doctors were working. Unfortunately, there were too many men on board who wanted to know what was going on down on the planet. It was easy for him to fork in some mashed potatoes between sentences, but he didn't have the concentration needed to cut his steak into mouth-size pieces while answering their queries. Finally, after a half hour of failing to transfer his food to his mouth, an announcement came over the PA system.

"Specialist Malone, please report to Command Central immediately." Then it repeated twice more.

He grabbed the dinner roll on his plate, pulled it in half, and stuffed the remainder of his steak between the two pieces of bread. "Sorry, guys, I gotta go." He got up from the long bench he'd been sitting at and hurried to the door before anyone could intercept him. Knowing he'd be excused from returning his tray if anyone pushed it.

Command Central was a fifty-foot sphere in the station's central core. Normally it was a zero-gee facility so the admiralty could leap to any point in the spacial battlefield to get a true understanding of what was going on. Right now, it had a floor pulled across its midsection, since the command staff only had to deal with a two-dimensional front.

Malone walked up to the Officer of the Watch. "Specialist Malone, reporting as ordered, sir." He snapped a salute as the shorter officer turned to acknowledge him.

The officer returned the salute, so Malone could drop his hand. "Colonel Vermillan is waiting for you in the General's office. I suggest you make haste, the General does not like to be kept waiting."

"No, sir." Malone quick-marched over to the Command Office which was off to the right and slightly forward of the Information system of the Command Central. He knocked on the door and waited to be called before entering.

"Malone, good, now everybody is here. The briefing can begin," the colonel said from his position behind the general's desk. "We have decided to drop another platoon onto Lankmere. This one will be a recon unit.

"We seem to be doing a mopping up effort at this point. We got lucky with those first three towns, but I don't want to trust to luck. I want to know what they're up to. Why are they killing all the Lankmerans? And why are they only targeting them or us? They're ignoring the structures and fields of the Lankmerans, why? They don't even hunt the animal life down there. I need to know what's going on. Your mission will be to get in front of those killer aliens and find out what their plans are. Disrupt where possible, but get me some answers. Who are they? How did they get here? What is their ultimate goal?

"Major Demmings here, will run you through what we have managed to discover about them from here. Major?"

The room went dark as the projector mounted near the door was turned on and sent the TeleFlex logo to the screen mounted on the far wall. The Major focused the image before beginning. Once the letters were crystal sharp, he clicked on to the first image. "This is one of the weapons sent to us from the first soldiers to encounter the Narnians, that's what we in the counter-intelligence division are calling these guys until someone can give us their actual name. As you can see," the image on the wall began to rotate, "there is no barrel, just an emitter rod. The composition of the rod is still under analysis as it is no single compound but some kind of non-metallic alloy. The rod is wrapped in a carbon fiber sheath. The wrapping is able to radiate heat away from the center rod to prevent it from overheating in case of extreme rapid fire.

"And by rapid fire, I mean a single shot every second. The rifle has a recharge time of one second after each discharge, so unlike your EE-19's which can fire forty rounds a second, it is much slower in its rate of fire. While this is a electro-magnetic discharge weapon, you cannot sweep an area with it. Unless you have the weapon set on maximum power, then you can do a one second sweep. Otherwise, it must be focused on a single area to get enough power discharged to do any damage."

He stopped the rotating image and zoomed in on the area right above the trigger complex. "It has a variable power setting. From what we've seen of the weapons that came up from our first encounter with them, the Narnians had their weapons set on minimum strength. Minimum strength is enough to drive a cauterized wound through unprotected flesh. It was why some of the Lankmerans were killed by the Narnians, and the discharges did not affect our troops. Our bullet-proof jackets will protect us from anything up to and including setting four. Setting five will burn through our Kevlar and skin. The weapon burns a hole through the victim that is cauterized in its wake, so unless the Narnian hit a vital organ, you should be able to survive a direct hit.

"But enough about their weapons." He clicked the presentation; the slide changed to a picture of a standing alien. "There are a few anatomical differences you need to be aware of. The most important to your efforts is that, while they have a mouth, they do not make any communication sounds from it. The gases they breath inside those helmets is almost exactly the same as what we do, except it has two additional components. Two specialty gases are added to the outside air that are unknown to us. Their helmets have a special apparatus to deliver these gases to them, but without these gasses, they can still breath. As was demonstrated when you burst several of those helmets without effecting the warrior underneath. We don't know what they're for.

"For targeting purposes, their heart or blood-pumping organ is on the opposite side of their chest. Otherwise, their organs are in about the same places as ours. But..." He clicked his remote, and the next slide appeared. It was one of the aliens' uniforms turned inside out. "Since they are using weapons that cauterize wounds, they only defend their vital organs. Hence you will only see pockets for armored plates over their heart and lungs. They haven't taken bleeding to death into account. And those armor plates won't stop the copper-jacketed rounds we're using."

The lights in the room began to come back on as the projector shut itself down. "Are there any questions?" the Major asked. He looked over the room as no one rose to the occasion. "Good, Lieutenant Latifi, you and Sergeant Malone, get your troops ready. I want you planet-side before you lose all the daylight down there."

"Sir," Malone raised his hand. "I'm only a specialist. I'm not a sergeant."

"You are now, son. You have enough recommendations in your file to justify the promotion, and you know the enemy. We need that in your platoon right now. So you've just been promoted. Now get moving, we've got a planet to save," said General Chi as he walked in his back door, motioned the Colonel to get out of his chair and was sitting down by the time Malone and Latifi made it to the office's front door.

"Let's get back to Command Central." Colonel Vermillan led the way to the main door. "I'll show you the area we want you to patrol." Malone, who held the door open, held it for the Colonel to march through first

"A sergeant just because Captain Nilssen sent me up here," Malone said under his breath.

"Actually, Nilssen sent you up here at our request," Colonel Vermillan responded quietly back. Malone let the door close behind him as he was the last one through. Their stride increased as they walked across the room and around the central consoles mounted in the middle of the room. He went up to the largest of the monitor banks and turned to the computers directly across from them. With a few key strokes, he brought up a map of Lankmere. Then he enlarged the view down to a two thousand mile representation.

"That's where we're going to drop your team. It's about a thousand miles from the dead city you found, Malone. But that should put you ahead of any incursions by these Narnians." He used a laser devise to point to the right edge of the map. "There's Pantropolis," he moved the green light to the middle of the map, "and that clearing is where we intend to set you down. As you can see, cover is not far away in case the area becomes a hot zone. But we don't expect it to." He turned and looked at the two men. "The most important thing you can find out for us, is where these people are coming from. There have been no space ships landing on this planet since we arrived, nor any entering the system. So how are these guys getting here? If we can find that out, we can keep them from getting any more reinforcements. We can't interrogate them, so you'll have to catch them in the act. Find out. Let us know. And if you think you can stop them, do so. But only after you've accomplished the first two objectives. Am I clear?"

"Yes, sir," Malone snapped a salute.

"Yes, colonel," Latifi answered.

"Good. Now you have your mission. Collect your men and get started. Dismissed." The colonel began reaching for the console he'd used to bring up the map, then stopped himself and straightened back up. "And good luck, gentlemen."

* * *

"Jarhead" Simmons was one of the few pilots in the Earth Forces willing to fraternize with the enlisted men of Bravo Company; Malone knew him well and felt comfortable with him flying the platoon over what Malone figured was enemy-occupied land. He had no way to know it was enemy-occupied, but based on the briefing they'd just gotten, he felt it was a good assumption.

He had unfastened his restraints and moved where he could watch their descent through the cockpit window. They broke through the high clouds about a hundred miles from where they were planning to set down. A moment later, something hit the right booster engine and shut it down. The shuttle lost power, the left engine wasn't strong enough to sustain flight. Malone could feel the vehicle falling from the sky. Malone saw Simmons switch on the gravitational controls and stop their descent.

"I'm killing the left booster or this baby's just goin' around in circles," Simmons said to Latifi sitting in the co-pilot's seat. He turned his head enough to address the lieutenant, then he saw Malone in his peripheral vision. "Harry, make sure everyone's strapped in back there. Something hit us and if we lose gravitational control, we're goin' down hard."

Malone turned and quick stepped through the area where the shuttle's sensor equipment was mounted to get to the back of it where his troops were waiting. "Everyone buckle in. Store everything not strapped down tight. We might be going down the hard way." He grabbed his seat, just beyond the bulkhead leading to the cockpit and pulled his harness over himself. Then he scanned down the rest of his troops and saw only a couple of them having to tighten their harnesses. Only one sitting on the far side of the shuttle was sitting back up after placing something in the storage box below his seat.

Damn, I wish I could remember their names, Malone thought, *like who that soldier is.*

They were all strapped in when something hit the left booster and then the middle of the shuttle. The last one drove its way through the floor, into the personnel section of the craft and through one of the rifles mounted on the rack between the two groups of soldiers.

"Whose rifle was that?," Malone asked.

"Mine, sarge," came a response from the soldier five seats down from Malone.

"Make sure you grab a new one on the way out. Peterson, right?"

"Peters, sir."

Malone let the sir go. They had plenty to worry about now. He could feel the ship dropping. He used his communicator to call up to Latifi. "Lieutenant, did we just lose…"

"Gravitational power is gone, along with our other booster," he heard Simmons responding. "Brace yourselves, this time we're really goin' down."

The seat cushions and the floor were beginning to inflate as the crash containment system began activating. Malone looked up and saw the padding in the roof had also swelled in size. He had just enough time to push his head against the padded neck rest before he could hear the shuttle crashing through a series of trees, then smashing into the ground and halting its descent. It came to rest at a twenty-five-degree angle. The back of the shuttle was lower than the front and there was a slight tilt from side to side.

"Humphlett, get the ramp down."

"Humphrey, sir." Damn, it was going to take him a while to get all these new names down.

"Everyone grab your gear and get out of here. Humphrey, you and Lee go forward, on the outside, and see if the two Lieutenants need help. And everyone, stop calling me sir, especially when the real brass is around." He worked with everyone to get their gear and work their way out of the shuttle. He made sure he was the last man out.

They had been planning on landing in a clearing five times the size of the shuttle and so would have enough space to get things rigged up before moving out. They landed in the middle of a grove of trees dense enough to not show where the nearest clearing was.

Malone did a quick inspection of the landing site. Several large trees had broken off to their lowest and thickest sections. He tried rocking the shuttle and it did not seem to move. "We're secure," he called back to his men in the rear of the shuttle. "Start stripping this thing. Anything we can use is going with us. Peters, see if the long range radio can be removed. Our portable units are supposed to be able to reach the Command satellite, but I'll feel better if we had a backup." He walked up to the front of the shuttle.

As he got there, Specialist Lee was just rappelling down a vine he had pulled away from one of the unbroken trees. "How're they looking up there?"

Lee looked over to acknowledge Malone before turning his attention to the cockpit a good fifteen feet in the air. "Lieutenant Latifi took a gash to his leg as a thin tree drove its way through the cockpit. I got it bandaged up, and he should be coming down momentarily. Lieutenant Simmons should be down already. The front of the shuttle scraped against several trees on the way down. I don't think we'll find anything useful in it."

Malone turned his attention to where the door leading from the co-pilot seat would open and saw Lieutenant Latifi emerge and begin climbing down the vine that Lee had a tight grip on.

Simmons came through the collapsed trees and grabbed onto the vine to help Lee stabilize it. Malone noticed Latifi was climbing slowly. "Everything okay, Lieutenant?" he called up.

"Leg hurts a bit. I'm not risking infection on my way down. The troops ready to go?"

"We will be in a few, sir." Malone turned and headed back to see how the cannibalizing of the shuttle was going. When he got back to the unloading ramp, he climbed back into the loading area and looked up through the passage to the cockpit to see if the sensor suites were salvageable. Something had jarred the whole corridor on the way down. The equipment on the left side had come detached and fallen into that corridor, blocking enough of it to make Latifi and Simmons rappel down from the cockpit.

Malone turned back to the troop section of the craft, as nothing was usable forward. As far as he could see, the platoon had stripped everything of value out of the ship and were in the process of organizing it on the forest floor behind the shuttle.

He stepped off the shuttle in time for the lieutenants to come around from the front. "We'd better get packed up and moving," Simmons said. "If the enemy could shoot us down, they'll be coming after us. At least to make sure they got us."

"Pack all the survival gear we've got," Lieutenant Latifi instructed as he found a broken tree trunk he could sit on and rest his leg. "We'll have to hike back. Maybe gather a bit of that intelligence the Colonel wanted while we're here. But we have to survive, so focus on food, water and shelter. Sergeant Malone, I know we didn't need to, but did we pack any tents?"

Malone looked over at the piles of equipment sorted on the ground. "It looks like we have about a dozen one-man tents, sir. Not enough for the entire platoon."

"First place we camp, build some lean-tos strong enough to tow equipment. They can double as shelter when we need them to. We probably have about an hour before the enemy can zero in on our location, so I want us on the move in thirty minutes. Get a quick sled constructed and pack the heavy equipment on it. We can rebuild it once we camp tonight."

"Okay, men, you heard the lieutenant," Malone began. "Peters, you take a detail and get that sled built. Lee, rig the shuttle's self destruct system with a few extra charges of explosive." He turned to Jarhead. "You do plan to blow up the shuttle, don't you, sir?"

"You know the drill, Malone," Simmons smiled as he realized this soldier knew what had to be done without being ordered. "See that mound about a hundred yards from here? Set up the detonator behind it. I'll see if I can catch a few of the enemy when I set it off."

Malone turned back to his men. "The rest of you pack up everything you can carry. We need to be on the move in thirty minutes." Malone turned to Specialist Lopez. "Check out Lieutenant Latifi's leg and get him moving as soon as you can."

"Now wait a minute, Malone. I can carry my weight in this platoon," Latifi objected.

"And you can carry it best by being safely away from any action right now so we don't have to spare men to rescue you. Lopez, get him moving."

"Right away, sarge," Lopez responded. "Now, let's have another look at that leg and see if I can't keep you off a stretcher."

* * *

"Everyone's ready to move out, lieutenant," Malone said to Simmons a minute before Latifi's deadline. "What direction to you want us heading, sir?"

Simmons rolled onto his back from the mound he was hiding behind. "We were coming in a northwesterly direction. So don't head back southeasterly, try a direct easterly line." He pulled his satellite tracking monitor, which was in constant communication with one of the six positioning satellites they had dropped into orbit when they arrived at Lankmere. "It looks like we're really close to the twenty-fifth parallel. I'd say follow that until we can all get caught up."

"Peters, you stay with the Lieutenant. Lee, you've got point. Check your directional finder and get us headed for that 25th parallel. Everyone pick up your gear and let's head out." With everyone beginning to weave through the trees, Malone contacted Lopez. "Miguel, do you copy? Head for the 25th parallel and follow it eastward. We're moving out and should be at your position shortly. Specialist Lopez, did you copy?"

"Roger, sarge," came over the communicator. "See you soon."

* * *

They found a spring after marching for about four hours. It had taken them about a half hour to catch up with Lieutenant Latifi and Specialist Lopez, which slowed down their march forward. It took an hour for "Jarhead" Simmons and Private Peters to catch up with them, after Malone had heard the explosion of the shuttle.

The rations they had brought required no external heating, so they didn't build a fire that could give away their position. It had never gotten really cold at night in all the time Malone had been on-planet. They spent their time pitching the few tents they'd brought and constructing lean-tos/sleds. He remembered the dampness of the early morning, so Malone was going to be prepared to stay as dry as possible.

He looked over his shoulder at one of the new, right-out-of-basic privates they had assigned him. The knots the kid had tied looked tight, so he patted the kid on his shoulder, stood up from his squatting position, and went over to check on his commander.

"How's he doing, Miguel?" Malone asked as he pulled aside the tent flap. He looked down and saw Latifi was sleeping so he dropped his volume half way through his question.

"I'm a little worried about the wound in his leg," Lopez whispered back. "It looks like infection might be working its way in. I've started him on a broad spectrum antibiotic, since we have no idea what this planet might throw at us. Oh, and I gave him a sleeping pill. It's sometimes hard for the person in command to let themselves go so their bodies can heal themselves."

"Good. Get some supper, I'll watch him while you eat."

Lopez climbed out of the tent that was too small for him to stand up in. "Thanks, I'll be back as soon as I'm done." Lopez stood up as he climbed out of the small tent. He stretched and headed over to where most of the platoon found logs to sit down on and have an evening meal.

Malone climbed into the tent and sat facing his Lieutenant. Though he was practically in the middle, his head brushed against the Rylon of the roof. He looked down at his commander, relaxed a bit and let out a sigh. It must have been louder than Malone thought, since Latifi began to stir.

He placed his hand on the Lieutenant's shoulder. "Take it easy, sir." He watched his eyes open, look up at Malone, and then felt his body relax under his hand. "We've got everything under control. The electronic sentries have been placed. I've got a duty rotation for human guards to keep an eye on things throughout the night. And we've got enough lean-tos built to keep everyone dry through the morning."

"The shuttle?" Latifi was barely able to ask. Malone could tell Lopez's sleeping pill was working hard to send its patient back to sleep.

"Simmons said it went up spectacularly. About five of the enemy had climbed into it and another six were outside. He got them all in the explosion. Didn't you hear it?"

"Yeah, you are right. I forgot. It was so quiet." The lieutenant closed his eyes again and Malone watched as his face relaxed back into sleep.

After about fifteen minutes, Lopez pulled aside the tent flap. That was Malone's cue to exit the enclosure. As he passed the field medic, he saw Lopez had his sleeping bag with him. He was thankful the man would spend the night watching Latifi. Malone walked over to where some of the troopers were still eating and grabbed a bag of chow before he, too, decided to turn in for the night.

"Hey, sarge," called the trooper sitting across from Malone on the log circle someone had organized. He was another of his men that he hadn't learned the name of yet. "What exactly are we doing here?"

"Yeah," began the guy sitting next to him. Someone Malone thought was Humphrey but he wasn't sure. "I thought we were here to set up basic relations with the peoples of this here planet. Why is we out here fightin' 'um?

Malone swallowed the scoop of potatoes and set his biodegradable spoon on the remains of his side dish. "It was our mission to make contact with the Lankmerans. Which we did. Members of the diplomatic team had been slated to come down and begin talks with them about a permanent base, once we'd found out where their capital city was. Only they don't have one. The Lankmerans don't have any centralized form of government. They've developed a sense of respect for each other and when one of them steps out of line, they hold an intervention for them, or if necessary, that person is exiled from their community. They have a communication system between all the cities so that person can't just go and start again in another one. But it's my understanding, they haven't had to resort to that degree of action in over a hundred years."

"But why did they turn on us?"

"They didn't. We are still friends with the Lankmerans, in fact we are trying to defend them from whoever these attackers are that are trying to kill them. An enemy who looks wholly different from the cat-like Lankmerans. An enemy we haven't been able to communicate with, and therefore, don't know why they're killing everyone."

"Maybe they just don't like people?"

Malone turned his head to look at the man on his left who had spoken. "What?"

The man continued, "Maybe they're xenophobic. Maybe they just don't like other sentient beings."

"I just wish the guys upstairs would find a way to communicate with them so we can find out why they're doing this. Remember, if we capture any of them, they have a button on their right arm that will flood their helmets with a lethal gas. Something new, the guys in the lab say. I can't possibly remember the name they gave it. It'll sicken us, but kill them. You have to stop each one from deploying it. And the best way to do that is twist off their helmet or destroy it."

He looked at the remains of his dinner, now cold, and began getting up from his log. "Sunrise is in six hours. Get some sleep. Without transport, it's going to be a long way back to civilization." He stepped over his log and dropped his meal tray into the hole in the ground Landsby had dug for biodegradable waste disposal. It was only a few more steps over to his tent and sleep for the night.

The Diversion

Malone wanted to take point in the morning. He wanted to get a feel for the land they were crossing before the rest of his squad got there. He had to settle for every-five-minute reports from Lee and Humphrey. Fortunately, everything was quiet so far. The two of them were staying about five hundred yards ahead of the main body. It would give the main body time to hunker down if they did run into something.

Despite the antibiotics, Latifi wasn't getting better. When Lopez had changed his bandages this morning, the reddened area around the wound had spread. When the Lieutenant tried to stand up, his leg wouldn't support him. So one of the lean-tos Malone had planned to strap to someone's back was being used to pull the Lieutenant along.

"I've been in touch with Doctor Lattimer this morning. He wants me to continue the antibiotic regime, but get the Lieutenant to a secure area as quickly as possible so he can be extracted and treated upstairs. But they're not risking another shuttle coming over this part of the planet again," Lopez reported.

"Can they give us some idea how far away that is?"

Simmons was standing next to Malone. "About another fifty miles of this forest, then a hundred miles of open farm land. And that farm land is where I'd worry the most. No cover."

"Command, come in, Command. This is Spec... Sergeant Malone, I need to speak to someone in Surveillance. Command, do you read me?"

"Patching you through now, sergeant."

A few seconds later, "Sergeant Malone, this is Surveillance. What can we do for you?"

"I need you to pinpoint our position and tell me how far away the enemy positions are." He looked over to Simmons, "Maybe we can avoid enemy patrols by going further north. They seem to be more focused on extermination than recon."

"Surveillance to Malone. They seem to be attacking a city about five miles directly south of your position. We read another town completely dead about fifty miles southeast of your position. If you keep following the twenty-fifth parallel, you should be able to avoid them."

They stuck to that route the entire morning until Malone called the platoon to take a break. He called Lee and Humphrey as he planned to change out the point people. Everyone got issued a mid-day meal ration pack and found a place to sit, to get some food, and rest. Lopez had two men drag the Lieutenant's sled up against a tree so he could examine the wound.

"The infection is still spreading," he told Malone and Simmons. "After thirty-six hours, I would expect the antibiotics to have some effect. I don't think the Lieutenant will last until we get to that secure landing site. We need to get him to sick bay immediately."

"They won't risk sending another shuttle this close to enemy lines," Simmons said.

"What if we go to the city they've already finished with?" offered Malone. "They don't stick around once they've cleared an area. If I'm right, we should be able to get the lieutenant there by nightfall. Then they could bring in a shuttle under the cover of darkness."

"But how do we know they'll have left?" Latifi wasn't completely out of it. He was still trying to contribute.

"We send a couple of squads back and engage them in the city they're attacking right now. Give them something other than the rescue team to focus on," Malone decided. "We don't need to take back the city. All we have to do is make those guys think we're trying to."

"I'm not ground combat rated," Simmons began to object.

Malone knew his idea would work, but it would be up to him to carry it out. "I'll lead the attack. You're going to be needed to help bring the rescue shuttle in."

"I don't care what you guys do, but we have to do something now, before we lose the lieutenant," Lopez said.

"Sergeant Malone, they're your men. Divide them up. I'll get the lieutenant to the dead city." Simmons extended his hand to Malone. "Good luck with your diversion."

* * *

The two squads of soldiers Malone had taken with him circled the woods that ran right up to the town's western edge. There was less than fifty yards of grassland to the nearest building. They could see the enemy troops rounding up and killing Lankmerans from behind the trees they were using for cover. The street they stared down led directly to the town square, where the Lankmerans were being executed. With the nearby buildings cleared, Malone split his two squads between the two homes nearest them. Four men into each building.

"Slowly move from building to building until you've got nothing between you and that town square. But stay under cover, don't make any sound, we don't know what kind of hearing those guys have. Now spread out, find cover, and wait for my signal."

He took four soldiers into the house on the left. They searched every room in the dwelling before moving from the back door of the house to the back door of the next. They repeated the clearing process and moved forward. When they went through the empty tailor's shop, the large front window gave them a good view of the city's open commons area.

Malone pointed to four of the men with him and motioned them to stay put. "Okay, you four," he whispered as he pointed at two pairs of his troops. "Pick out spots by the windows fronting on the town square. "Wait for my signal before opening fire. We need to make ourselves sound bigger than we are." He went over to the building on his right, a bakery, to check on the troops there.

The door was unlocked and he slipped into the shop. The four troopers working the same side of the road were just coming in the back door of the establishment. Individually, he sent the three men and one woman over to different spots around the front window where they could hide under the display boxes that still held pastries and cakes the vendor sold.

105

Something they'd done must have alerted the enemy, several of the enemy soldiers in the square turned their attention to the bakery. When they started moving towards it, Malone knew he'd wanted to be better prepared for them. Several Lankmerans were still kneeling at gun point in the city park.

Looking around, he focused on Specialist Wilkins. "Wilkins, come with me, We're going to widen our firing line by going over to the next shop." The two men went through the bakery's kitchen to its side door. It opened on an alley. They ran across and into a bowling alley. They quickly went to the alley's far corner and found concealable firing positions.

Malone activated his communicator without removing it from his pocket. "On my command, everyone open fire. Now!" His EE-19 fired seven-round bursts at the approaching enemy combatants, shattering the bowling alley's small window. His burst was followed by those of the rest of his people.

"Roger, sarge," Wilkins said as he followed suit, though his rifle was still set for triple bursts. Immediately, the dozen enemy soldiers in the park dropped to the ground and held their positions.

"Get out of there," Malone yelled at the Lankmerans still kneeling. Then he spotted the other side door for the establishment and dashed out into the park to help the Lankmerans get up and head back to the bowling alley.

"Sarge, you okay?" Malone heard Wilkins call over to him as he returned to the bowling alley and slammed the door shut. He'd managed to lead three Lankmerans back with him.

This was the first chance Malone had had to scan the business since he and Wilkins had entered. Several Lankmerans were left where they'd been shot along several of the bowling lanes. But what drew Malone's attention was the body of one of the enemy soldiers bent over the counter with part of his chest torn out. "What happened back there?"

"We were rounded up and taken into the square to be shot," one of the Lankmerans began saying. "Barlon T'wan was just coming from the back room when he saw what was happening and went berserk. He clawed the alien you see there before the rest of them shot him down."

"Good for him," Malone said. "But we have to get back to work." He keyed his platoon's circuit again. "We have to assume word got out that we're here. That means more of these guys should be on their way. So brace yourselves and prepare to repel the enemy. We have to hold out until Lieutenant Latifi is clear." Malone turned his rifle around and used the butt of it to clear out the glass from the window he'd been firing through. Then switched his rifle from septuple-round to triple-round burst so he could lay a more controlled stream on the approaching soldiers.

After a few minutes, he pulled his communicator from his pocket. "Simmons, come in, Simmons. Are you guys off the ground yet? We've got these guys tied up, but I'd love to abandon this position as soon as possible. Simmons, do you read?" He dropped it back into its pocket and tried picking off a few of the soldiers appearing from around the buildings on the other side of the park. He got two of them before the rest decided to find cover behind some of the park benches.

"Malone, we've made it to the city. We're just waiting for a shuttle to get here so we can load up and get out. Repeat, we've got a shuttle inbound, but we're not aboard yet. It should be here in fifteen. I hope you guys can hold out that long."

"Simmons, let us know as soon as you're airborne. I'm sending you some Lankmeran refugees. We can't hold this position forever, get everyone and get out." To emphasize the point to himself a hole appeared just to his right and chipped some plaster from the ceiling. He slid his thumb through the frequency settings until he had the platoon again. "They've upped their power settings. Everyone make sure you're under cover. Let's hope these buildings' construction can cut their power levels down as the lasers burn their way through." He turned to get behind a solid wall and yelled out, "Every Lankmeran who can move, get up and head out the back. Follow the Earth Force teams and head for the extraction point. Don't worry, they'll guide you. Just get out of here."

He stayed behind the wall and got to his feet. He wanted to get a better look at the enemy position than looking through his electronic view finder afforded him. He auto leveled his rifle about five feet off the floor and used the gravitational stand to hold it in place so his hands were free to control the view finder.

The closest of the enemy troops had hunkered down, hiding behind benches, bushes, and even trash containers. But about three dozen more were running across the town square to back them up. Malone electronically switched his rifle to continuous fire and opened up on the advancing soldiers. They were within easy range, so he got over a dozen of them before the rest hit the ground. Malone ceased fire to conserve ammunition and set his rifle back to triple round action. He also dropped back down to the floor, having his rifle keep watch.

The enemy wasn't coming any closer. It was like the stalemate they'd had at Anora, but a stalemate was just what they needed, one that would keep the enemy busy while the shuttle got away.

Every so often a helmet would begin to emerge from behind an obstruction. "Watch this," Cho said in the room he was occupying. He fired off a single round that shattered the helmet. "Once you pop that top, you can't stop." He then fired a triple burst into the bushes nearby that he had seen an enemy soldier jump behind.

Malone frowned at Cho's levity, but let it go. As long as they didn't do something stupid, he'd allow them to blow off steam however they could. Another hole appeared in the wall near him. He looked through his view finder and thought he saw someone behind an aluminum trash can. He dropped a three round burst through it and quickly followed it up with another. A figure dressed in red fell out from behind the can.

"How we doing on ammo?" he radioed his squads. He got responses of one or two spare clips. They'd each brought ten, meaning they'd gone through a lot of bullets. *If Simmons doesn't get off soon, we're going to have to bug out to retrieve the supplies we left in the woods,* Malone thought.

"Sergeant Malone, come in, Sergeant Malone, over," came from the small speaker in his chest pocket.

He dropped behind the wall even further. "Malone here."

"Lieutenant Simmons here. We're off, Sergeant. Thanks for the distraction. Now get your men out of there."

He rapidly went back to the platoon channel. "Alright, everyone. I just got the word. Rig a couple of grenades to the doors of
these buildings and get out of there. Head back to the woods west
of town, where we left our extra supplies. Get your equipment and
keep heading west. Regroup about a mile from the edge of the
woods. Malone out."

"Sarge, we have a problem. Specialist Sato took a hit in his
leg. It keeps folding under him. We're going to have to help him
out."

"Carry him, if you have to. Forget the traps, just take care of
Sato. We'll wait at the rendezvous point. If you run into trouble,
holler out. I want you men alive, not dying like heroes."

He wired a pair of his grenades to the front door. If anyone
came through, they would drop to the floor and explode three seconds later. Then he turned to the rest of his troops, "Seven round
burst from each of you. One at a time, starting with Cho. As soon
as you've fired, get out the back door and head for cover. Let's go."

Malone ran to the back door and held it open as the other three
came running through. They jumped the back fence and headed
down the street. Everyone made it to the woods before the sounds
of explosions could be heard from the shops they'd just abandoned.
Lee stopped, turned, and looked in the direction of the noise as
Malone caught up with him.

"Keep moving, soldier. Even if we didn't get any of them,
those blasts should slow them down while they look for any others
we might have left them. Now move." Malone gave Lee a moder-
ate shove to get him moving. Within two steps, he was racing after
the rest of his comrades. Malone smiled as he followed suit.

The March

A hundred yards into the woods, they found the cache of supplies they hadn't wanted to carry into a combat situation. They strapped Sato onto one of the lean-to gurneys and abandoned the rest. "Lee, Peters, Cho and Wilkins; carry the gurney. Don't drag it. It'll be easier to hide where we've gone if we don't leave ruts behind us. Humphrey, divide up the supplies Sato had between everyone. I want the only thing we leave behind is wrecked carrying sleds." With that, Malone took the lean-to segment they had not mounted Sato to and broke it into pieces. When he was done, it just looked like typical forest debris.

"As we move out, I want the lead man to pivot left and head due south. Travel about one mile along that course then proceed to rendezvous along a line heading due south." Malone took his GPS display out of his pants' pocket to check where they were. " Longitude 11.5158° 25 seconds. When you get to that meridian, keep heading south. Everyone try to meet up ten miles from here. "Now let's move out."

The four assigned to carry Sato got in the middle of the line and before an hour had gone by, turned off to head south. Malone brought up the rear of the march to make sure his squads did what he'd told them to. He went about a hundred yards further than where he was planning to turn off. He turned around and walked back, inside his own footprints before heading south. He double-timed his pace in hopes of catching up with members of his platoon.

He had to stop a few times and pull thorns out of the leather of his boots. He had to wonder how the duroplastic soles of them were doing, most of the thorns seemed to come from ground-based vegetation. He was going to have to scrape them clean in case they had any contaminates, like the stuff that infected Lieutenant Latifi.

It was starting to get dark when Malone found his platoon. They'd decided to set up camp and wait for stragglers. Malone was the last one to arrive. They had the tents and lean-to ready and were just burying the remains of dinner when he arrived.

"Hey, sarge, ready for supper?" Cho called as he came around the last tree into the small clearing. He stood up from the stump he'd been sitting on and offered a fresh meal to his commander.

"No, you keep it. I have to scout the area before I can settle down for a meal." Malone drifted past his men into the forest to the east, quickly disappearing from sight. He turned, examining the surroundings. Despite the small size of the clearing, it wouldn't do any good if it were easily discovered.

It looked good. At a hundred yards away, nothing showed. He circled the perimeter of the camp and found it secure in all directions. He walked back in to have supper. Afterwards, he assigned guard shifts, crawled into his tent and drifted off to sleep.

* * *

"So what exactly is our objective now?" Wilkins asked Malone while they were walking south.

"We still know squat about the enemy. Where do they come from? Surveillance swears they didn't fly into the system. There's no evidence that they've lived on this planet and are just now taking vengeance on the Lankmerans. So who are these guys? They don't talk. Unless the linguists can get them to learn sign language, we may never be able to communicate with them. If we can find their headquarters, we might learn something about these guys. If they've got a written language, the boys upstairs would like us to swipe a few of their books."

"So your basic smash and grab raid. Good thing Sato's injury was superficial enough so he can walk again."

"If it wasn't, we'd have to pull out of this mission for lack of personnel. It's about time for Lee to take a break; go relieve him on point. I have to check in with the Nyumbani anyway." Malone watched as Wilkins double-timed it up to the head of the column and patted Specialist Lee on the shoulder. As they began talking, Malone pulled his communicator and called upstairs to the station.

"Malone to Control. Sergeant Malone to Control."

"Control here. You got anything new for us, Sergeant?" came back through his reciever.

"We're still making our way south. So unless you want a detailed biome report, I got nothing."

"I've got your position fixed. You guys need to move about ten miles to the west and continue in your southerly direction for another seventy. We're showing some activity in that area. I'm sending you the coordinates now. We've been picking up enemy activity; the bulk of it is located in a building at that location. If you can get there and see what's happening, we'd really appreciate it."

"Enough for some virtual home leave?" Malone knew the enemy couldn't hear anything through their helmets but it didn't stop him from stepping around the larger sticks on the ground to avoid making any noise.

"Don't push it, sergeant. You know how the Big Man gets."

"How far is it to where you picked up Lieutenant Latifi?"

"We need you to get us that Intel. We have to find out how the enemy is getting their troops onto Lankmere. If they are resupplying them or if this is all we have to worry about."

"And we will. But I have a wounded man who could use evac. Where can I send him to get him off this planet?"

"Oh. That's different. Give me a second."

"By the way, how is the lieutenant doing?"

"They say he's stable. Maybe when you finish up down there, he'll be ready to entertain visitors. Good luck, sergeant. It looks like you're about fifty miles due west of the location where we picked him up. How quickly can your team make it to that location?"

Malone had to run the math through his head. *Fifty miles, they were doing about thirty miles a day before Sato's injury, now they were down to around twenty.* "If they push, they could make the site the day after tomorrow, after dark."

"Sarge, I can keep going. You guys need me," Malone hadn't noticed Sato catching up to him or how long he'd been listening.

"We'll have a shuttle waiting. Surveillance signing off. Good luck."

"Hold on a second, Surveillance." He turned to face Sato. "Are you sure that leg is good enough for you to go back into combat? Let alone the grueling march we have to do to get there?"

"I'm not a fresh-out-of-boot-camp recruit, sarge. I can contribute to this mission."

"Okay." He activated his communicator again. "Cancel that pickup, Surveillance. We're good to go."

"Well, good luck, Recon."

They were planning on taking their lunch break in two hours, Malone felt it would be a good time for the main body to alter course and start in the southwesterly direction Surveillance wanted them to head in. "What's up, Sarge?" one of the privates Malone hadn't yet learned the name of asked.

"Command wants us to check out a cleared city to the southwest. Sato says he can handle himself, so we're going to pick up our pace." He raised his voice so the entire platoon could hear him. "We'll pick up the pace to normal marching speed. If Sato can't handle it, then we can slow back down. But if he can, we'll just get this mission done that much quicker." He stopped and watched his people break into a brisker step and after the last man passed him, he fell into line behind him.

If Sato couldn't handle it, he didn't want the man left behind.

Planning The Raid

It had been over eight hours since he had checked in on Lieutenant Latifi, so after his mission to collect Specialist Sato had been scrubbed, Lieutenant Simmons walked over to the recovery ward, room number Five, where they were keeping him.

He knocked once on the door before pushing it into the wall and entering the room. Latifi still lay in the bed he'd been in before Simmons left. But this time he had a couple of doctors, Doctor Lattimer was one, but Simmons couldn't remember the other doctor's name.

"Yes, it looks like the infection is beginning to go down. What was in that salve you administered to the patient?" asked the doctor that Simmons couldn't remember the name of.

Simmons moved along the back wall so he could see the doctor across the bed from the others. "It's an old herbal remedy. While the source of his condition comes from the lichen that grows on the vines, the leaves of three bush plants growing in the same vicinity, when ground together and made into a paste, they have the properties of drawing the poison out of the body. The Lieutenant has been infected for about four days, so it will take that long again for the salve to restore his health. I assure you, gentlemen, he is on the road to recovery," M'lora explained to them.

"How are you feeling?" Lattimer placed his stethoscope on Latifi's chest to listen.

"I'm feeling better than I was yesterday. But the leg still hurts whenever the pain medication wears off."

"More or less than before?" Lattimer took his stethoscope out of his ears and picked up Latifi's wrist.

"It feels stronger if I wait too long to ask for my meds."

M'lora replaced the sheets over the wound. "Good. That means your body is healing itself. The lichen's poison has the ability to anesthetize the area to get its victim to ignore the pain and not look for treatment. Even though we run daily PSAs on this stuff, we still have patients dying of it every few weeks." She looked down into Latifi's eyes. "I'm glad we were able to save you, young man. Normally, we have to shave the patients we treat for this infection, but you humans have no fur covering your skin."

Simmons remembered Latifi having some of the hairiest legs he seen since leaving Earth.

The doctor Simmons couldn't remember turned and began heading for the door. "Shall we continue our rounds? There are many more medical techniques we promised to show Dr. M'lora here." They were out the door a moment later.

Simmons walked over to the bed. "So you're getting better," he said as he leaned on the rail designed to keep patients from rolling out onto the floor.

"That's what they tell me. But until that Lankmeran doctor said something about it, I thought they were going to have to amputate. The pain was getting so bad."

"I hear your guys are going south to check out a town the enemy are actually using as a base."

"My first real command in the field, and I get side-lined by a plant."

"I know the feeling. Nothing like sitting on your ass when others are taking all the risks."

"Hey, whose side are you on? Aren't you here to cheer me up or something?"

"Nah. Colonel's orders. I'm supposed to make you as miserable as possible. It's why I brought you these." Simmons pulled a couple of bags of amber ale out from his back pocket. "But if you aren't interested?"

"Not interested." Latifi made a grab at what Simmons knew was his favorite beer.

Simmons tossed the pair of bags on Latifi's chest before he could grab them. Then he pulled a third one out of his pocket for himself. He pulled on the drinking tab, straightened it into a straw and took a pull from the bag. "I suppose it could have been a bit colder, but those doctors kept talking and they keep warming up in my pocket."

"Damn. After two weeks, these guys are just fine. Thanks, Jason."

"Just trying to do my part. I need you back on drinking duty."

"When I get outta here, it's back to the planet to spy on our nasty friends down there. Hey, could you do me a favor? Could you check and see how they're doing? I can't get any information out of the staff here. I didn't even know about that mission you mentioned earlier."

"Sure thing." Simmons turned to go and remembered he couldn't carry a beer bag through Sick Bay. "You might as well finish this." He handed the bag over to his friend and left the room.

* * *

Simmons' scheduled meeting with the surveillance officer was in five minutes, and it was a ten-minute walk to the other side of the station. He had to apologize on the run to two higher ranking officers as he darted through the hallways and down the stairs. He didn't feel he could afford the time waiting for the elevator.

The chronometer in his contact lens told him he was a minute late as he opened the door to the Surveillance department's receptionist room. *Maybe I can blame my tardiness on the secretaries*, he thought until he saw the single seat in the waiting room vacant.

All he could do was go up to the main desk and report in. "Lieutenant Simmons to see Major McGivens," he said to the receptionist.

She looked up for a second before returning to the report she'd been reading. "Oh, yes, he was just asking where you were. Go right in."

He slid the single door into the wall and stepped into the Surveillance Center. He walked past the rows of monitors displaying the feeds from satellites monitoring the planet and the banks of soldiers sitting at their stations listening to the communication traffic coming to their facility. He crossed the room without looking at any of the devices the teams of analysts were using to evaluate the incoming data and knocked on the door to Major McGivens' office on the opposite side of the room.

There was a click before Simmons heard, "Lieutenant, get your butt in here," coming from the other side of the door.

McGivins' office was relatively small; however, it was connected to a larger conference area used for classified briefings. Especially for briefings involving those that couldn't be removed from the department.

"Take a seat, man. Three crises could have blown up while I've been waiting for you." The small man did not get out of his chair. The only nod he gave to Simmons' entry was to toss the report he was reading on the corner of his six-foot-long desk. "That platoon you dropped into enemy territory may be in trouble. The area Colonel Vermillan sent them into, looks like it could be an embarkation point for the enemy troops. Therefore, we need to devise an extraction plan for when they complete their mission." He pressed a button on the opposite side of his desk and leaned over to talk into a surface-mounted speaker. "Vincroft, get in here." He straightened back up to address Simmons. "Our idea is to send you into the area with an attack shuttle so you can extract them and offer air support, if needed."

The door behind Simmons opened and another lieutenant walked into the room. "Lieutenant Vincroft reporting, sir," the new officer snapped to attention as he approached the desk.

"He's a combat vet, Conrad, not one of Chi's lackeys. No need to be formal."

Simmons rose from his chair and offered the other man his hand. "Lieutenant Jason Simmons, but friends call me Jarhead," he said as the other man took it.

"Lieutenant Conrad Vincroft, at your service, lieutenant." They both seated themselves after the introductions. "Have you briefed him on the descent plan, Major?"

"That's why I called you in here. You've got all the maps keyed up and ready to go. I therefore wanted you to brief him."

Vincroft rose from his chair. "If the two of you will join me in the briefing room, I'll call them up for the Lieutenant's benefit." He walked into the adjacent room without waiting to see if he was followed.

By the time Simmons and the Major had taken seats in the twenty-four person meeting room, Vincroft was displaying a large map of the area where the recon team was located. "We're calling this city Central, since we think it's central to the enemy's plans.

"You can see the buildings of Central are still standing. We still do not understand that. Why does the enemy kill everyone in the city, and leave the buildings standing, then just leave the area? Until we found them here, they'd just been killing everyone and leaving. Never actually using the buildings for anything. So why here? We're hoping Latifi's team can get us some answers."

While Simmons was watching the map, two dozen figures emerged from the largest of the building in the image. "Those can't be our guys, can it?" He watched as they moved over to another large but smaller building and entered it.

"No, lieutenant. We believe those are enemy troops leaving the main building and heading for the one they will be staging out of. That second building, we see troops entering and leaving. But we never see troops entering that larger building, they only leave it. We have no idea how they get into it. They must have some underground means of getting in there we can't see. We're hoping the recon platoon you dropped there can get us those answers."

"Just how many troops have they got in that city?"

"We're not entirely sure," said the Major, "but since they haven't sent any out in a while—they're still attacking the city to the north and west of their position—we know that number is increasing. It's why we want to send you in with an attack shuttle. Provide Recon platoon with air cover."

"If you go in," Vincroft began again, "fly along this line and hug the trees until you reach the farmland around Central, then drop to about six feet until you reach the forested area north of the city. We'll contact Latifi and have him meet you there."

"You guys do know that Lieutenant Latifi is currently in Sick Bay. He's got Sergeant Malone commanding those troops. And, I might add, Malone is a newly minted sergeant."

"Mr. Vincroft, it looks like you'll have to go down with Lieutenant Simmons, here, and take command of this mission."

"But, sir."

"And do we have any more combat troops we can send down?"

"Just the five soldiers I brought back up, the ones that helped transfer Lieutenant Latifi," Simmons replied.

"But, Major, I don't have any combat experience," Vincroft cried.

"Then it's time you earned that particular stripe. Get your gear together, you know all the questions we need answers for, Vincroft. Simmons, round up those men you mentioned, and get them ready to move out. I'd like to see you launch in an hour so you can get there and be waiting for Malone when he arrives. Gentlemen, you're on the clock. Move it."

Establishing The Ground Game

Jason "Jarhead" Simmons, the only combat shuttle pilot on this mission, walked around the shuttle he planned to drop down on the planet with. His munitions operators were busy loading all the ordinance they were going to need for the mission. The extra belts of explosive rounds could come in handy keeping the enemy from trying their lasers on the underside of his craft again. The dozen stored missiles could take down any tower they tried to shoot him from. No, his boys knew what he wanted, and he would have it when needed.

After he contacted his flight team to prepare the shuttle, he went to tell Latifi what was going on with his platoon. Next he went to Operations to contact the members of Recon Platoon he'd brought up and have them get ready to return to the planet.

Everything and everyone was loaded up in the shuttle by the end of Major McGivens' deadline except his staff member. "Hey, Vincroft, you on your way?" Simmons said over the intercom so the entire station could hear him. "You never know where the good lieutenant could be," he said to his gunner sitting in the seat next to him.

The doors of the hanger bay parted as Vincroft puffed his way through them. He ran up the ramp and tossed his backpacks to the soldiers strapped in waiting for liftoff. They promptly pushed them back on the floor as they were ready to go.

"Good of you to join us, Lieutenant," Simmons said over the shuttle intercom. "Now stow your gear and strap yourself in." The ramp was rising even as he spoke. "I'm taking off in, three, two, one." The shuttle lifted inches off the floor as the back hatch hissed shut. When the boosters kicked in, Vincroft was thrown to the floor while trying to lift his first backpack up into the storage compartment above the only seat the rest of the soldiers would let him use. Somehow, they had read 'green horn' all over the Lieutenant.

As the shuttle cleared the hanger doors, Private Oshinko unbuckled his harness, tossed both of the Lieutenant's backpacks into the upper compartments. Despite the rapidly banking turns Simmons was making, Oshinko stayed on his feet while the Lieutenant fell over twice more. Oshinko hauled the Lieutenant up and pushed him into his seat, then buckled him in as the rest of the troops forced themselves not to laugh.

Simmons raced into the atmosphere at twice the speed of the other shuttles; this was a combat vehicle and had engines twice as powerful as the rest of the fleet. He buzzed the town of Anora at just five hundred feet. Then he dropped to one hundred, the height of the tallest tree visible. As they approached the farmland west of Central, he called back to the people sitting in cargo. "We're going really low, so keep your arms and legs in the vehicle at all times until we come to a full and complete stop." He dropped the vehicle to just five feet above the ground and headed for his rendezvous point with Recon Platoon.

* * *

"Sergeant Malone of Recon platoon. Sergeant Malone, do you read me?" It had only been a couple of minutes since the last time Simmons tried to raise the men he was here to meet. But he had to keep trying. If he couldn't make contact, his whole mission would be wasted. The flight down had been uneventful, just the way "Jarhead" liked it. When he arrived at the appointed destination, he found a gap in the foliage that allowed him to hide the shuttle like he was parking it in a garage. He just had to find Recon platoon. "Sergeant Malone…"

"Malone here. Is that you, Simmons?"

"Damn, am I glad to hear from you." Simmons looked over to his gunner and smiled. "We've got a new set of coordinates for you to head for. It's only a mile north of the original ones. I'm sending them to you now." He opened the file with the new coordinates and sent them to Malone.

"Received. Hey, you're closer than we thought. We'll be there in about a half hour. I'm sure going to like getting those men back. Hold tight. We'll see you soon."

* * *

121

The five men Simmons sent ahead to recon the enemy-held city returned minutes after Malone brought his troops up the ramp and seated themselves. By the time they arrived, his people were breaking out their evening meal.

"Boy, it's good to have an actual chair to sit in after all this marching," said Watkins as he twisted his butt into the cushions of the seat just behind the sensor suite of the shuttle. He tore open the bag with his evening meal, and cursed when he saw he'd have to heat it for another five minutes. After breaking the chemical heating unit to ignite it, he set the bag on the storage rack in front of him, then leaned back into his seat and folded his arms in front of his chest. Malone could hear the growling of the Specialist's stomach.

"Boy, am I glad to see you guys again." Malone was out of the seat he'd spent less than a minute in and helped the missing members of Recon platoon back into the shuttle. "How's the lieutenant?"

"Last we heard," Cho said as he grabbed Malone's hand to be pulled up the ramp. "He was recovering fine. The Lankmerans had a salve to treat the infection. The doctors said it was working, but that they want the lieutenant on bed rest for the rest of the week."

Simmons was up, helping the next man in. "So, what did you find in town?"

"Sir," answered the last man to step into the shuttle. Someone Malone hadn't seen before. "It seems to be a larger city than the Lankmeran villages we've dropped men into. Several industrial buildings are at the far edge of the town. Most of them are dark and unused. The largest, though, appears to have troops leaving it, but we never see them going in. Since they're not landing anyone on the building's roof, we ran sonic sensors along three sides of the building and detected no underground activity. They don't seem to have tunnels allowing them passage, either. We weren't there long enough to time it, but a large light flashes occasionally, and twenty minutes later, a group of one hundred troops leave that building to go to the one across the street to the east."

"Did you find an entrance into the large building?" Malone asked.

"Oh, sorry," Simmons broke in. "Sergeant Malone, this is Sergeant Iona of Army Intelligence. He's down here to help us find out something about these guys." Simmons threw his thumb in the direction of the city.

"I'm glad to meet you, Sergeant Iona. I could really use your experience down here."

"From what I've heard you're doing quite well down here. But to what you were asking, the south side of the building is completely sealed, either with stone or downed tree trunks. There's no way in on that side. But they seem to have ignored the north side, and especially at ground level. I think there are a few broken-out windows that could lead to the basement of the facility. If we strip down to mission critical equipment, we should be able to enter the structure there." He turned to Malone, "I was given your record in my briefing for this mission, Sergeant Malone. They are your men. Specialist Keahi and I are only here as advisors; technically, we are under your command." He turned to Lieutenant Simmons, "And your orders are to stay with the shuttle, having it ready to give the Sergeant any support he needs when the situation demands it."

"Yeah, that's what McGivens told me. So how are we gonna play this?"

"Let's give my boys a chance to rest up and go in after dark. Sergeant Iona…"

"Call me Tamar. Not your men, just you."

"Thanks. Tamar, do you think you and Keahi could lead us back to those windows without being seen? I'd like to take the entire squad, in case we run into trouble."

"As long as your men bring their night vision equipment."

The Wormhole

They looked at the building they were about to infiltrate. Malone held up his hand and clenched it to bring his troops to a halt. "One more thing I need to tell you guys," Malone turned his head to look at Sergeant Iona, but was speaking over the platoon's channel. "Do not try and silently kill one of the aliens. They have some method of communication, they know if something happens to one of them, even if you don't make any noise. In the last encounter we were in, we killed one out of sight of the rest, and the next thing we knew, they were pouring down on us."

"Good to know," Tamar replied. "That might be something they can use upstairs when we get back." They made their way through several of the city's streets until they were hiding behind a building next to the one they planned to enter. "Those are the bricks," he pointed to the black opening at the base of the building, "we need to move a few more of them and we should be able to crawl into that building."

"Peters, Watkins," Malone said to the two men crouched behind him. "Make your way over to that hole in the building and see if you can widen it so we can get through."

"It'd be a lot easier if chubby here would lose some pounds," Watkins said as he passed Malone.

"Enough. Just get a move on," Malone responded. "I'll see you both on the track upstairs when this thing's over."

The two men hesitated at the edge of the building, looking in all directions to see if there was anyone who could spot them, including up. They dashed across and dropped into the darkness the building provided from the quarter moon shining down. They lowered their night vision glasses into place and peered into the window that was partially bricked in before attempting to move any of the small bricks positioned in the gap. They had not been mortared in, so were easily moved aside. They stacked the bricks to the right side of the opening as they removed them. In minutes, they had the opening restored to its original size and were slipping through.

"We're in, sarge," Peters said over his communicator. "You can bring the rest of the squad in now."

"Thanks. Okay, everyone," he radioed his men, "buddy up. I want everyone crossing in pairs. Sergeant Iona and I will bring up the rear. Once you see the team ahead of you disappear into the building, count to five and make it across. But do not risk being seen."

A half hour after the initial team cleared the opening, Malone was watching Tamer slip through the entryway before passing him his rifle, grabbing one of the extended bricks above the window and slipping feet first through the opening. Tamar and Lee grabbed his feet as he came in and pulled him the rest of the way inside.

The greenish glow from the night vision goggles showed them to be in a large room being used as a storage facility. Several crates were stacked against the walls, leaving the window and door areas open. The west side of the room had crates stacked two deep.

Keahi opened the door just enough to get a probe through and see what was beyond. "Clear," he announced and pulled the door fully open before being the first man across the threshold.

The rest of the troops followed him, with Tamar and Malone bringing up the rear. They found themselves in a corridor. At the end of the east passage was a large double door. Before that there were only a couple of smaller doors on either side of the corridor. Malone could not see the end of the corridor going west. "We'll break into two teams," Malone said. "Sergeant Iona will lead one heading to the east side of the building, and I will lead the other heading west. Count off."

The men quickly ran through a count. "Okay, odd numbers go with Sergeant Iona and even numbers are with me. Let's move out." He pushed his way west through the men until he emerged in the point. "Let's go, evens." He continued forward down the hall until he came to the first door. It was on the inside of the building. He was reaching for the door handle when Oshinko pushed his hand away.

125

"Sergeant Malone, you are in charge and should not be taking this risk. Let one of us open the door, with your person several steps away."

Malone looked into Oshinko's face with an angry stare. Then realized the man was right. He was too new at being in command. As a Specialist, he just did things when they needed doing, not have someone else risk their lives. He smiled at Oshinko and stepped back, allowing his soldiers to step between him and the door. Oshinko placed his hand on the handle and twisted it before pushing the door inward.

It was an empty room, except for the benches mounted against the walls and in a circle in the center of the room. With all the electrical receptacles mounted into the wall, it looked like the Lankmerans were setting up a control room in here and never had the chance to finish.

"Okay, nothing here." Malone said. "Let's move on. Lee, there's a door up ahead on the right. I think it's probably another store room. You and Watkins check it out. Everyone else keep moving forward."

The corridor kept going. They passed and checked two more doors on their way to the back wall, both rooms were empty. Neither crates or consoles. But mounted to the back wall was a staircase that lead to the upper levels. Malone was given the option of going up the stairs or following the corridor that ran south of their position.

The urge to find something was getting strong. He knew whatever was going on in here had to be at ground level or above. But he couldn't leave an area behind his men that might contain enemy forces. He decided to send four of his men down the corridor to hopefully work their way around to Tamar, while he took the rest of his men to the upper floors.

Still not knowing what the enemy might be able to hear through their helmets, Malone had his troops quietly make their way up the stairs one level before coming to a stop on the next floor. A few feet in front of them was another set of stairs going further up. Much as he wanted to keep going up, Malone knew he had to search this floor first and not divide his team any further.

Three corridors ran east into the building from their position. He picked the one to the north and began their exploration. There were several rooms on either side of this corridor, most empty, some with furniture, though nothing more than desks and a few chairs. But they eventually came to the end of the corridor.

The corridor just ended. They could just barely see the far wall in the distance, but where they could walk did not stretch over to that wall. There was another corridor that ran from where they were to where Malone knew the middle or far corridor had to be. *No, wait,* Malone thought, "It's not a corridor. It's destroyed rooms. They're busted up enough to look like a corridor." *But why?*

In front of them, the floor just ended. They looked out on a large cavernous space stretching from the basement, where they had entered, and the top of this building six additional floors up.

"It's just one big open space," Malone said without realizing he'd spoken. "One big open space."

"What do you suppose it's for?" asked the man standing behind him.

He couldn't even look behind him to see who'd spoken. His eyes drifted upward and saw that the floor above him didn't even extend as far as the one he was on. With the floor above that backed into the building even further, before starting to return on the floor above that one. "I don't know," was all Malone could think to say as he stared across the openness that had engulfed him. "Sergeant Iona," he called. "Do you read me, Sergeant Iona?"

"I think I can even see you. Are you on the upper floor towards the back of the building?"

Malone looked down and thought he could see a man waving up at him. "Yes. Do you see this? What the hell's this for?"

"I don't know," Tamar replied. "But stay where you are and we'll be up there in a few minutes."

Malone just stared at the empty space for several minutes before Specialist Lee spoke up. "Hey, sarge. Do we just stand around here or is there something you want us to do?"

Turning to face Lee broke the spell the emptiness had cast over him. "Do? We should check out the rest of this floor. Lee, take the men and search down the other two corridors of this floor.

I'll wait here for Sergeant Iona's squad. Hurry back; we're going to need you guys going up."

"Okay, but be careful, sarge. This thing has some kinda grip on you." Lee turned and motioned to the rest of the squad to follow him back down the corridor so they could check the rest of the rooms.

Malone was alone. Yet when he turned to stare out into the abyss it didn't seem to have the same hold over him. "Cho, have you finished searching the basement rooms?"

"One left, sarge."

"Well, get it done and get up here. I'm down the northern-most corridor."

Lee took a few minutes longer to get to the edge of the middle corridor. Watkins was sticking his head around the far corridor shortly thereafter. Malone thought he heard a sound, a slight sound, maybe felt would be a better description then heard. He turned to look back down the corridor he was in and saw Tamar and his team heading his way. "So what do you think this thing is?" he asked as Sergeant Iona peered over the edge both down and up.

"What do they need such a large space for? Especially if they're not going to put anything in it." He turned to look at Malone. "You guys didn't find any tunnels down below, did you? I'm still trying to figure out how the enemy gets into this building."

"No, no tunnels. Why do they have a ledge overlooking the basement mounted to the front door?" Malone pointed over to part of the floor that had not been removed, leading out of the building but above the basement.

"Something weird is going on here," Sergeant Iona said. "I think we need to set up a stake-out until we can find out what they're using this space for. How many meals did we bring with us?"

"Only a day's worth," one of the soldiers reported.

"If we spread out, covering all floors, we can wait for something to happen. If nothing happens in twenty-four hours, we can send out for more supplies. Malone, send a couple of your men to watch the front, as well as all the side doors. I don't think the enemy is coming into this building the way we did, so forget the windows. Arrange the rest of your men to cover each of the floors that border on this hole. Keahi and I will be on the top floor looking down."

It took about a half hour for each of the teams to acknowledge that they were in position. Since Iona called back first, Malone assumed they hadn't searched the top floor. He sent Lee and three others to search it and stay with them as backup.

Malone went with the group to the floor directly below the top floor. It seemed to be a production floor with several unconnected conveyer belts hanging from their rollers. There were no other rooms on this floor. They made their way to the far side of the room. The steel bars that held the rollers in place came to an abrupt end at the cavern, like they had been sliced off at that point. The belts were disconnected, some hanging over the edge while others just sat on the floor, too short to drape into the open area. Others just sat on the top of the rollers. It was like something had come in and sliced a section out of the building from the inside.

Once Malone had everyone's position, he asked Iona for instructions. "Have your men get comfortable. We have no idea what goes on here or when. It could be in five minutes or five weeks, but we need to know what the enemy is using this building for. Over."

There was no point in having his men stand around. "All personnel; divide your groups into pairs. Find furniture in the empty offices and make your positions comfortable. You all heard Sergeant Iona, we could be here a very long time. Outdoor units, sing out if you see any enemy activity."

His team had to drag several office chairs up from three floors down, competing with two other teams who were also on floors without offices on them. They finally got hunkered down and sat watching the cavernous hole.

"I thought this was going to be a simple contact mission when I volunteered," said Private Ivanov.

"Nothing ever goes as planned, son," Malone responded. *Son! The kid can't be more than a couple years younger than me. Is this promotion going to my head?* Malone felt age creeping up on him, despite not having grown any older.

"But how long are they expecting us to be deployed to this planet, sarge?" asked Private Smythe.

"We're here until the situation settles down. I'd expect reinforcements should be headed our way, but don't expect to be pulled out when they get here. We still don't know who we're fighting or why."

"But I just got engaged before we left," Specialist Hines said.

"When we get back from this assignment, see what the Chaplain's office can do for you. Maybe a VR wedding. At least she'd get spousal benefits while you're here." *How is my wife handling this deployment? This is the longest I've been away from her since we were married three years ago.* He shook his head. Thoughts like that had no business on this mission. He needed to focus. "Anybody bring their bedrolls?" Two of the six people he had with him put their hands up. "Good, roll them out and the two of you get some sack time. We don't know how long we're going to be here, so we'll take turns sleeping." He hoped the other teams had someone suggesting that also.

* * *

"Sergeant, sergeant." Someone was shaking his shoulder. He turned onto his back and opened his eyes. It was Specialist Hines. "Something's happening down there." He pointed over the edge of the floor they were on.

Malone blinked twice, took a deep breath and let it out before trying to get up off the mat he'd been sleeping on. He looked at his watch, he'd gotten three hours sleep and given the other two rest periods he'd already given his men, it meant they'd been on watch for fifteen hours.

He looked over the edge and saw a blue glow shimmering around the entire cavity except in front and back. He shook his body, driving the remaining fatigue from it, and headed off to the front of the building, jumping the three conveyer belts between himself and it.

The blue glow extended to within ten feet of the front door and swallowed the ledge extending from that door. He was thinking about reaching out to touch it, when a spark crackling off its side convinced him not to. He waved the rest of his troop over to his position. Less to give them a better view than to keep an eye on them. He had no idea what this thing was or what it could do.

He heard a crackle and smelled burned plastic wafting from two floors below. Someone must have tried touching the glow with their rifle. "Everyone, keep back from this thing," he called out over the ledge he was standing on.

Sergeant Iona reinforced his warning, "We don't know what this thing is or what it will do to us. So stand back." Then Malone heard over the platoon channel, "All outdoor units, something is happening in here. Be on the alert."

As they waited, the shimmering of the structure began to solidify until it finally looked like a large can ready to disgorge its contents. After a few more minutes, alien soldiers began marching out of the can in a single-file line. They opened the front door and left the building.

"Specialist Cho, here. Several enemy troops are emerging from the building. They appear to be heading across the street to what looks like a warehouse."

Iona was back on the radio. "Cho, keep a count on how many there are. Everyone make a note of how many of these guys are coming out."

Everyone watched in silence as a hundred alien soldiers marched out of the device bringing them to Lankmere. Following the last alien soldier to emerge from the device was a sled with rifles and crates. It floated several inches off the floor and headed to the same place as the arriving alien troops. When the sled passed through the building's front door, the blue can they had come through dissolved and the space was again vacant.

"What the hell was that, sergeant?" Smythe was saying over Malone's shoulder.

"I have no idea. Damn, I didn't think to get a picture for the boys upstairs. I'm just not cut out for recon."

"Did you even have a camera, sarge?" asked Hines, "We normally don't carry them."

He turned to look at his men. "Well, on a recon mission like this, I should have known to."

"Isn't that what our recon advisors are for? If they'd thought you needed a camera, wouldn't they have told you to bring one?"

"You know, you're right, Hines. That's their responsibility. We just need to get back and report." Malone keyed his radio. "Sergeant Iona, do you have everything you need? Can we get out of here? Over."

"We just need to sneak across to the building the enemy is assembling in, get some pictures, then blow it up. I'll meet you in the basement. Have your men assemble there. Over."

* * *

The window they had entered through, and now left by, was on the northern side of the building. There were still no enemy soldiers patrolling the area as they made their way out. Sergeant Iona knelt down on the ground, pulled his backpack off and started pulling round disks out of it.

"Specialist Keahi will get pictures of what's going on in that building. I want the rest of you to mount these disks every six feet along the outside of this building. They're self-adhesive. Once you do, stick one of these control pegs in each one. I've got six for each of you. That should do the job on a building already as crippled as this one. Once Keahi is back, we'll do the same to the other building. Now get moving, I want to get back to the shuttle before the sun comes up an hour from now."

* * *

The sky was starting to brighten as Malone was setting the final charge on the back of the smaller building. He pushed the igniter into the putty as his eye caught movement coming around the far corner of the building. Someone was leaving it via the front door, and was blocking his route back to the shuttle.

He'd sent the last of his men back moments ago, telling them he'd place the last charge. Now he scanned his surroundings for another avenue of escape. One that would not reveal his presence to the enemy. If one of them found out, they would all know. There was an empty lot directly behind him. Several shops running to the north and south along the street that backed up this building. But he was nowhere near the woods he needed to make his escape.

He pulled his scope off his rifle and set it on the ground just beyond the edge of the wall protecting him and pulled up what it saw on his viewfinder. More than one of the enemy soldiers was coming around the far corner, but were not headed his way. They were lining up facing away from him, towards the facility they had emerged from. Almost like they were assembling there.

Help, he had to get help. He contacted Iona, "Sergeant Iona, the last charge is set. But I am pinned down in the back of the building by enemy forces. Over."

"Is there any way you can get five hundred yards away from the building? Over," Tamar said over the radio."

"Not quickly or without being seen. There's a vacant lot behind the building here."

"Large enough for me to bring in the shuttle?" Simmons asked over the radio.

"Easily. Over."

"Sergeant Iona," continued Simmons, "you got everyone onboard?"

"The last one is coming up the ramp now. Over," Tamar responded.

"Then strap in, and let's go cause some carnage."

"Roger that, Lieutenant. We're ready when you are. Over."

"We're not landing, Malone. Be ready to jump in when we get there."

Malone could hear the faint whine of the gravity drive as it lifted the shuttle from its position. Then the roar of the thrusters burst from the forest to the north of him. That was when the lineup of enemy soldiers turned their heads, almost in unison, towards the noise.

"They can hear," Malone said under his breath.

The shuttle briefly closed on the town and began opening a barrage of explosive bullets into the buildings until it came to the largest of them. Simmons launched two of his missiles, throwing debris everywhere and breaking up the precision lineup of troops in the street. He then turned the shuttle east and flew across the street. He cut his thrusters and brought the shuttle down on its gravitational drive until the bottom of the landing ramp was a foot off the ground.

Malone took this as his cue and raced into the vacant lot. He was jumping towards the ramp as several small holes began to appear on the metal all around him. Something burned in his foot as he hit the ramp about half way into the shuttle. The door was closing behind him as he felt the thrusters kick in. Lee and Peters unstrapped, grabbed Malone's arms, and hauled him deeper into the trooper bay.

He lifted his head to look up at Sergeant Iona. The Intel Officer smiled as he lifted a clear lid covering a red button, that he then pressed.

A loud explosion sounded outside the shuttle from the direction they had departed. Then the shuttle rocked slightly before Malone felt it turn upwards at an angle steep enough that Lee and Peters had to hold onto something while keeping him pinned to the floor. They were going home.

Wormhole Debriefing

"It's going to take three to four weeks for that foot to heal, sergeant." Dr. Lattimer hadn't made the trip back down to Lankmere since coming up to work on Lieutenant Latifi's wound. "Since it won't bleed out on you, if you feel comfortable walking on it, you can continue your duties."

"Thanks, Doc," Malone said as he pulled his sock over the bandaged foot. "I've got a hell of a lot of debriefings I have to attend." He slid his foot back into his boot and watched the sides pull themselves together. He jumped down from the examining table after they'd finished and made his way to the door. "You planning on going back planetside anytime soon?"

"Your Lieutenant should be ready to return to active duty tomorrow. I was planning on going down with him."

"I just hope I get done with my reports by then." Malone waited for the door to retract into the wall before passing through the entryway. He tapped his wrist and the time was displayed on his right contact lens. He had ten minutes to get to his first session in the planning office. And General Chi was not a man one kept waiting.

General Chi, however, was one who didn't mind keeping others waiting. Malone took a seat in the conference center's waiting room and watched as the big brass of the task force entered the conference center. Including Captains Palmer, Nilsson and Pangestu, along with Lieutenant Latifi being wheeled into the room. Sergeant Iona sat in the chair next to him.

"I see you were summoned, also," Tamar said as he settled into his seat.

"I'd hoped our reports would be good enough."

"They like to question the preparers of those reports in person," said the secretary, handing a name badge to each of the officers gathering for the meeting.

"What're the badges for?" Malone asked the sergeant sitting behind the desk. "Don't these guys know each other?"

"They each get a small storage augment. It contains all the reports on the incidents they're going to be discussing. Reports are fed to their ocular view screens in the contact lenses they wear, along with a scrambler so no recording of the proceeding can be made." He pulled out another badge to hand to General Chi as he approached and stood up to salute with his other hand.

Malone and Iona stood to salute also. The General acknowledged the salute of his desk sergeant before disappearing into the room.

"At least he saw we were here before he was," Tamar said. "I hate his reaction when he thinks we're keeping him waiting."

"I keep thinking this promotion isn't worth it," Malone said as he sat back down.

"Give it time," Tamar replied. "It'll grow on you."

They sat there for half an hour waiting to be called in. Finally, the desk sergeant turned to them. "Take these." He handed them each a badge with no names. "Put these on and go into the conference room. They're waiting for you."

The two men did as instructed and each pulled one of the double doors exiting the small waiting area for the conference room, which was easily five times the size of the room they had just left. A large oval table occupied the center of the room. Malone saw that it was made of the programmable material, allowing it to dissolve into the floor when not in use. The chairs surrounding it also looked to be of the same material, and could not be moved away from the positions they were molded in. At the far end of the room, a wall-mounted monitor currently displayed the city where Malone and Iona found the aliens' troop delivery system. The city appeared on the monitor as it looked after Malone and Iona's men had destroyed it. Colonel Vermillan motioned the pair to go to a podium standing to the left of the monitor.

"These are the men responsible for destroying the enemy outpost?" General Chi asked as he motioned for his aide to refill his water glass.

"Actually, sir," Tamar began, "Lieutenant Simmons also had a hand in its destruction."

"Why isn't he in here?" the General raised his voice slightly. "I wanted all those responsible for yesterday's action present." He stopped talking for a moment and used his arm control to scroll through something. Malone assumed it was the reports he had stored in his badge. "I can't find an action report from him. Where's his action report?"

The door to the center opened and the desk sergeant walked in. "Get Lieutenant Simmons in here, pronto," the General said.

"Yes, sir." The sergeant was out the door.

"Well, we might as well get started with you two," Colonel Vermillan said from his seat next to the General, sitting at the head of the table. "Sergeant Iona, you're Recon. Please take the podium and recount what happened."

Tamar gave a half-hour presentation, complete with slides projected on the monitor. He recounted the activity starting when he joined Malone's platoon through the time Simmons returned them all to Nyumbani station.

"Thank you, Sergean Iona," began Colonel Vermillan. "Please take a seat." He pointed his hand over to the other side of the monitor, where a chair was rising out of the floor. "Sergeant Malone, do you concur with Sergeant Iona's report?"

Malone began to nod.

"Sergeant, would you please take the podium and place your right hand in the black circle?" Vermillan asked.

"Yes, sir." Malone slid behind the podium he'd been standing next to. He looked down on it and saw a large black circle on its top. He placed his hand on it. A small electrical charge passed from it through his hand. It was not a large enough charge for him to pull his hand away, just enough to let him know he'd completed some circuit. "Yes, sirs. I concur with the report Sergeant Iona has just given."

"Do you have anything to add to it?" the Colonel prompted.

"Yes, sir. It was my estimate that the building the enemy was mustering in contained over a thousand troops. Unlike the troops I'm familiar with, while waiting on a deployment, they were standing completly still. They were not moving around or fidgeting. They almost seemed like statues."

"Thank you, sergeant. You may take a seat." As he approached the chair extruding itself from the floor next to Tamar, "We're asking the two of you remain for the completion of this meeting, as your platoon will be affected by it."

Vermillan continued with the briefing. "Dr. Bykov is having limited success teaching the enemy sign language." He pressed a button on the table and a video began playing.

A picture of Dr. Bykov appeared on the screen. "The enemy soldiers are beginning to accept the hand gestures I have been making in front of them are actually a method of communication. For the first week, they'd been ignoring them. We believe they didn't look on the gestures as a form of language. They are now accepting it as such, and are mimicking the moves. We are using written language and pictures to reinforce the hand signs, but it is slow going. We still have not discovered how they communicate with each other, but we believe it has something to do with the helmets they wear. They seem isolated and listless without them. Some have even tried attacking one of their fellow soldiers if he'd had it off for a long period of time. Attacking him like he was an intruder to their collective. We still do not understand their...''

Vermillan pressed the button again, ending the video. "We aren't going to be negotiating with these people very soon. The testimony these sergeants presented gives us a plausible explanation for how the enemy is getting to this planet without being spotted. Our scientists are speculating the blue tunnel is a wormhole that's allowing a certain number of their soldiers to pass through at set intervals. We should be thankful they can't send an entire batallion through at each opening."

"Gentlemen," the General began speaking, "our first priority is to determine if they have another one of these devices somewhere else on this planet, and continue monitoring for one, in case they attempt to establish another beachhead somewhere else. Next, since we have no idea why this alien race is trying to kill all the Lankmerans, we need to bring the population together so we can adequately defend them."

"General," began Captain Palmer, "we've trained some of the younger Lankmerans in the use of the enemy weapons we've captured. Perhaps they should also be included in any plans to defend the populace."

"I'm assuming you feel you can trust the Lankmerans not to turn those guns on us, Captain Palmer," Colonel Vermillan said.

"Overall," Major Jerkins of Intel added, "we've found the Lankmerans to be an extremely peaceful people. I'm surprised Captain Palmer has gotten any of them to pick up a gun. When they hunt for sport, they use their claws."

"Well, not the older ones," Palmer continued, "They want nothing to do with the rifles. They're willing to wait until the enemy comes within their attack range and spring on them with tooth and claw."

"Still," the General redirected the conversation, "we need to round up the population where they can be protected. Do we have any idea of the total population of this planet?"

"They haven't industrialized yet," Major Jerkins continued, "so we're estimating a worldwide population of only 400 million people."

"That's still a large number."

"About the same number as we have on the ringed colony around Titan or Ganymede."

"We don't have time to build that size space structure. We have to find a place on the planet to house them."

"Major Miller, you're in charge of logistics. Make this happen," the General decided.

"Yes, sir," the man sitting closest to the monitor replied.

"We also need to destroy any Lankmeran structure large enough to house another of those wormholes. Captain Ramirez, I'm dropping you and your artillery company down on the planet. Major Jenkins will send you the coordinates and you're to destroy anywhere they can hide a wormhole. Lieutenant Latifi, your men will be deployed further out from our beachhead to look for more of those wormholes or structures that could contain them. Sergeants, I hope your men know how to ride anti-grav bikes, because you're going mobile. Now let's get to work. Dismissed."

The Sign Language Revolution

"Take it easy on those guys, will you, Henry?" Sergeant Singh surveyed the training field his platoon had set up to get the Lankmerans proficient in using the captured enemy firearms. He hadn't noticed the obstacle course Specialist Phillips had created over the last couple of days until this morning. "These guys hunt already. And they do it using their bare hands. What the hell do you think you can teach *them* about physical conditioning?"

"But, sarge, this is just the same stuff my drill instructor put me through."

"You're not here to get revenge for the necessary workouts you were given. You're here to bring these guys up to speed on firearms safety and utilization. Now get them back to the rifle range and teach them to use those lasers."

Watching from about 5 yards away, Mayor L'mere turned to the army officer supervising the drill. "I am still uncomfortable with the idea of our youngsters being trained in the use of these devilish weapons, Lieutenant Angelov. Can't we find another way to defend ourselves?"

"You saw what the enemy did to your town in just those two attacks. How many of your people were able to get within claw range to defend the town?"

"But guns?"

"With all due respect, Madam Mayor, distance weapons have to be dealt with by distance weapons. You can't take a claw to a gun fight. Even we have to find shelter and wait for them to get close enough. Their lasers even out-range our rifles. We need to hold them back."

"What about traps? Devices to slow them down and hold them in position where we can approach them for personal combat."

"We've been over that. We can't be certain where the enemy will attack from. No, we need to be able to turn in the direction of their attack and instantly repel it. We need to get your people trained on how to defend yourselves if we have any hope of holding off these invaders."

"I watched our young people shoot at the paper targets you set up for them. But I don't know if they can shoot at a living being, shoot at something they can't look in the eye and accept the gift of their life."

"They'll do fine. Even our troops have trouble the first time out. I think we can count on your people to do the right thing when the time comes."

L'mere turned back to the buildings and looked out on the temporary housing going up beyond them. She bowed her head before speaking, "It's bad enough you're restricting our freedom by forcing us into a community in the middle of this continent. Lenora City does not have the resources to house all 400 million of us. Do you expect us to cram into buildings together or sleep on the ground?"

Angelov was patient, but even she had her limits. She had been over the same points with the mayor for the past several days, but L'mere insisted on bringing them up at every available occasion. "The Engineering Corps is erecting several temporary housing units. Some families will have to double up, but I don't think conditions will get as bad as you think."

"What about the damage you did to Latonia? You destroyed several buildings there. Why did you destroy them?"

"We had to destroy the enemies' beachhead. If we let them keep..."

Just then a large noise came from the field hundreds of yards west of the town. The mayor jumped high enough that Angelov thought about catching her on the way down.

She landed on all fours before standing back up. "What was that? You seemed to be expecting it, what was it?"

"Artillery practice."

"What?"

"Very large rifles with very long range and explosive firepower when they hit their target. Just something to take out the enemy's range advantage. We can blow them out of buildings if they get established in them."

"And just how do they do that?"

"One of those mortar rounds hits a building, the whole structure's coming down. Usually on top of the enemy."

"Now you want to destroy everything we've built." L'mere dropped to all fours and ran back to city hall.

Angelov just watched the mayor go, not understanding how the mayor interpreted what she had said.

* * *

"Lieutenant Mason," came over the company's general channel. "Lieutenant Mason, could you come up to the POW encampment. The prisoners are doing something very odd."

"On my way." Mason leaned forward in his chair and started to get up. "Want to accompany me, Lee?"

"A chance for something to do? Of course." He was standing a second behind Mason but beat him to the door of the Anoran building they were using as a command center. They watched the mayor of the town run into City Hall as they emerged.

"I know I'm reading too much into this," Lee said. "But she looked upset about something."

"You probably are. Let's get to the shuttle."

They were airborne in under ten minutes and dropping to the landing pad next to the POW compound fifteen minutes after that. They exited the shuttle through the co-pilot door as Lieutenant Dae-Jung had sat in the surveillance seat on the way up.

The main gate disappeared long enough for the two men to walk through it and reformed behind them. The MP Commandant of the camp, Lieutenant Leonard van Walters, was exiting his field command center as they approached.

"I'm glad you guys could get here so quickly. I wanted to confer with someone and get their take on this before I reported to the Nyumbani. With all the Captains up there currently, I called on you guys."

"So, what 'ya got?" Mason asked.

Dae-Jung stared over at the prisoners congregating outside of the barracks. They were making strange gestures with their hands.

Not all at one time, but it almost seemed like the gestures were in response to gestures another prisoner had made. "Hey," he turned and tried to get the other men's attention. "What are the prisoners doing over there?" Pointing to the prisoners he'd been watching.

"That's what I called you guys about," van Walters started saying. "I don't know sign language, but it looks to me that they're making those kind of hand gestures."

"I've got a deaf trooper in my platoon, so I've learned a few phrases," Mason offered. He stared at the prisoners for a few minutes. Then he turned to his fellow officers, "Damn. I recognize a few gestures. They're signing English."

"What?"

"I'm telling you, Lee, their using American Sign Language."

"How is that even possible?"

"They started making those signs shortly after the last batch of POWs came down from the Nyumbani. A day after their arrival, I noticed some of the new arrivals linking arms with the prisoners already here. After which, they began making those signs to each other. They've been doing that now for the last two days," the Commandant explained. "Should we call up to the station?"

"Without question," Mason began. "Lee, see if you can get some footage of their signing. Leo, you got a video connection here?" When van Walters nodded, he continued, "Well, let's get it fired up, so we can show the brass what's going on down here."

The Tanks Roll In

Major Bancroft got his orders just that morning, and by 1400 hours, he was unloading his company of mobile artillery onto the farmlands surrounding Lenora City. It took about six trips to bring all the troops down to the planet. Bancroft ordered the troops to the southern side of the town, regroup, and set up to receive situational information from Surveillance.

Terran tanks had two modes of mobility, flying and crawling. They could rapidly move from point A to point B on the battlefield by using their anti-gravity drives. The problem with anti-gravity drives is inertia or the lack thereof. If they fired either of their two cannons while in anti-gravity setting, they would be blown backwards with the same amount of force as their projectile, and at the same time, reduce the range of that projectile by absorbing some of its momentum. So a secondary drive system was installed for combat situations. Old fashioned treads were used by the tank operator while engaged in combat, they disengaged the anti-grav system and landed, because treads would anchor them to the ground. Pushing Newton's third law of motion into the ground.

The four dozen tanks now sat on their treads waiting for Major Bancroft's arrival with the last several tanks of the company. The quiet of the anti-grav drive was soothing to Bancroft's ears as the wind through his hair put a smile on the major's face. His face shield would protect him from debris flung his way at the one hundred mile per hour speed his tanks were making. It'd be a matter of minutes until he met up with the rest of his command.

"Sir, we have instructions from Nyumbani," called the communications officer from inside the tank.

"What have you got, Charlie?" The major squatted into the body of his tank to hear his operator without the distortion of the wind. He leaned back into the tank commander's chair after he cleared the hatch opening.

"We're to pick up Sergeant Malone's Recon Platoon and head for these coordinates." He tore a slip of paper off the pad next to the radio and handed it up to the major.

"Did they happen to mention where this Recon Platoon is?"

"Sergeant Malone, to tank company Sword. Are you there?" Bancroft could hear the communication, now that the wind wasn't whistling past his ears.

"This is Sword tank group, sergeant. We read you."

"I just got a call from Surveillance to have you guys pick us up at these coordinates."

The radio operator handed the coordinates up to the Major, who promptly gave them to the tank driver. "Tell the sergeant we shall be there in ten minutes." He activated the communication circuit around his throat, it was a dedicated line to the rest of his tanks. He liked what he'd seen in old movies and had one contructed for himself. "Wheels up, everyone. We have a platoon of grunts to pick up. Then it's off to the action."

* * *

With each member of the Recon platoon safely stored in the passenger seat of the individual tanks, Major Bancroft's company sped to a city that was five hundred miles southeast of Lenora City. This town had a direct road connecting it with Lenora City. With nothing to get in the way, Bancroft ordered his tanks to move single file at full speed.

"What do you want us to do once we get to Macnenium, major?" Malone leaned over in his chair to talk to the major. Under anti-grav power, the noise level in the tank made conversations possible.

"We're going to drop your platoon off at the northern edge of the town and make our way around to the southwestern side. Your platoon is to start infiltrating the city. Command has assured us that all non-combatants have been removed to Lenora City, so anyone in, what did they call that town again, Magnesium?"

"Macnenium, sir."

"Right. Anyway, once your team has reached the towns' first buildings, send up a flare. That will be our signal to begin our attack. If you sweep east and head for the town center, we should be able to trap the enemy between us."

"Let's just hope they're still there when we arrive, major." Malone lifted the metal cover over the viewing slit by his seat and looked out at the passing farm lands. "Once they discover all the Lankmerans have left, what's to keep them there?"

"The desire to hold the land they've taken. Oh, they'll move on soon, but not before fortifying their conquest."

"If that's what they want, sir. They haven't stayed in any other cities, they just kill everyone and move on. Except the one they used for their beach head."

"Exactly. And they'll be wanting another."

"Sir, coming up on Macnenium," said the communication's officer. "There are no EM emissions coming from the city."

The Major looked down from the perch he was sitting on. "Of course, son. We've evacuated all the Lankmerans and the enemy doesn't use any communication technique we are aware of." He sat back in his seat and reached up to open the outer hatch. "Signal the rest of the company to go to tread mode from here on." Then he stood up to survey the area they were approaching.

The wind was brisk as he rose out of the tank, but quickly died down as the vehicle dropped back to a comfortable forty miles an hour. Farm land still surrounded the road they were traveling down. Off in the distance, he could begin to see the outlines of the larger buildings in the town.

"Drop us to thirty until we are within a mile of the town," he pressed the connection in his throat microphone. "Then bring the column to a halt at about a quarter mile out. Malone, we will disembark your troops there. Everyone copy?"

"Yes, sir," came the staggered responses.

The tank column roared ahead. Malone wished the major would close the top hatch, the racket was so loud it was hurting his ears. The sound dampeners in the tank could deaden the noise, but only if the vehicle was sealed. He wished the major wasn't so used to it. He could use the dampeners in his helmet, but the major was on a different circuit than the one built into his helmet. Five miles out, he'd have less than ten minutes to endure the sound.

As the tanks ground to a halt, a whistling began to pervade the inside of the tank. Malone worked to figure out where it was coming from, though it didn't seem to bother the other tank operators. As it stopped, he finally figured out where it was coming from. Outside the hatch. Major Bancroft was whistling a tune Malone had never heard before.

The major pulled himself out of the body of the tank before calling down. "Okay, Malone, this is where your men form up." He pulled his communicator from his vest pocket and activated the Recon platoon channel. "All members of Recon platoon, please disembark and follow your Sergeant's instructions."

Malone climbed out of his seat and over the Commander's chair before he could pull himself out of the hatch. He stepped onto the back of the tank where the major was also standing. It was four feet to the ground, so he chose to jump down rather than use the steps mounted into the side of the vehicle. He received a slight twinge in his left ankle as a reward for his macho behavior. As he stood up, the major was passing his rifle and then his pack down to him. There'd been no room to crawl through the hatch wearing them.

"Thank you, major," he called up after standing his rifle against the tank so he could sling his pack on his back. He keyed his communicator, "Recon platoon, please form up on the right side of the road. These tanks need to get moving ASAP. So get a move on!"

As he walked over to the roadside, he could see his men. Some hustling, some barely moving, but all getting to the edge of the road in a few minutes. Malone walked up the line of men doing a head count. Once he finished, he looked over to the major standing inside his tank, watching their activity. Malone waved to the major and talked into the com unit, "Everyone accounted for, sir! Thanks for the ride. Over."

"We'll be waiting, sergeant." A moment later, the tanks began rolling down the road before turning and crossing a field.

"Okay, everyone gather around." He waited a moment for everyone to form an imperfect circle with him at its center. "We have to get from here, a quarter mile out, into the city," he pointed to

Macnenium. "Sato, can you get me eyes on it? I want to know if any of the enemy are on this side."

Sato patted one of his chest pockets and made his way over to a climbable tree between the field and the road. He climbed up to a safe height, about a third of the way up the trunk. He wrapped his arm around the trunk and pulled out his binoculars from his chest pocket and scanned the city.

"We need to get into the city as far as we can before engaging the enemy, we are the diversion for the tanks coming in. Then we need to drive the enemy to the center of the town and deal with them."

"Sarge, does that mean…"

"Yes, Ivanov. Capture if we can, kill if we have to."

"Sarge," Sato called down from the tree. "I can't find any enemy activity. It looks like nobody's in town."

"Get down here," Malone replied. "Okay. everyone, columns of three. We may as well march right in, if there's goin' be no resistance."

It took them ten minutes to form ranks and make their way into the first street of the town. "Last rank, break off and search the house on the right. Next rank, take the house on the left. Once complete, move on the homes on either side of you. Third rank, the second house on the right. And keep breaking off while you can." Malone pulled a flare gun from one of his lower pants pocket and fired a green flare into the sky.

Moments later, he could hear the rumble of tanks polluting the quiet afternoon air. He imagined them breaking into the city and smashing through the houses as the sounds they made changed. Why was the Major destroying this community when he was facing no resistance?

Recon platoon moved further into the city. When they reached the first of the city parks without resistance, Malone broke the three man teams into pairs to cover more ground. Then he had them turn to cover the homes further out from the strip they'd already covered.

An hour into the search, Malone radioed Major Bancroft. "Major, we're not finding any enemy soldiers in this city. They must have entered it, found no one here and left. I don't think their plan involves occupation. All they want to do is kill the Lankmerans."

"Sergeant, make for the park in the center of town. Surveillance has given us another target. We need to get on the road immediately."

"Roger that, major. We're on our way."

* * *

After an hour flight, the tanks rolled to a stop. They could hear screams and shouts in the distance, moving closer as the minutes ticked by. The noise wasn't close, but it was approaching them.

"We'd better get in there and save what Lankmerans we can," Malone said as he jumped down from Bancroft's command tank.

"Now don't get any heroic ideas, sergeant," the major said as he watched Malone start moving to his men. "This is a Search and Destroy mission. Nothing more," he hollered down as Malone turned to look at him.

"But, sir?"

"No buts, Malone. Your first priority is to kill the enemy." The major disappeared back into his tank, pulling the hatch closed behind him.

Malone spat on the ground as the tanks began their maneuver around the city. Their initial job had been to establish good relations with these people. Not let them die. He walked over to where his men lined up. "Divide into teams of four this time and go house to house. Make sure they're clear before moving on to the next."

"What if we encounter any Lankmerans, sarge?" Hines would have to ask.

"Well, I can't stop you if you send them on their way to Lenora City. Nor can I take the time to stop you from helping them get started. Now, let's move out. This looks like an active city." He grabbed the first three men in line, which included Hines, and headed for the home directly across the road.

They hopped the two-foot fence bordering the back of the house two at a time. Then rapidly made their way to the back door. They were getting ready to kick the door down when Malone caught up and placed his hand on Oshinko's shoulder hard enough

149

for the soldier to turn and look at him. Malone moved past him and tried turning the door knob, opening the door.

The four rushed in and stationed themselves at each of the three doors leading from what looked like a kitchen. Malone joined Hines at the large opening leading to the front of the house. He looked in and found three Lankmerans crouching behind a couch-like device. With its four different heights of sitting positions, it was nothing Malone would have used.

He motioned his men to remain, then ran into the room and dropped behind the family. With his rifle slung behind him, he touched each of the adult cat-people on their shoulders and brought his finger to his lips when they turned to look at him. He motioned for his men to stay put and ran over to the family behind the couch. They jumped back a little, but settled down quickly.

Malone touched the on switch of his translator and began talking. "We're not here to hurt you. We'd actually like to get you out of here. Are there any more of you in this house?"

The male crouched even lower but the female spoke to Malone. "You're one of those humans we've seen on the video."

Malone nodded.

"Our eldest son is still up in his bedroom. We've instructed him to shelter in place up there. It's against the back wall and away from the killing going on in the center of town."

"Hines, get in here." He duck walked into the living room, staying below the level of the couch. "You go with…" Malone looked over at the female Lankmeran.

"Karock T'wine."

"Mrs. T'wine, and bring her kid down here." As the two began moving towards the stairs, Malone turned to the male adult. "Are you okay, Mr. T'wine?"

"F'raq," he began to rise from his crouch but stayed below the top of the couch. "I'm Josoon F'raq."

"Okay, Mr. F'raq. Have you got any land transportation?"

"No. But our neighbor is a constructionist and has a utility vehicle," he said with trepidation in his voice.

"Rouse him and get it behind your homes. We need to load as many people as we can into it and get them moving towards Lenora City. We're using it as a sanctuary city, we're hoping to protect your people there. Now get moving." He helped the man up by his elbow and watched him dart into the kitchen before hearing the back door close.

Malone spun around and sat with his back against the couch. He switched to the platoon only channel. "Attention, Recon platoon, this is Sergeant Malone. By now you have probably encountered civilians in the buildings you're searching. Help them out of their dwellings and get them on the road to Lenora City. If they have a vehicle, encourage them to use it, and share it. If they have to walk, they have to walk, we'll see about air transportation later. We need to get these people headed towards safety."

He turned back and looked at the child still remaining behind the couch. "Oshinko, get in here and cover this room," he called to the kitchen without even turning his head. At the same time, Hines was returning down the stairs leading an older Lankmeran youth and his mother. "Hines," seeing his man approaching, "get these three out the back and ready to board the vehicle F'raq went to find. Then get them out of here."

"Yes, sarge."

"Sato, get in here. We're moving on to the next house." They opened the door. The screams became louder but there appeared no enemy activity in this area. They dashed across the street and into the larger home there.

"We're staying together on this search," Malone said. They'd found no one in the living room. "Kitchen," he waved his men to check out the kitchen. Again they found no one. What looked like an office of some sort or a 'man-cave', as Sato called it, was also empty.

They made their way to the stairs leading to the second level. Malone was going to take point, but Oshinko wouldn't let him. So Malone fell in behind Oshinko and the three of them moved upstairs. They found no one in the two small bedrooms at the top of the stairs. So they moved on to the one on the right side of the house.

It opened into a very large bedroom, which had a bath and a closed door on one side of the room. And what looked like a metal, floor-to-ceiling plate on the other wall. The bathroom was empty, opening the door revealed an empty closet, except for clothes. But it was the third wall that was covered by a metal plate that had Malone curious.

As he walked past the bed in the center of the room, something in the corner of the ceiling caught his eye. It was just above the plate and moved slightly, as Malone moved closer to the plate, the central black dot followed him. He had everyone back up to the far end of the bed and the dot stayed centered on them.

"Panic room," he said mostly to himself.

"Could be, sarge," Oshinko replied.

"Oh, sorry, I was talking to myself."

"Well, ask for some easier orders, when you reply to yourself," Sato said as he walked up to the plate and pounded on it. It sounded hollow on the other side. "Hey, anyone home?"

After the shock of his action lifted from Malone, he waited another minute, listening for a response.

None came.

"If that's a panic room, they're not going to open up for a squad of armed soldiers," Oshinko said. "We need to present them a friendly face."

"Like one of their neighbors." Malone turned and hurried from the room.

Once outside, he looked around for a Lankmeran family heading for sanctuary. He found one in short order. It took a moment to convince the young couple to come with him to try to coax the family out of their safe place. He lead the couple up to where the suspected panic room was.

"Yeah, the K'larens showed us this place," the male said as they entered the bedroom and walked up to the door. "He was really proud of that room, despite the fact he could never tell us what kind of apocalypse he was preparing for. They've got enough supplies in there to last the five of them an entire month. He's a bit paranoid. If you guys leave, we'll see what we can do."

"Thanks," Malone said. "Just get them to head for Lenora City. Okay, come on, you two. We've got others to rescue." He led his men out of the house and into the next one.

They moved forward through five more homes, finding people, and sending them on. They came to a large apartment building. Office complexes were still up ahead. As they walked into the lobby, they found the front desk deserted. Noise was coming from one of the back rooms on that level. They carefully made their way to a barricaded door almost near the rear of the building.

"Hello, inside," Malone announced their presence.

Nothing.

"We're here to help you," he continued. "We're with the Earth Expeditionary Force. We want to get you away from the soldiers who are trying to kill you. Can you please let us in?"

They could hear the sounds of furniture moving on the other side of the door, then the moving stopped. They heard a voice from the other side, "Can you prove who you say you are?"

"The fact that we're talking to you, shows we've taken the time to learn your language," Oshinko said.

Malone unslung his EE-19, pointed it at the floor and fired seven rounds rapid. "The people trying to kill you don't use weapons that sound like that. Now open up. We need to get you all to safety."

Furniture began scraping across the floor again. In a matter of minutes, the doors were being pulled inward, and Malone's team was admitted into the room. Ten Lankmerans were sheltering inside. Some with aprons, some in uniforms, some in suits like Malone had seen the Anora mayor wearing.

"Thank you for trusting us," Malone began. "We have set up a sanctuary in Lenora City, and we need to get everyone there. Once the Lankmeran population has been relocated, we're hoping we have enough troops to stop these killers. But we need to get you people moving."

"Is there anyone upstairs?" Sato thought to ask.

"This is a convalescence home. There are almost fifty patients here, most needing help to move," said one of the women in an apron.

"We hoped they would find us and leave our patients alone," said a man in a suit.

153

"No chance," Malone replied. "Do you have some way to transport them?"

"Normally we call on the city cargo van. We just wheel down the patients' beds and attach them to the restraints built into the van. Most of our patients could simply sit on the floor, but we have a dozen who are bed-ridden and will need to have their beds brought with them."

"Okay, where is this van?"

"In the garage next to city hall. But that's down where the sounds of fighting are coming from, about a mile from here."

"Get your patients out of here, wait for us outside your main doors. We'll get the van and be back." Malone turned and began walking towards the main door. Then he had a thought that just might speed up this rescue. "Can you call everyone else in this city and get them started down the road to Lenora City? I don't care how they travel, but they have to get away from here. They have to get to where we can protect them."

"We'll try," said the man in the suit again.

Malone was on the platoon channel as the three of them headed out. "Ivanov, Smythe, Hines, meet me on," he turned to Sato, "What street are we on?"

"Maltron, sarge," he replied after looking out the window.

Malone rekeyed his communicator, "Meet us on Maltron Street by the five-story building. We're going on a mission to rescue a van."

Get Them To Lenora City

Malone took his men deep into the city. As they approached the central park skirting City Hall, a hole was burned into one of the trees they were passing.

"Down," Malone shouted. His men dropped to the ground and crawled behind one of the park benches. They managed to get it overturned for protection while they tried to figure out how many alien soldiers had jumped them.

By Malone's count, there were twelve aliens firing at them. Sato and Smythe cut them down to eight after firing from either side of the bench. After that, the enemy took cover.

"We can't stay here and trade fire," Malone said. "Sato, there's another bench off to your left. Think you can get under it?"

"Pin those guys down, and it'll be no problem."

"Smythe, there's a large tree about ten yards from you. Are you game?" Malone asked.

"We go at the same time and you're covering fire for Jackson will work for me."

"Then get ready. Everyone else, pick an enemy sniping at us and lay down several rapid three-round burst on their position." Malone was hoping no one got killed in this maneuver, because he wanted to spread his team out even further. "Okay, now. Sato, Smythe, go!"

Both men took off in a crouch to their respective sites. About half way to the tree, Symthe dropped to the ground and began crawling towards it. "I'm okay," he hollered back when he got under cover. "They got me in the sleeve. They're a bit loose. I'll have to tighten them down when I get some leave."

He turned to the three men left. "Ivanov, I want you to move over to Sato's position. Then disappear into the brush behind him and make your way behind our attackers. Hines, same thing, only you use Smythe's tree as your starting point. So, that means we're going to have to lay down fire like there's a dozen of us here, Carl. Have you got enough rounds left?"

"Easily, sarge."

"Ivanov, Symthe, as soon as we start firing, go." Malone turned his attention to the alien soldiers ahead of him and without even looking at Oshinko, ordered, "Fire!"

The two men fired through the slats in the bench as the others ran to their respective destinations. Malone made sure they'd gotten to them before telling Oshinko to slow down his rate of fire. "We need to conserve ammo until they get around the enemy."

Oshinko nodded while watching for any of them to stick their head out. In a minute, one did and there was one less shooting back at them.

"Major Bancroft, Major Bancroft," Malone called over the tank company's circuit.

"Bancroft here. Where are you Malone? You should have met up with us some time ago."

"Right now, I'm pinned down in the central park, trying to make my way to the city garage. We could use some help getting the city van out of it to retrieve medically incapacitated survivors. Over."

"I told you to leave survivors alone. We are here to decimate the enemy, Malone."

"Sir, I need a couple of tanks to cover us while we acquire the van and get it back to the nursing home where the survivors are waiting. We have discussed this with the staff and this van is designed to transport them." Malone was having trouble keeping the anger at Bancroft's lack of empathy out of his voice.

"No, I can't… What? Malone hang on a minute." The channel went quiet for a few minutes, while Malone counted the bursts Oshinko was firing in the enemies' direction. He heard the rounds the others were spending, but only counted Oshinko's.

"Malone, what the hell did you do?"

"Do, sir? Over."

"Lankmerans are erupting out of everywhere and streaming toward our tanks. The first one to get here are hailing us. They seem to think we're some kind of saviors."

"Well, sir. I may have suggested that some of the people we saved call their friends and tell them to get out of town. Head for Lenora City, where we can better protect them, sir."

There was dead air for a moment. "Two tanks are on their way to City Hall. Use them as you need. But this isn't over, sergeant."

"Roger that, sir." Malone started to raise his hand to victory pump it, then realized it would take that hand above the protection of the park bench and stopped himself.

A few seconds later, gunfire erupted behind the enemy position. Then stopped before sounding again. After which, Hines called to them, "All clear, sarge."

The garage was across the park from where they were. It was across an open field. It was not an area Malone wanted to cross. Going around the outskirts might be the safer course, but no matter which direction he chose, the enemy had positions behind the obscuring brush. There was probably lighter fire to the west of where they were, but he chose to go east.

"If we can cut a gap in the enemy lines, it might make the major's job a bit easier." He looked over to the area the tanks had already rolled through. "And maybe save some of the civilian building. Let's move out. Single file, about two yards apart, but within sight of each other. Sato, you lead."

Jackson Sato slung his rifle on his back, moved out from behind the bench where they were hiding and crept on all fours until he reached the bushes. He then stood up and waved the others to follow while he brought his rifle into a firing position.

"Oshinko, you're next. Go."

After all of his men had made it to the bushes, Malone followed suit. They shortened Malone's suggested distance as they pushed the bush aside so they could hand it off to the man coming behind them. It caused less noise as they moved around the park.

They were about a third of the way around when Malone found his men had stopped. When he went to ask why, Sato simply pointed to an enemy soldier laying under a scrub up ahead of them.

Specialist Smythe whispered in Malone's ear, "I could take him silently before he even knows what hit him, sarge."

"No, we tried that already. They have some way of knowing when one of them is killed. No, we'll have to go around him." They started to move out, when suddenly the enemy soldier looked over in their direction. One of them must have made a noise. Before he could move his rifle, a knife was sticking out of the alien's mouth and he fell to the ground. Malone was shocked enough by the visuals that he'd failed to register the sound of the man's helmet breaking.

"What, he saw us," Smythe said.

Malone smacked him on the head as Smythe was pulling his knife free and wiping it on the leaves of the bushes. "Good throw, though."

They covered the rest of the way to the street where the garage was without incident until they came upon a dozen enemy soldiers lined up under the bushes, some laying on the ground, some firing from a kneeling position. Malone looked over, they had one of Bancroft's tanks pinned down. The tank's tread had been sliced by their laser fire, and they were keeping the tank crew inside, unable to climb out and fix it.

"Fan out," Malone whispered to his men. "Take up firing positions. Raise your hand when you're ready." It took almost two minutes for his men to get into position. He watched the hands go up, then return to holding their EE-19s in firing position.

"Now," he called out. All of his men plus himself fired triple shot bursts into the enemy. One of the enemy soldiers had time to turn before being cut down and was able to get one un-aimed shot off against the Earthmen. Ivanov's combat helmet was smoking where the paint had been burned off.

"Okay, that cleared the way. Get to the garage as fast as you can. Run," Malone instructed his men. A bush behind him exploded as its trunk was shattered by a laser bolt the moment he took off.

They broke from the cover of the bushes to make better time. Malone could feel the laser blasts going past even though he knew he shouldn't be able to feel them. The sensation was only in his mind. They kept firing triple shots at the enemy as they overran their position. They didn't bother with the couple of alien soldiers that were left there, their objective was the van.

As Malone made it to the street, Sato was opening the garage doors. In front of him, Malone saw Smythe stumble. Without breaking stride, he grabbed his trooper by his arm and helped him the rest of the way and into the garage. Where, by now, everyone else was.

The van was just inside the door, pointed to be driven out. Malone used the front end of the vehicle to set Smythe down against. There was a hole in his upper right thigh. "No wonder you stumbled out there."

"Thanks, sarge. If you hadn't caught me, I was going down for sure."

"At least with their laser cauterizing everything, we don't need to bandage it," Malone said. "Feel up to a ride?"

"Then a month's recovery on Nyumbani, of course." He pushed with his right hand and his left leg trying to stand up. Sato grabbed him by his left arm and Oshinko by his right. They lifted him to the side of the van. Malone opened the side door and pulled out a ramp that went all the way to the floor. They loaded him in and secured him to one of the seats. The seats were in the back of the van while there were several empty spaces for beds to be secured into the vehicle towards the front.

Ivanov quickly climbed into the cab. Malone, seeing that Oshinko and Sato had Smythe, jumped on the running board and looked over the dashboard. It was obvious what the large wheel in the center of the seat on the van's left side was for. But there was no place to insert a key to start the thing. Several buttons presented themselves on the panel behind the wheel, but none of them were labeled starter, and there were four pedals on the floor.

"We don't have time to figure this thing out," Malone said as he jumped back down. He went to the front door and waited until a Lankmeran family was running past. He whisked them into the garage where he could safely talk to them.

He stared at the male Lankmeran. "You know how to drive?"

"No, he doesn't," said the woman. "But I do."

"Ivanov, get over. We've found a driver," he called up to the van. "Lady, would you please take the wheel? Sir, get the rest of your family into the back of the van. We need to make a stop at the nursing home on the other side of town, then you're off to Lenora City."

They all piled into the van taking the vacant seats. Since it had no barrier between the driver and the back end, Malone called up, "We're ready. Let's get on the road. There should be a tank escort for us somewhere."

As they pulled out onto the street, one of Bancroft's tanks was firing towards the western side of the park. The lady turned the van to the east and after reaching the end of the park, to the north. She gunned it fast enough that the tank, in combat mode, had trouble keeping up with her.

Three laser bolts burst into the side of the van, at different times, and out the other. Otherwise, the trip to the nursing home was uneventful.

* * *

Once the patients were loaded into the van and the rest of the space was filled with others trying to get to Lenora City, Malone pulled his platoon back together on the southeast edge of the park. "Major Bancroft, do you copy? Over."

"Yes, Malone, I'm here. Did you send my tanks back?"

"Sir, there was only one waiting to escort us. He's on his way up the highway escorting the caravan of refugees. Over." Malone knew that wasn't going to sit well, and was not surprised by the silence he was greeted with. He knew the major was calling his tank back.

"Okay, Malone. where are you and your platoon? I need some support. The enemy has figured out how to stop our tanks."

"We know, sir," Malone radioed back. "We had to stop an enemy patrol from holding one of them in place. Could that have been the other tank you promised us?"

"Don't get cheeky, Malone. It's your platoon's job to support us."

"Yes, sir. We're on the southeast corner of the central park."

160

"Work your way to the southern part of the city. Find where the enemy is hiding and flush them out."

"You will let us know before you blow up the buildings we're in, won't you, sir?"

"If you keep up a decent pace, you'll stay ahead of our artillery."

"It's his busting through the front door that I'm worried about." But Malone didn't say that over the communicator channel, only to his men. "Roger that, sir. We're on our way."

With a tank company barreling down on him, Malone decided to break his platoon into six-man teams and cover the houses from east to west, south of the park. He hadn't come onto dead Lankmerans yet, and he hoped he could find more survivors to send to safety.

As they were crossing from the third house to the fourth, Sato spotted some of the enemy soldiers headed their way. Malone's group was working the home closer to the park, diverted from the home they had planned to inspect and went to the one Sato's team was entering. They almost had the house cleared when they stumbled onto an elderly couple still in bed.

"Oshinko, get those two on the road to Lenora City. Everyone else, find a window and get ready." He activated his channel to Major Bancroft. "Major, come in, major."

"Bancroft here."

"Major, we're about to be attacked by an enemy patrol. We don't know their numbers yet, but I'm guessing once we begin firing, the sound will draw a whole lot of those guys to our location. How far are you away from our position?" He pressed the button to acquire his GPS coordinates and send them to the Major.

"Sarge," Oshinko approached him. "This couple can't leave. The man has a chronic breathing disorder. Unless you can find some transport. It's why they didn't leave when their neighbors did."

"Malone," he heard the major call back. "We can be at your position in ten minutes. Can you hold out?"

"We have to, Major. We have civilians needing transport in this house. Can you take up a position in front of it? Once you're here, we can support your positions from behind the tanks." He released his on switch and addressed Oshinko. "Check out the empty houses we've cleared and see if there's transport in any of them. If not, I think there was a car in the City garage. Now go, man, find them a way out of here."

Malone dropped behind one of the living room windows, before trying to get a look out of it. "Does anyone have an idea of how far away they are?"

"They're about three blocks back, sarge," Ivanko called from the dining room. "But it looks like they didn't see us. They're still going through each home looking for Lankmerans."

"Well, we still have some time, then. Did anyone bring remote grenades?"

"I've got four, sarge," offered Sato.

"Get across the street and set up a staggered pattern. Then get back here. Ivanko, where are our friends now?"

"They've just entered the bakery down a couple of blocks, sarge."

"Sato. Go!"

Through the window, Malone watched his man dash across the street and place four grenades in various spots in the grass. Once he was done, he turned to look at the building the enemy had just entered. Malone wasn't sure if any of the aliens had left. He said under his breath, "Sato, get your ass back here."

Ivanko looked at him but didn't say anything.

Sato burst through the front door several moments before the enemy soldiers emerged from the bakery. He'd gotten back unseen.

Malone looked at him as he came into the living room. "Plant yourself in the middle of the room, away from this window and wait for my signal," he told him. *Who would get here first,* Malone thought, *our tanks or our enemies?*

Across the street, beyond the home directly in front of them, looking into the back yard of the one behind it, Malone saw bubble-headed soldiers emerging from the next house they inspected. It looked like the tanks would have another few minutes to arrive.

Saving Rain From The Sky

Captain Nilssen had taken her platoon into the large metropolis on the southern border of Continent 1. The soldiers called it Anceroferdon. They had to call it something, because the Lankmerans didn't have a name for it. Since she had given up trying to figure out the Lankmeran's naming scheme, she just referred to the city as This City whenever they entered a new one.

The enemy hadn't invaded it when they'd entered, which meant they made good time getting the citizens of the town loaded on the boats in the harbor and sent them around the continent to the north, where they would make landfall in the coastal community of Raschon. From there, they would travel by road to protection in Lenora City.

She'd found a bell tower that stood ninety feet above This City, the highest structure within it, and set up an observation post. She'd divided her company by their platoons and had each one working from a corner of the city inward. Except for the southeast corner, closest to the docks. Once her crow's nest was established, she went there with an electronic megaphone and broadcast an announcement about the evacuation.

As the Lankmerans began arriving at the dock, she turned logistics duties over to her staff and headed back to her perch, to keep an eye on things. It was when she got back that things started going south. She saw the domed helmets of the enemy peeking out of the windbreak east of town.

She grabbed the microphone off the desk rather than reaching for her personal one. "All units, all units. Drop what you are doing and make your way to the east of town. Prepare to repel invaders. There are several goods depots there, rally at those locations and make a stand. The aliens are on their way into this city, so move it. Over."

Then there was a noise. The enemy soldiers had gone into the home across the street as a lone car pulled up in front of the house Malone was occupying. It was Oshinko.

These houses had no driveways, very few Lankmerans owned a vehicle. Sato and Ivanov ran to the bedroom and scooped up the old man, carrying him to the front door and outside. The female Lankmeran followed them out. Oshinko had the door open, ready for them to place the man inside. He was back behind the steering wheel before they were setting him down. The woman began running to the other side to get in.

Several laser bolts came from the window of the adjacent home, one catching the woman in her right arm. Sato jumped over the car's trunk to help her in. Ivanko swung his rifle off his back. Before he could lay down covering fire, everyone still in the house opened up on that large window.

As soon as Sato closed the back door, Oshinko took off up the street to get away from the firefight. Sato ran for the front door to get back in the house as Ivanov fell back to the lawn of the home and dropped to a firing position on the ground.

As Sato slammed the door behind him, Malone evaluated Ivanov's position. Classic firing range gunnery position, he should be safe from the enemy fire. He could leave the man out there for now. Besides, he thought he heard Bancroft's tanks rolling down the street.

He looked over at Sato as the man walked back into the dining room. "Sato, stop," he called to the man as he came to the arch between the two rooms. After staring at his back for a moment, Malone continued, "Strip down to your shirt. You've got several holes in your backpack."

But the shirt was clean. Enemy fire wasn't strong enough to punch through Sato's pack and Kevlar. "You're okay. Take up your position." Malone went back to the window to wait for the tanks to arrive.

Within a couple of minutes, the first tank came rolling down the street. It stopped just east of the house, then turned ninety degrees to face the homes where the enemy fire was coming from. Then the next tank arrived and did the same thing. With a six foot gap between the two tanks, Malone heard the second one switch to anti-grav drive and close the gap to a foot. Followed by a thud as it switched back and hit the pavement.

Within ten minutes, a row of ten tanks were pointed at the buildings across from Malone. Each of them pumped explosive shells into those structures.

"Okay, everyone. Get out there and behind those tanks," Malone called to his men. "Take up firing positions."

The radio buzzed on the tank frequency. Malone switched to it, "Sergeant Malone, once your men are in position, we can roll down these line of houses. The major says that if our guns don't get them, our treads will."

"I really don't want to be destroying all the Lankmeran homes, Commander," Malone pleaded with the tank commander whose voice didn't sound like the Major's. He emerged from the house and looked for a position behind a tank that was available.

"Orders, sir. Nothing is to remain to give the enemy shelter."

Dammit, we'd come to make friends with these people, not destroy everything they have. He looked over at his men, now protected by the tanks in front of them. "Okay, Commander, we're in position. You may proceed." Maybe he could appeal to the General when this operation was over.

The tanks began moving forward. The houses with fences lost them immediately. As the tanks approached the actual homes, Malone could hear the tank drivers increase the power of their engines, explosive shells were fired into the structures, producing explosions the tanks could just ignore, and then they rammed their way into the building.

Malone and his platoon tried to fire at the fleeing enemy soldiers as they bolted from their hiding places. They hit many of them, but a lot more got away. Within an hour, the tank patrol had cleared a corridor a block wide and a mile long. They came to a stop as they reached the edge of town.

The City of Chinook

It was rescue time, as far as General Chi was concerned. Captain Palmer had taken Bravo Company into the city of Chinook to make sure all its inhabitants had left before the enemy could make its way there. He had Headhunter platoon clearing out the southern part of the town, Listener platoon the middle section and Coverfire platoon working the northern part. He and his three Lieutenants made their way to the central square with the bullhorn that the tech department of the Nyumbani had designed. It was a device that would not only allow him to holler out to the nearby Lankmerans, but any recieving device that was active would recieve his words.

"People of Chinook. We of the Earth Expeditionary Force, in our effort to protect you from the invading aliens, need to move all of you to a safer location. We need all of you to move to Lenora City until this crisis is over. Pack what you can carry. If you have a vehicle, we urge you to use it. It's several hundred miles from here and the sooner you get there, the safer you'll be. Take one of the three roads leading north out of town and we'll have men to help you along the way. If you know of any infirmed individuals, let one of my soldiers know, and we will make arrangements to transport them there. Please, this is for your safety." He tossed the bullhorn to Lieutenant Angelov and began walking into the town's green space.

"Very rousing speech, captain."

"Suck it, Mason. I don't need your toadying going on right now."

"Yes, sir."

"Captain Palmer, Captain Palmer, this is an emergency. Please come in." His and all of his Lieutenants' devices spoke.

"Palmer here, go ahead."

"What is your mission status?"

He looked at his three Lieutenants before answering. "We're about half done clearing this town."

"Captain, you have a large squad of enemy troops heading for your position. They are approaching from the south and are about a mile out. We suggest that you start fortifying a defensive position there immediately. We're sending a company of artillery your way to assist. But get hunkered down now."

"Roger, base." He turned around to look his lieutenants in their eyes. "You heard the man. Get your men down to the southern edge of town and prepare them. Mr. Mason, have one of your platoon squads continue the search, working from the town's southern edge north."

"Right, sir." He was just a step behind the other Lieutenants as they headed to meet up with their platoons, each calling ahead to their men to have them ready to move out.

This was an extraction mission, Palmer thought. *What am I going to do with an artillery company?*

Palmer looked over the skyline of the city to find the tallest building, closest to where the action would be. He spotted a four-story structure a few blocks north of the city's edge and made his way over to it.

As he approached the building, he found the front doors of the establishment facing north and locked. He pulled out his pistol and unlocked the door, then he made his way into the lobby where a room with multiple tables set up on one side, and a dining room set up on the other. He marched up to the man standing behind the main desk.

"Didn't you hear my announcement about leaving this town?"

"Sir, we've heard about the Earth forces and what they're trying to do. And how deadly this enemy is. But we have patients here who are not ambulatory." Palmer gave him a quizzical look. "They're bed-ridden. They can't walk. And this home doesn't have any means of transporting them."

Great, Palmer thought. *How do I get these people to safety? A* ... "Surveillance, this is Palmer. I need a shuttle down here to pick up several Lankmeran patients."

"How many are we talking about?"

Palmer looked over to the Lankmeran desk clerk. The clerk checked the registry. "We have twelve, sir."

"There's twelve of them. Can you set down in the central park here?"

"We've got a shuttle on the way. And use the artillery transports when they get there, if that doesn't have enough space."

"Roger and thanks." He turned back to the man behind the desk. "Can you get those patients to the park north of here?"

"You're going to fly them out?"

"Only if you get them there. Can you?" When the man nodded, he continued, "Then move."

The Lankmeran wearing a white nursing uniform turned and ran up the stairs with Palmer following. The care-giver stopped to give instructions to another white-uniformed figure before continuing on to the next floor, passing Palmer in his haste. The new individual ran down the hall and rounded up other staff members. Palmer kept going to the top floor so he could keep an eye on his troops.

Palmer reached the top floor. There were no patients present; only a laundry, food lockers, and storerooms. There was also an observation lounge up there allowing Palmer southern and northern views of the streets below. He couldn't see the bulk of his troops; however, he observed a few still making their way into the houses skirting the fields surrounding the city. He didn't know anything about what kind of organized games the Lankmerans played, but the fields they played them on offered his men an open area to the trees lining the farming country.

Looking down through the northern window, Palmer saw a number of ambulatory patients making their way out of the facility. "I hope we have enough time to move everyone before those bubble-heads get here," he said to himself.

He pulled his communicator out of his pocket. "Nyumbani, this is Captain Palmer. What's the ETA on those rescue shuttles?"

"Williams here, Captain. Chen and I should be at your location within fifteen minutes."

"The patients should be waiting for you when you get here. Coordinate with the facility staff when you arrive. They will be wheeling the convalescent patients out on mobile beds."

"Roger that, Captain. We'll make sure nobody gets left behind."

"And we've got bubble-heads on the way, so keep low." He would have preferred "Jarhead" Simmons, but Gevona and Bao were competent pilots. It would be his boys' job to keep the bubble-heads too busy to fire at the shuttles.

The bark of an EE-19 pulled his attention back to the southern window. Bubble-heads were beginning to emerge from the treeline and one of his men had jumped the gun. One of the aliens had fallen to the ground, but the rest that had stepped into the open area were retreating behind the trees.

"Lieutenant Mason," Palmer called. "What's your status?"

"Private Marlon jumped the gun when the enemy broke through the tree line. They're still within easy range of our rifles, Captain. What's our mission here?"

"Keep your men under control, Lieutenant. We're to hold the bubble-heads back until we get additional orders from on high. Just keep them too busy to notice the two shuttles coming in to pick up Lankmeran patients." Palmer pulled his binoculars out of his vest pocket to get a better view of the fighting. The sound of rifles could be heard popping now from where he was.

"Roger that, captain. I hope they come up with something soon, or we could be in for a long stalemate."

"You and me both, lieutenant. Take care of your men." He dropped his communicator into his vest pocket and brought his hand up to steady his binoculars. "You and me both," he added to himself.

The battle looked one-sided for about ten minutes, you could only hear the firing from the Earthmen's weapons, since alien lasers were silent. Then, "Captain Palmer, this is Lieutenant Angelov. We're taking fire from the buildings on our left side. It appears..."

"Captain Palmer, this is Lieutenant Dae-Jung. The enemy appears to have moved to the buildings on our right. We are taking fire from them."

Damn it, Palmer thought. *They've figured out how to surround us.* He grabbed his radio, "Everyone, retreat. Repeat, everyone pull back about three blocks and see if you can spread out enough to keep those guys from flanking you. There's an open field to the east that should give you unrestrictive fire."

He didn't have the men to hold the whole city. "Surveillance, this is Captain Palmer. Surveillance, do you copy?"

"Captain Palmer, pull your men out of the city. Make your way into the hills just north of town. Set up a spotter position there. We're sending in an artillery division to level the town and deny it to the aliens. Link up with Major Williams when you get there. Over."

"Blow up the town? We're here to protect the Lankmerans, not to destroy everything they've built."

"Captain, you have your orders."

"They're still loading the shuttles, Surveillance. We need to give them cover."

"As soon as those shuttles are in the air, you get out of there, Captain."

"Roger that." He released the unit from his trembling hand, letting it fall back into the pocket he carried it in. "I just hope we've had enough time to get everyone out of the city," he muttered to himself. It'd taken a lot of effort not to tear the communication device out of his vest pocket and hurl it across the room. He had lived with these Lankmerans, gotten to know them, liked them, and now he was asked to be a part of destroying their lifestyle and leaving a lot of them to die.

But his men came first. There was no way they were going to beat back this alien incursion, they had to retreat. "Bravo Company, this is Captain Palmer. Begin an orderly retreat out of the city. Pull back to the shuttles and find positions to protect them until they're airborne. Once they're gone, we'll regroup in the hills about a mile to the north. Do not leave anything for the enemy to use, and take care of each other. Lieutenant Mason, take command of the company. Surveillance asked for a spotter for the artillery they're sending in. I'll be staying in the nursing home. It's the tallest building and I can act as a spotter as well. Get the men to safety, Andrew."

He was tempted to turn off his radio; he knew his men would call him to try and talk him out of it. To offer to exchange positions with him. But he couldn't allow it. There were no other tall structures outside the city he could spot from. He knew he would be right in the middle of the target area when the shelling started. He couldn't ask anyone else to make that sacrifice.

He continued contemplating his dilemma while watching the shuttles land and begin loading the bed-ridden patients on board. The shuttle crew and orderlies loaded six patient-beds in each shuttle. Fortunately, to Palmer's relief, there was also room enough for the hospital staff. Everyone would be evacuated safely.

"Captain Palmer," one of the several messages coming over his communicator sounded more like a query than a plea. "Captain Palmer, this is Specialist Yang requesting direction. We heard the recall order a few minutes ago, but we have a dozen more blocks of houses to cover. What should we do?"

"Yang, get your men out of there. We need to be clear of Chinook before the artillery gets here. Now move."

"Right away, sir."

Distracted by the call, Palmer didn't notice the sound of footsteps climbing the stairs until two soldiers were standing in the room with him. He turned and demanded, "What the hell are you two doing here?"

"Sir, Specialists Weber and Becker here. We're relieving you."

Weber stood at attention while Becker walked to the large picture window, cut a hole in it, and watched as the glass shattered on the sidewalk below. "I told your Lieutenants I would be the spotter," Palmer said.

"That you did, Sir. But the Lieutenant decided what was really needed up here were snipers, not, and I quote, 'toothless officers'. We can spot for the artillery and slow the advance of the alien enemy," said Weber, standing in front of the Captain.

"If we can slow them enough, the artillery may not even have to shell this building," said the man kneeling by the window. He'd set his EE-19 on the floor and was adjusting his longer sniper rifle. "Sir."

"So if it pleases the captain," said the first sniper. "Get the hell out of here and let us do our job. Sir." He didn't wait for the captain to respond, but went up to the far side of the picture window where his partner was working and kicked his steel-toed shoe through the glass. "Wilhelm, I got a bigger hole."

"Just don't cut yourself on those edges," replied the other.

"Sir, what are you waiting for? Get moving."

One thing they never taught you in Officer Training School but you quickly learned, if you were an effective field commander, was never overrule a man when he's doing the job he'd been trained for. Experience trump's rank. "I want to see you men when this is over, you understand?"

"Yes, sir," they replied almost in unison.

He walked over to the stairs and took them two at a time before he got to the ground floor and walked out the front door. Lieutenant Angelov was waiting for him there.

"Just so you know, those two volunteered. I'll even bet you they used the same arguments on you they did on me when I was going to traipse up there and take your place."

"Let's see if we can keep Williams from shelling this place."

"Roger that, sir," she replied. "The shuttles left a few minutes ago and as far as I can tell, everybody else is north of our position."

"So we'd better hurry before the bubble-heads overtake us."

"You know you're the only one calling them that. Their helmets are a long domes more than a bubble."

"Long-dome-head, just doesn't have the same ring to it, lieutenant. Now I think it's time we did our annual mile run." He took off before the Lieutenant could respond, since last year when they did their qualifying runs together, she beat him by a lap.

As Palmer topped the hill overlooking the town of Chinook, Major Williams stood on the far side of the ridge with his hands clasped behind his back, watching his men. They were still pulling the last couple of anti-grav pallets which had three foot tubes that were made of metal over two inches thick mounted on them. They looked like they would be quite heavy, if the Higgs field around each of them hadn't been negated. A short wiry lieutenant, whose cleanly pressed uniform made him look like he was straight out of the academy, was directing the artillerymen where to set up. Four units had already been dropped into position, their gravity restored, they dug into the earth under them. One unit on the end had its gunnery team connecting the five round magazine into the top of the barrel.

"Randy, even when you cheat, I can still outrun you," said Lieutenant Angelov as she stood up from resting with her hands on her knees while she caught her breath. She finally looked around the hillside. Seeing the major, she tried to slink off to her platoon that was sitting under a group of trees behind where the guns were being set up.

"Captain Palmer, a word," said Major Williams as he saw Captain Palmer come over the hill. He was still standing straight as an arrow, hands clasped behind his back as the sweating, out-of-breath Palmer approached. "You're not setting a good example, man, if you let a subordinate beat you like that."

"She ran the marathon in last year's Olympics, sir," Palmer said between heavily-laden breaths. "But she's slowing down, I almost caught her twice just then."

"More likely she was keeping an eye on you. You have your spotters in position?"

He looked back at the city he'd just run through and picked out the nursing home. "Sir, that four-story building. The tallest one, just south of the center of town," he pointed in the direction he wanted the major to look. "We left Specialists Weber and Becker, two snipers, on the top floor. They're going to try to hold back the enemy advance while spotting."

"Smart move," the Major replied.

"Actually, they volunteered, sir. I had originally planned to stay behind myself."

"And what good would that do? It would only deprive this army of a properly trained Captain. No, sacrifices like this are for our troops to make."

"Sir, we are going to retrieve them?"

"If we can. But our primary goal is to level this city to deny the enemy of its use. As soon as these guns are in place, we'll be firing test rounds to see where they're landing. Then when your boys say we homed in on our targets, we're going to bring this city to the ground."

"And all the work the Lankmerans did to create it. Sir."

"We're saving their lives, Mr. Palmer. Isn't that enough?" He turned to look for his own subordinate. "Lieutenant, how soon will we be ready?"

"We're ready for the test rounds now, sir." His voice even had the freshness of the academy.

"Do so immediately."

"Gunnery team One. Take a reading on the farthest line of houses and target them. You may fire when ready."

A minute later, the silence of the hill was shattered with the explosive sound of the big guns firing for range. It was impossible to follow the trajectory of the rocket-driven round as it sped over the city. But the crash and thunder of it hitting the ground announced it was at its destination.

"Specialist Weber, here. Your round overflew the city by about a hundred yards," came the field report.

"Again, Lieutenant."

"Adjust and fire." A moment later, a second round launched itself into the air. This time everyone could hear the splintering of the home it had just destroyed.

"You're on the last line of homes," came the spotter's report. "The enemy has moved much further into the city, though." The sound of a rifle round came over the channel. "I would suggest coming further north by about five hundred yards. We're trying to hold them there."

"Everyone adjust your trajectories and fire at will." The Lieutenant walked behind his line of fifteen cannons and watched as they began their bombardment. It took the first cannon a minute to go through its remaining three shells before they had to pull the magazine and insert another. The others pounded the back end of the city for almost a minute longer.

"Sirs," came another report from the spotters. "The enemy seems to be retreating. They're moving south, out of the city."

"Team one," said the major, "use your earlier settings and pound that last line of houses. Pan west with each round."

"Yes, sir," the team responded before launching the rockets in the magazine they had just loaded.

Palmer noticed the shuttle that had held the artillery pieces was still in the field behind the gun emplacements. "Sir," he went up to address Major Williams. "If we take the shuttle, we could use its guns to drive the enemy back the way they came and find out where they are based."

"Son, our orders are to wipe this company of soldiers out. And we will do exactly that. But as the enemy gets behind that line of trees, our spotters can't tell us where they are. Your shuttle idea might be a good one. Lieutenant Chen, power up your shuttle. Captain Palmer, load your platoon into it. I'm sending the two of you behind enemy lines to cut them off. Between my artillery and your rifles, we'll destroy them."

"Right away, sir," Palmer answered and turned, facing where his men were resting. "Okay, boys, grab your gear and head for the shuttle. We're going to be dropped behind the enemy to pin them down."

"Sirs," Specialist Becker said over the communicator. "The enemy has some kind of weapon on the far side of the tree line. It's just burned a hole through a couple of trees before destroying three homes running south to north. Those homes are now on fire. If I had to guess, they've got some type of really powerful laser out there. It's behind the trees, so I can't give you its coordinates. But it's got to be huge."

Palmer turned from his men and climbed back up to where Major Williams was looking out over the town. "Sir, we can't send the shuttle into that. A smaller version took one down earlier."

"Are you refusing my order, Captain?"

A call interrupted. "There it goes again. They've taken out the next four houses in that line. We're pulling out of here before that thing gets a bead on us."

"We're going to have to deal with that thing before we send people into the air, major."

"Captain, send your men around the eastern side of the city. That should be closest to whatever that thing is. Find it. Destroy it. If you need artillery support, call it in."

"Yes, sir. We're on our way." He trotted back to his men, all geared up and awaiting further orders. "We're going around the eastern side of the city. We're going to take that laser-cannon, or whatever it is, out."

* * *

The trek around the city, without transports, took Palmer and his troops just under an hour to arrive. In that time, the aliens had burned down over a quarter of the city. As they crept around the tree line protecting the alien machine, Palmer got his first look at it.

It was currently not in use. The enemy, having burned their way through another strip of Chinook, were moving it along the berm they'd created to elevate the device to clear natural hazards and have an unobstructed firing line. It took four alien troopers to get the cannon moving. Its weight had to be tremendous. Forward of the platform, with six wheels mounted below it, was a three foot barrel. Balancing that on the platform was a very large black box that was almost completely vented. Several dozen other enemy troops were standing on the far side of the berm, watching their companions move the device.

"Weber, Becker. Do you think you can take out the guys pushing that thing?"

"It'd be our pleasure, Captain," Becker said. The pair of them began pulling their long-range rifles off their backs and found positions to set them up on their tripods to make the shots.

"Everyone else get ready. Once they fire, that crowd of bubble-heads'll know we're here."

"Far side first, Hans?"

175

"Agreed, Wilhelm. That should stop the thing in its tracks, then we can get the other two." The two men's rifles spat at almost the same moment. The enemy cannon stopped its motion a second later. The entire squad of enemy soldiers looked in the direction of the rifle shots. That's when the snipers dropped the other two men pushing the cannon.

Bravo Company opened up on the alien soldiers, who were trying to get to their laser weapons. Several aliens ran up the berm trying to get in a position where they could push the cannon forward. Weber and Becker picked them off as quickly as the aliens took up their position. They were a harder target to hit, since they were laying on the ground with about a dozen of their fellow troopers giving them support.

Palmer backed away from the confrontation to call Major Bancroft. "Major Bancroft, come in, Major Bancroft."

"Bancroft here."

He tapped the button on his computer pad to call for the location of the aliens in front of him and fed those numbers into his radio. "This is the coordinates of the bubble-heads' cannon. And these," he fed another set in, "are where the rest of them are. If you can…"

"Have your men take cover, captain."

Within seconds, the whine of incoming projectiles could be heard coming from where Williams' artillery was stationed. "Get Down! Take Cover!" Palmer barely had time to scream to his troops as the rounds struck.

First the immobile cannon exploded into millions of tiny pieces, then explosions rained down on the troops sitting behind the berm. After the first barrage hit, the aliens not killed were running around, trying to figure out how death could drop from the sky on them. The soldiers of Bravo Company easily picked off the stragglers.

Enemy Ambush

"Major Bancroft," came down from the Nyumbani, "this is Surveillance. We have a new destination for you. Alpha Company is trapped in the town of Larvesta. We need you to take your tank company and the Recon platoon to these coordinates and provide relief."

"Roger that, Surveillance. We understand and comply." The major ducked back into the body of his tank and addressed his navigator. "Plot a course to Larvesta, Mr. Riley. Mr. Le, bring us to a halt until we know where we're going. Henderson, signal the other tanks to hold their positions."

"Aye, sir," came the response from two of the men.

Riley looked up at the major and asked, "Where is Larvesta?"

After contacting Surveillance again and getting the coordinates of the town, Sergeant Riley plotted the course, fed the numbers into the tank's navigational computer, and waited for it to give him a course they could follow.

"Recon platoon," Malone called to his platoon. "We're going on a rescue mission, guys."

"I've got the directions, major. It's about six hundred miles from our present location." He worked a few controls on his computer. "I've sent the coordinates to all the other navigators and drivers."

"Very good, Mr. Riley." He touched his throat, where he still kept the microphone for tank communication. *For tradition's sake*, he'd told General Chi when the old man had asked. "All units, make haste to the coordinates you've been given. We have another squad of grunts to save. Bancroft out." He leaned towards his unit's driver, "What are you waiting for, Mr. Le? Let's move out."

"Mai mai, sir." Malone felt the tank begin to move. He imagined it lifting to over the treetops, then he felt the speed kick in as they began racing the six hundred miles to Larvesta.

"English, son."

"Aye, sir."

Malone slumped down in his chair a bit. The half hour trip he'd been expecting had just turned into almost two hours long. As he learned in basic training, catch shuteye whenever you can. The continuous sound of the thrusters lulled him asleep in minutes.

* * *

A jolt woke him back up.

"Le, what's the problem?" Bancroft called down from his command chair.

"It's the lead tank, sir. Something hit it. It's falling to the ground. The column came to an immediate stop."

Bancroft swiveled his chair to talk to the navigator. "Riley, get a hold of that tank and find out what's wrong."

Another explosion, this time much closer, like it was the tank in front of Bancroft's. He popped the hatch and stuck his head outside.

The tank in front of his was now falling to the ground, like the anti-grav unit holding it aloft had stopped working. He could see the first tank shattered on the ground with its crew beginning to climb out of the wreckage.

"Everyone, descend to ground level. Repeat, return to the ground, immediately." Within moments, the entire remaining column was descending, searching for a non-wooded spot to set down.

"Sir, what happened?" Malone had gotten out of his chair so he could look up into the open hatch and talk to the major.

He dropped back into the tank, Malone giving him room. "The most vulnerable part of these tanks is the anti-grav unit. We mount it under the chassis so it can't be gotten to. When we're in the air, we're usually moving too fast and too high for anyone to hit it."

"Unless they have speed of light weapons."

"Unless they have speed of light weapons, like the people we're facing do. We don't know they shot down those lead tanks, but we need to find out what brought them down before we can go any further."

"Are the men alright?"

"The tanks are toast, but they're designed to allow the crews to survive. They may be banged up a bit, but they should still be alive."

The rest of the column landed without incident. After the Recon platoon scrambled out of their respective tanks, they scoured the area to see if it was safe for the rest of the tank crews to emerge.

There was no one in the woods for over a hundred yards. Major Bancroft had his tank personnel pull out their field equipment and set up a camp for everyone, while Malone's Recon platoon walked into the woods following the route the column had taken to find out what had brought down the two tanks. Malone suspected it was something like the lasers that had taken down the shuttle a couple of weeks back. Unfortunately, he hadn't seen those, either.

They fanned out, covering several hundred yards across, and walked forward. About a mile in, Malone decided to turn his troops and see if a laser came from either side of the column. They pivoted on their central point, which happened to be Malone himself, and marched to the left.

About a half mile in, they came upon a clearing that had movement in it. They crept up to its edge. The clearing was an oblong-shaped circle, with several enemy soldiers working the largest laser rifle Malone had ever seen. While it was over twelve feet from the end planted in the ground to the tip of its emitter, it did not stand taller than the trees surrounding it. The upper part of the barrel was supported by a large tripod, and instead of a rifle's trigger, there was a control panel on the side of it, where three of the aliens were working.

Malone counted six soldiers in the clearing with rifles, the rest were tending the machine. Malone turned to look at his men. As each turned to catch his eyes, he motioned them to take out one of the armed targets. Where he could, he assigned two of his men to each of their adversaries. He also needed to take out the technicians quickly.

As they all took aim. Malone drew in a deep breath, mentally counted to three, then said, "Now."

Human gunfire erupted on the unsuspecting aliens. They all went down in the solo seven-round volley each human unleashed.

Malone held up his hand and announced, "Cease fire." Then he marched into the clearing, followed by his men. "Spread out," he ordered. "I find it hard to believe there isn't another patrol around here someplace. I know I wouldn't leave something like this undefended."

He began walking up to the enemy artillery piece. "Carl, I want you to have a look at this thing."

"Sure, sarge."

"What's the best way to destroy it?" Malone ran his hand over the reachable sections of the barrel while Oshinko bent down to get a good look at the thing.

"Yeah, it's too big to drag back to base camp, and I don't think we can get a shuttle in here. I think we can wreak some real havoc on it with the grenades we have. A dozen should make a real nice explosion. Unless you want to bring one of the major's tanks in here."

"That'd take longer than I want to be here. Someone had to hear our gunfire. Start rigging your explosives while I document this thing for Surveillance." Malone touched the side of his helmet and activated the camera in the faceplate Surveillance had added to his helmet after he couldn't get any pictures of the alien wormhole. He walked all around the big laser, taking about a dozen photos. He went around collecting more grenades for Oshinko when he'd finished.

As he was handing his trooper about a dozen more grenades, Oshinko said, "That's more than enough. But the extras will make for a bigger boom. I'm rigging the grenades to explode on a radio trigger, so we can get away and know they'll all go off together."

"Good thinking."

"I'll be done here in five minutes. You can start pulling everyone back."

"Okay," Malone hollered at his men walking around the clearing's parameter. "Head back to our entry point."

All the men got out of the clearing as Oshinko finished rigging the explosives. Finishing up on the far side, Oshinko stood up to head out of the clearing, when he screamed and dropped away from Malone's sight. Several aliens broke out of the other side of the clearing and began firing at Malone's men.

"Damn, he's down. And with the detonator," Malone said quietly. He turned to his troops, "Open fire. Cover me. I'm going out to get Carl."

He set his rifle against a tree and dropped to his belly. He crawled out onto the clearing and established a pace he could arrive at the gun, a hundred feet away, unfatigued. He made his way to the control panel and hid behind it.

"Carl, Carl, are you okay?" he called around it.

"I'm hit in the leg and shoulder. I'm tossing the detonator over to you."

"No. Keep it. You're coming with me." With bullets sailing over his head and invisible laser beams somewhere up there also, Malone inched his way around the back of the gun and caught Oshinko's arm that was holding the detonator. "I said, keep it." He curled Oshinko's fingers back around the tube-like device and grabbed him by his wrist. He pulled the wounded man under the gun to the other side.

Once there he got Carl up slightly, so he could hold him up by the shoulder of his wounded leg. Fortunately it was his other shoulder that had been wounded, so Oshinko had the strength to hold on. He contacted his people on the platoon channel, "Suppression fire at least five feet high. I need to run across this field with Oshinko."

As the volume of fire increased, becoming continuous, he lifted Oshinko up into a running crouch and ran across the open field until he could fall into the surrounding woods with him. They'd made it into the tree cover.

"How far back do we need to be?" Malone asked his explosives expert.

"About another hundred yards," he replied as Sato came over to take one side of him and Watkins the other.

They carried him away from the clearing. The rest of the troops ran to get far enough away from it. Oshinko almost dropped the detonator once but grabbed his right hand, that had been holding it, with his left to keep it secure.

Once they had gone a hundred yards into the woods, Oshinko pressed the detonator without waiting for anyone to stop. The explosion behind them was tremendous. Several yards of trees were destroyed and a few more yards of them were uprooted. The blast did not affect the pace the troops were running at.

"Hines, get the men back to Major Bancroft and wait for me there. I need to make sure the enemy artillery is destroyed."

"Roger that, sarge."

He watched his troops form up into a marching line and head back in the direction indicated by Hines' check on the tank column. Then he turned and walked back to the clearing.

The gun had been red, completely painted in red. Now there were only red pieces of what it had been constructed of scattered about the six-foot-deep crater in the center of the clearing. Malone took a few more pictures and contacted the tank column for directions to return to them.

She dropped the hand unit back onto the desk and turned to look out the opening on the eastern side of the tower. The enemy was moving into the city faster than she had expected. They'd searched a few of the initial houses very quickly; Captain Nilsson was hoping that the aliens hadn't found any Lankmerans still in them. After the third row of homes, they stopped their search and simply began marching in. They reached the row of receiving warehouses before her troops did.

Over the radio she heard, "Captain Nilssen, this is Sergeant Warren. The aliens are already here. They've taken up positions in the warehouses. Do you wish us to drive them out?"

"No, sergeant," she said from the microphone on her vest. "Back off and rendezvous with the rest of your platoon. Over." Then she spoke to all her soldiers. "All units, the position I sent you to has been compromised. Rally in the market just west of the warehouses. Hold the line there." She raised the binoculars slung around her neck to see troop movements.

Remora and Switchblade platoons were coming from the west, behind the Lankmeran markets, made their treks fine. Sword platoon had to come from the north, though; a few of its members were exposed to enemy fire. Since Nilssen couldn't see the light beams of the enemy lasers, she could only tell when those men were hit by the way they staggered afterwards. One of them dropped. The urge to call for a status report was strong, but she knew better than to distract her men from their rescue efforts. She watched them back up a block and make their way forward in a wide circle. They weren't going to give the enemy any more clear shots.

The end of a report from Sword platoon's lieutenant included, "...three wounded and Private Kane killed in the move."

"Get your men into positions of safety. And Larson, bring those three wounded men up here to the crow's nest. Lieutenants Bhembe and Diaz, I want you up here, also. Sergeant Myers, stay by the docks, get those refugees loaded and out of here. Have the ships head south before turning east."

"Understood," said Captain Nilssen's aide. "Stay away from the enemy's laser weapons. Got it."

Captain Nilssen went back to watching outside. It looked like a standoff, much like that in Bergland, where they had initially made landfall. Only this time, they hadn't stopped the aliens in the surrounding field, the aliens had gotten into town and undercover. *What could her people do?* she asked herself.

She noticed her lieutenants emerging from their market cover and moving over to help Larson with the wounded soldiers. "I'm glad those laser rifles of theirs only wound if they don't hit a vital organ. Otherwise, we could have a real mess on our hands. It'd take weeks to get reinforcements out here."

She turned as she heard military boots making their way up the spiral stairs of the bell tower. "Are those men okay?" she asked as the new arrivals came into the room.

"That's the only good thing about the enemy's lasers, they cauterize the wounds so you can't bleed out," Lieutenant Larson said as he sat the first man against the western wall of the tower's bell room.

"Good," Nilssen replied. "Now we have to figure out how to get the rest of our men to safety, and the rest of the citizens of this city to Lenora City."

"It looks like we have to remove the enemy soldiers from Anceroferdon first," said Lieutenant Bhembe.

"Mindy," Lieutenant Larson used Captain Nilsson's first name by accident. They'd been lieutenants together for years before this mission. "A frontal attack would be suicide."

"Too bad we can't call for air support," said Lieutenant Diaz.

Captain Nilssen stared through her binoculars at the battle in progress between her troops in the market, and the enemy in the warehouses. Quiet descended on the room for several moments, the only sound being the rifle rounds from below. "Maybe there is a way," Captain Nilsson broke the silence. She pulled the binoculars from around her neck and offered them to Bhembe. "How far would you say the warehouses are from the markets?"

Dingane Bhembe took the offered glasses and dialed the distance gauge inside it. "I'd have to estimate about sixty yards." He placed the glasses into the hand Lieutenant Diaz had extended to reach for them.

"Which is well within the accuracy of the missiles on the Nyumbani. Diaz, get the coordinates on those warehouse. No, just behind them. Let's give our boys a little fudge factor." She keyed the communicator she pulled out of her vest pocket, "Captain Nilssen to Surveillance. Captain Nilssen to Surveillance."

"Surveillence here, Captain. What can we do for you?"

"We have the enemy dug into a position down here and they have our boys pinned down. We were hoping, once we gave you their positions," she motioned for Diaz to hurry up and send them, "you could drop a couple of your precision ordinances on them."

"I'll check with the General's office and get back to you."

"Well, let's hope we can survive until they make up their minds," Diaz said.

"I just hope the walls protecting our boys are strong enough to stop those lasers," Larson said as he stared down on the market buildings. It was his turn again with the binoculars. "They have side entrances down there." He turned from the open area to the others. "We could have mounted a flanking attack on those warehouses."

Nilssen held out her hand for the binoculars to be returned. "We don't know the layout inside those warehouses. We could get into a quagmire. No, we'll wait for Command to bomb those bastards out."

Nilssen and her fellow officers waited fifteen minutes before the answer came. "Surveillance to Captain Nilssen."

"Nilssen here."

"Your request has been approved. We have the coordinates for the missile launch. Keep everybodies' heads down."

A moment later, a thundercrack came from above them. Followed by the shrill sound of something pushing aside the air to reach its destination. Finally, in a split second, they saw the streak heading towards them, then overhead to reach out for the far side of the warehouse. The missiles struck about two hundred yards on the far side of them, keeping the markets where Nilssen's men were hiding just out of the blast radius, but between the two missiles sent down, the group of warehouses, as well as half the city, was destroyed.

Nilssen's men walked out of the market shops and inspected the devastated area. Not a single enemy soldier remained. Their pieces were so scattered that they couldn't even be visually identified from the rest of the area's debris.

"Okay, people," Nilssen was back on her radio. "We still have a job to do. We have to see if there are any Lankmerans left in town."

They found a couple of truckloads of Lankmerans still hunkered in Anceroferdon, and a couple of trucks to send them on their way to Lenora City.

The Other Continent

The planet Lankmere had two large continents separated by a vast ocean. Citizens occupied both continents and someone had to take on the job of rounding up the Lankmerans on the distant continent and move them to safety. General Chi selected Charlie Company for the unenviable task.

Captain Latief Pangestu stepped off the shuttle on the northern side of the coastal community he and his men had been dropped near. Using the link Surveillance had established with the radio and television equipment on the planet, he'd let the citizens know his men were coming and what their purpose was. The mayor and a small delegation waited for Pangestu as he stepped off the shuttle and made his way to the bottom of the ramp.

"I welcome you to Onama, good sir. I am Arouna Z'tor, Mayor of Onama. How may I be of service?" Latief thought this Lankmeran was slightly taller than the other members of their species and a bit more muscular as well. The other four members of Z'tor's delegation were shorter and thinner.

"Greetings, your honor. As I mentioned on my way in, we're here to help you. Alien invaders have appeared on the other continent of Lankmere and are killing your fellow Lankmerans there," Pangestu began.

"We are getting daily reports from Sargron, out sister continent. We are told the invaders have no means of transportation to travel such large distances, so we believe ourselves safe here." Z'tor looked puzzled. "Are the reports in error?"

"The reports are accurate; however, the aliens have a method of accessing this planet from theirs that we do not completely understand. We would like to bring the entire population of Lankmere to Lenora City so we can offer all of you protection."

"What you seek is a grand endeavor, but I think unnecessary," the Mayor continued. "We have very few centers of population on this continent. Spread out enough that the enemy would find it very hard to round us up."

"We don't know why they are hunting your people, Mayor Z'tor," the Captain began.

"They are not hunting us. The way they attack is not that of a hunter. They are exterminating us, if I read the accounts from Sargron correctly. It is what we do when the vermin population gets too large in the city. Only we drive them together using fire and burn them. We do not know why, but this is an extermination effort by these aliens."

"All the more reason to get all your people in one place so we can use our forces to keep these invaders away from you."

The Lankmerans standing next to the Mayor leaned over to him and began talking in whispers quiet enough that Pangestu's translation unit couldn't pick out enough words to translate.

The Mayor turned back to the Captain. "It seems that your arguments have concerned my fellow city leaders enough to have them agree to your proposal. How do you suggest we cross to Lenora City?"

"We saw some large ships in your harbor as we came in. Could they be used to transport your people close enough to Lenora City for you to walk there?"

Z'tor turned back to his gathered friends and conferred. Then again facing the captain, "We have four ships in the harbor and can carry six thousand or more of us on the trip. We have three more out sailing, which we could call in and unload to make room for more of our population."

"Great. Bring them in, load as many of your people as you can and get them going to Sargron. I'll take my men out to the other cities and see about escorting them to safety." He began to turn to head towards his waiting men. "Let's hope you're right and we don't run into any aliens here."

* * *

Using the shuttles they'd arrived in, Charlie company was able to visit three large towns in as many days. Each time, the remaining residents became fewer as the warning about the aliens had reached them. More Lankmerans were on the road to Onama.

189

"I certainly hope they have enough ships," Private Anzo said as they were flying to their fourth town early on day four.

"We'll make it work," Pangestu replied. "Even if we have to use our shuttles to get these people to safety."

"We should have time, Captain," Specialist Carbello added. "We haven't even seen any of those helmeted bastards yet."

"And let's hope we don't," Pangestu said as he felt the shuttle descending. "Okay, time to gear up. We're landing."

The shuttle bay fell silent as everyone waited for the familiar bump. It was lessened this time. The ramp dropped and a poof of dirt came off the spot where it hit. "Lieutenant Simmons found a recently plowed field to land in," Pangestu said mostly to himself.

"They do make for a soft landing," his First Platoon Lieutenant, who'd been sitting next to him, replied.

They were off the shuttle in less than five minutes, standing behind each of their kits. Three rows of men were waiting for him. First Platoon in front, Third Platoon in back, and Second Platoon between them.

Pangestu looked to the city, noticing it was a bit smaller than the last one. The homes were a bit more spread out and there were several silos skirting its edge. He estimated his people should finish searching by noon.

Turning to face his men, he said, "Same as last time. First platoon take the northern third of the city, Third platoon take the southern third. And Second platoon, you guys go down the middle. Lieutenants, you have your orders. Move out."

There were very few Lankmerans, just as it was in the last town the troops had cleared. With so few Lankmerans left, the soldiers moved quickly through the town. They were approaching the last few rows of dwellings when one of them noticed several glass-domes in the woods surrounding the area. He opened fire and the rest of the troops did the same.

Captain Pangestu was searching the town's library when he heard the sound of weapons fire followed by a call alerting him to the incursion.

"Everyone, get into those homes," Lieutenant Michaels said over the company circuit.

"Medic, I have a wounded man over here," called Sergeant Fournier.

"What's going on?" Pangestu was out of the library and heading towards the sounds of gunfire.

"We've got an enemy force pinned down in the woods on the western side of town," responded Lieutenant Fischer. "Not sure of its size, we caught them emerging before driving them back."

"Damn," Pangestu said. "This is just like Craymon all over again. At least this time they appear to be in range." He made his way close enough to see what his soldiers were firing at. The road running along-side of the town couldn't be more than ten yards across.

He stopped a few blocks away from the fighting. "Well, it worked the first time," he said to himself. Keying his connection to his troops, "First platoon, make you way back. Leave the buildings you're in safely and regroup next to the…," he looked around for a land mark. "The fire station four blocks from your position. Lieutenant Boucher, get your snipers in place. Lieutenant Fischer, spread out Second platoon to cover the area First platoon was covering."

It took a few moments for members of First platoon to begin arriving. Pangestu waited patiently at the large garage doors of the fire house for Lieutenant Michaels to arrive. He wrapped his arm around the First platoon's officer's shoulder, "Bill, I want to try that flanking maneuver we used in our first engagement with the enemy. I want your men to go to the northern edge of the city," he pulled his arm off the lieutenant's shoulders and pointed due north. "From there, follow the tree line around until you can engage the enemy forces. Pinning them between two attacks should jar them loose."

"Right away, sir." He quickly saluted his captain and went off to rally his men to head north.

I'll give him fifteen minutes before something kicks loose, Pangestu thought. *Fifteen minutes and I'll have the rest of the troops make a push into those trees.*

He waited his fifteen minutes and heard nothing. He reached into his vest pocket to call Michaels to get details on what was happening before realizing if he contacted them, he'd be giving their position away to the enemy. He pulled his hand out of his pocket. Waiting was hard.

A few minutes later he got the call he was waiting for, "Captain Pangestu, this is Lieutenant Michaels. The enemy was waiting for us. They set up an ambush, triggered by our rustling of leaves. They were firing before we could see them. I have two men wounded and I don't think Private Mackenzie is going to make it. What do you want us to do?"

"Damn, there goes my forward push," Pangestu said to himself. He needed Intel from his troops, "How close did you get to the enemy position, lieutenant?"

"We can't tell sir, the foliage is too dense."

He thought for a minute. "Lieutenant, have squad one fire a continuous burst forward, sweeping through the foliage about two feet off the ground. Have your other two squads see if any of the enemy reacts and try to gage their distance by the noise they make."

"Roger that, captain."

Off in the distance, to the left of his position, Pangestu began hearing the continuous fire he had called for. It sounded like his men had made it a quarter of the distance back from the edge of town before encountering the enemy. Now was the time for something from their front.

"Lieutenant Fischer, I want a dozen grenades lofted into the enemy position. Can you comply?"

"Twelve grenades will be in the air shortly, sir."

After the massive explosion ended, "Captain Pangestu, it looks like we got within fifty yards of the enemy. I think we dropped a half dozen of them in that barrage, sir."

"Can your men get a few grenades into their line, lieutenant?"

"We will try, sir."

As he let his communicator fall back into his pocket, Second platoon's grenades began going off. From the edge of the tree line to six yards beyond, explosions shattered the foliage protecting the enemy. As they began to stand up from the explosions, Pangestu could hear the single rounds from Lieutenant Boucher's snipers putting them back down.

Before he could issue another command, the grenades from First platoon began sounding in the woodlands. Then the sound of EE-19 rifle fire moved southward. Now was the time.

"Second platoon, advance on the enemy position. Repeat, advance on the enemy position. Third platoon, lay down suppression fire as they advance. Let's wrap this thing up."

He entered the fire house and got to the sleeping quarters on the second floor to get a look at what he had set in motion. Through his binoculars, he could see Second platoon emerge from hiding as continuous rifle fire erupted from Third platoon. As Second platoon crossed the street bordering the woodlands, one man dropped to the ground and another grabbed his right arm, but kept pointing his EE-19 at the enemy, still using it. He watched as two men swooped down on the man laying in the street and carried him into the woods. "He must be alive if they're risking their lives to save him," Pangestu said to himself.

Pangestu watched until Second platoon entered the woods. As they did, he called to the leader of Third platoon, "Third, cease fire and move up to assist Second platoon!"

When Third platoon ceased fire, Pangestu noticed that the rest of his troopers weren't firing either. He folded his binoculars up and placed them in his vest pocket as he turned to make his way back out of the station.

When he arrived at the row of homes on the outskirts of the town, he could hear activity in the forest but no gunshots, it sounded like men wrestling. He didn't expect to hear any of the enemy's weapons being fired. He bent down and collected a bit of dust that he threw in front of him. No laser traces could be seen in the cloud.

He ran across the street to see what was happening. As he parted the brush at the entrance to the woods, he saw his men in a hand-to-hand struggle with the aliens. Most of their helmets had been either knocked off or busted, and while his men had combat knives in hand, the alien invaders fought bare handed.

As he walked into the melee, one of the alien soldiers made a leap at him. Instead of drawing his knife, Pangestu grabbed the man by his forward arm, shoved his left leg under the man's rear leg and redirected the leap to one of his men. One who had been finishing off another of the aliens and had turned his knife towards Pangestu seeking another target. The alien slid onto the knife the human soldier held, then the human pulled the knife upward, opening the enemy soldier's chest even wider. When he pulled his knife back, the alien fell to the ground.

By then, most of his other troopers were standing up after finishing with their opponents. "These guys don't do very well in a knife fight, sir," Sergeant Oldov, the man who held the knife that Pangestu had thrown his opponent on, said.

"I never thought to check," Pangestu said. "These guys don't carry any personal combat weapons. They only have those laser rifles."

"It looks that way," Lieutenant Michaels said as he brushed the foliage aside, walking over to the captain. Pangestu could see his other officers heading his way also.

"This could mean a change in tactics," Captain Pangestu said. "They have an advantage because of the infinite range of their weapons. But if we can get inside their range."

"They're not prepared to fight at close quarters," Lieutenant Fischer finished. He pulled a leaf off the tree next to him and finished wiping alien blood off his knife before sheathing it. "You know, with the claws the Lankmerans have and their hunting skills, it might give them a chance to defend themselves."

"Lieutenant Michaels, have the men collect up their rifles and strip the bodies. Lieutenant Fischer, detail your men to begin digging a burial pit. Lieutenant Boucher, assist Lieutenant Michaels and have both your platoons move the bodies into the pit Second platoon digs. I think we still need to train the Lankmerans in the use of firearms, but hand-to-hand combat might give them a fighting chance. They're proficient at that." He walked back to the city to give his men a chance to work while he reported back to Nyumbani.

Mayoral Dissent

Mayor Krisson L'mere and several other Lamkmeran mayors joined General Chi and his staff for a meeting aboard the Nyumbani. After a time, she felt she had sat long enough and stood with enough force that, if the chair had not been anchored to the floor, it would have been knocked over. Now she was just pacing the room.

"Mayor L'mere would you be so kind as to have a seat?" said Colonel Vermillan. The mayor's vacated chair was at the opposite end of the oval table from that of the General's. Seated to the General's right was the colonel, while two other staff members sat at his right.

She stopped right behind her chair. "Is this how you protect people, General? You ran a group of your tanks through the center of Macnenium, destroying almost a quarter of the city's buildings. Launched, what did you call them? Artillery? Right, an artillery attack on Chinook. Destroying most of the southern part of the town. Then there was the missile on Anceroferdon. Destroy. Destroy. Destroy. Is that all you do? When you came to us, your men helped us build our communities. Now you're blowing them up."

"Don't forget the central buildings in Racolndo, Krisson," said Mayor Z'coen.

"Yes, you even blew up an empty city, why? You drove off the invaders in Anora, Bergland, and Craymon without devastating our homes. And these devastation tactics of yours are just encouraging these aliens to bring out their own weapons of mass destruction. They have a laser now that destroys whole blocks of our homes in a single volley. I ask you again, is this your idea of protection?"

"Ma'am," Colonel Vermillan stayed in his seat as he addressed the mayor, who had begun pacing again. "This is war. In war, there are casualties. Not just people casualties, but material destruction.

We aim to minimize people casualties. So when we have to choose between destroying buildings and letting lives be lost, the buildings fall. Lives are more important."

"On that we agree," said the Mayor of Onama. "Please, Krisson, sit down. These men are only trying to help."

"But what they are doing to our culture, our society?" she said, hovering next to the chair she'd been assigned.

"They aren't even your cities. And you didn't lose the number of people we did in the attacks."

"Thank you, Mayor Z'tor." General Chi rose from his seat and walked over to the map of Lankmere projected on the screen behind him. "We are sorry for the destruction. The problem is that we did not expect to be fighting, let alone an enemy as fierce as the one we are facing. We came to Lankmere to establish a dialogue with your people, not fight a war. The problem with humans is that we can't just sit by and watch our friends be wiped out, which is what these aliens are doing to you. And we will use every means at our disposal to prevent that from happening.

"This enemy is a strange one. How is he getting to your planet? We've discovered the wormholes he's using. But how does he generate them, and more importantly, how can we stop him from continuing to generate these wormholes wherever he wants? How do they communicate with each other? They don't make any vocal sounds. And how do we talk to them? We're trying to teach them sign language, but our linguists seem skeptical of the results. We don't wish to destroy your culture, but we know so little, we don't even know when we can say this thing is contained."

"These aliens are trying to kill us," said Mayor D'thon of Craymon. "Is there any way we can help you deal with them? Can we help you hunt them down?"

"Your methods are fine for close quarters," Colonel Vermillan said as General Chi took his seat. "But those laser rifles the aliens use have a greater range then even our EE-19s. You'd be cut down before you ever got within claw range."

"We can hunt them," another Mayor said. "We have woodlands near most of our cities. We can hide in the woods and treat them like prey."

The rest of the mayors started expressing agreement with him.

"The problem is, how long would you people have to go living in those woods?" the Colonel said. "How would we know where the aliens would attack next, so you could be waiting for them? No, we'll continue our preparations at Lenora City and deal with the enemy when they come there."

"General Chi," the speaker in the far corner of the room's ceiling announced. "We have an incoming request from Captain Pangestu of Charlie company."

"What is it?" the general asked.

"They want us to drop a couple of guided missiles onto the buildings of the last city on Continent Two. They've found another wormhole set up there."

He looked over the Lankmerans sitting around the conference table. "Tell him we can't. He will have to use what he has to destroy that wormhole."

"Yes, sir."

"There you go. We'll start dialing back our response. There'll still be destruction, but maybe it won't be so massive."

"Thank you," an unhappy Krisson L'mere said.

Through The Looking Wormhole

"Okay, you guys heard the orders," Captain Pangestu said to the three platoons of his Charlie company. "We're to take that thing down with what we have and with as little collateral damage as possible."

"Do we have enough explosives to bring the buildings down around it, the way the Recon platoon did earlier?" asked Lieutenant Fischer.

"Okay, whose got any remaining magnomite?" the captain asked. The show of hands was sparse. Not all troopers were issued the stuff, only those who'd been trained on how to handle it. And then it wasn't concentrated with a single soldier. Four half-kilo bricks were stable enough for one man to carry, but above that, you risked a proximity explosion.

Three men from First platoon put up their hands and two each from the other two platoons.

"Okay, twenty-eight charges," Captain Pangestu said. As the hands fell down, one of the men in Second platoon kept his up. "What is it, Specialist?"

"I only have three, sir."

"And if we just drop the building down without the wormhole being active," said Lieutenant Michaels, "I suspect the aliens could just activate it later, probably at a location we don't know about. I think we have to take out the entire mechanism."

"Even then," Specialist Walters piped up, "I don't think we have enough explosives to take it down on this end."

The captain turned to focus on the man from Third platoon. "Meaning?"

"I think we have to go through the wormhole and attack it from its control complex. Wrecking the mechanism that generates this phenomenon should be easier than wrecking the actual phenomenon."

"That sounds like a mission we wouldn't be coming back from." Lieutenant Boucher commented.

"Coming back or not," said Captain Pangestu, "If we knock out their wormhole central control, we just might stop these things from coming through. When are we looking at the next opening occurring?"

"About an hour from now," said Lieutenant Michaels.

"Then we have an hour to get ready."

* * *

Fifty-eight minutes later, energy began crackling through the largest structure of the abandoned Lankmeran city. A moment later, sparks generated began to flow in a large circle almost four stories tall, increasing in amount and speed. There was a ledge built where the first floor would have been, which led over the opened basement. The outer cone was forming at the walls of the building and the ledge went six feet into the cone.

Staring into the opening, Captain Pangestu ordered his men forward to just outside of it, and watched as the wormhole began firming up. "Okay, here's the marching order. First platoon, followed by Second, then Third. The Seven explosive Specialists follow everybody else with me." It was getting harder and harder to see through the forming cone.

After another two minutes, the walls behind the cone could no longer be seen. "Go, go, go. Secure the other side of this wormhole. Move."

His men ran across the platform above the basement and disappeared before they reached the far end. Second platoon followed so close behind First that only the fact Pangestu knew which men were in which group allowed him to tell one platoon from the other. Third was quickly through, also. Now it was his turn, the explosives specialists hadn't waited for him.

A swirling of his vision took place as he reached the back third of the platform and the wooden planks that made up the ledge he'd started on became iron grating. The first thing he noticed was the sound of gunfire. His eyes hadn't adjusted yet, but his ears were perfectly functional. He ducked down and blinked his eyes several times to get them to reset.

It was darker in the chamber he was now in than the one he left on Lankmere, but this new chamber was large enough to have housed several of the buildings they had left behind. It was so vast and dark that he couldn't see the far walls. He was in the center of the room, standing on a raised platform, about ten feet from the chamber floor. His men had moved down the ramp leading away from the wormhole and taken up positions behind several of the control benches throughout the room.

He ran down the ramp and dropped behind the console directly in front of it. The rate of fire his men were putting out diminished until it completely stopped. He raised his head over the console to look around the room, but couldn't see any of the alien technicians he thought he had seen when he emerged from the cone.

He stood up to survey the entire room. There were three bodies dressed in grey uniforms on the far side of the nearby console. Looking over the dials and meters, it appeared to be a control station for the wormhole. His eyes were adjusting to the dim lighting, and could now see the walls twenty feet away. Along one of them was a series of panel boxes running from floor to ceiling. They held a series of meters that were reading about half way between one set point and another. There were also several switches under each meter, all in an upwards position. There were another six dead bodies, dressed in the same grey clothing, lying on the floor next to them. And several dozen alien bodies lined up like they were about to go through the wormhole, all dressed up like the troops that were killing the Lankmerans.

On the far wall was another series of panel boxes, but they only ran three-quarters of the way to the ceiling. Most of them had places for tape spools to be strung on them but the spindles were empty and a new bank had been installed in the middle box that had a shelf half way up with several small boxes plugged into the panel. There were no bodies there.

Against the wall between the two banks of panel boxes were two sets of stairs, one descending to a lower level on the right and the one on the left ascending to an upper level. From the floor above, the sounds of marching steps could be heard heading their way.

"Everyone take cover. I think the other part of the contingent they planned on sending to Lankmere is on its way. When they get to the bottom of the stairs. Take them out."

His men scrambled for cover while the gateway was still active behind them.

The door at the top of the stairs opened and the sounds of feet hitting the metal grating filled the large silent room. The alien troopers in their red suits and dome helmets began walking down the stairs. Half way down, they all stopped, and the alien leading the column looked over to the metered panels and pointed at the bodies lying about. He raised his laser-rifle and cautiously continued down the stairs; the troops behind him followed their leader's example and did the same.

"Open fire," roared Captain Pangestu from behind the cover of the central console. A hail storm of bullets flew up the stairs where the aliens were standing like so many rifle range targets. Many of them dropped, but several of his men were on the main floor, out in the open when the aliens appeared on the stairs. Some dropped to a prone firing position but about a half dozen spun around like they had been hit by laser fire, then fell to the floor.

The men did their best to clear the stairway of aliens, but more appeared at the top of the stairs, firing around the door. The enemy didn't have the wide coverage they would have on the stairs, but the door made an effective barrier to the humans' bullets. Those who had been hiding near the computer panels were still pinned down, but those behind the power-monitoring panels made their way around to the stairs without being seen.

Suddenly the aliens' tactics changed. Dead bodies began turning. Their chests or backs were pushed tight against the railing of the stairs. The barrels of the alien's laser rifles began appearing through the barrier they had created with their dead. Another three men went down, while two more lost control of one of their arms.

Specialist Adams had three men with him as he looked up through the grating under the steps. He was about to order his other men to open fire on the aliens. As he saw the aliens turning their rifles towards the humans, something snapped. Adams opened up with full automatic fire on the stairs. Enough of his rounds would get through to the oncoming menace or he'd die trying.

By the time the other soldiers realized what Adams had done, he was moving again. "Come on. We have to clear that door and secure it." They ran from under the stairs. More aliens were about to jump on the bodies Adams had just left. "Fire," Adams yelled. "And keep firing as we go up these steps."

Fortunately the steps were wide enough for two men to occupy each one with their arms spread enough to control their EE-19s. They stopped when they reached the alien bodies at the top.

About the same time, the aliens stopped trying to come through the door. The door was still ajar with two laser-rifle barrels preventing it from closing. The push from the other side appeared to have died some, the aliens weren't trying as hard to get in. Adams pulled his almost empty clip from his rifle and inserted another, then he switched the firing rate to three-round bursts. Turning to his men, he said, "Stay close, make your way to the door, get those rifles out of the way and get the door closed. I'll be covering you." He watched as the man next to him hesitated. "Go!"

The man placed his foot between the railing and the alien body, kicking it slightly to move it further away from the railing. The man behind him grabbed the alien by his arms and pulled him down the stairs and into the waiting arms of the next soldier. The troops of Charlie company, previously pinned down by alien troops, were working to clear the stairs of the dead and reach the door. They were stacking the bodies under the stairs.

Specialist Adams fired bursts towards the door at random intervals to keep the aliens from firing back at his troops. It took about fifteen minutes, but they cleared enough bodies to get three soldiers to the top of the landing. They had begun chucking the bodies into the far corner of the landing to get them away from the door.

As they were beginning to move the last body, one that had actually rolled into a position where it was blocking the door from opening further, the door began to be pushed open. They quickly drove their shoulders against the door. They would have gotten it closed, if it wasn't for the two gun barrels sticking out of it.

Without thinking, Private Amari grabbed the lower of the two barrels and pulled it as hard as he could. The person on the other end was pulled forward and a sound could be heard of him hitting something on the other side of the door. The rifle went slack and Amari was able to pull it all the way through. He spun it towards the floor of the control room and looked for the other barrel. It was no longer there. Two of his fellow troopers had pushed the door closed in that instant. "Pull those bodies over here. Pile them against the door. If one could stop them from opening it wider than it was, these half dozen should secure it completely."

They drug the bodies over and piled them against the door. The pile was two wide and almost a half-dozen tall against the door. They hoped this would be enough to keep the door from being pushed in.

Pangestu went over to Specialist Wilcox lying on the control room floor. He had taken a laser blast through his heart and lay dead. Privates Hino and Gorky were in shock, having taken blasts in non-vital areas of their chests. The two men that sustained arm wounds were up, they couldn't use their rifles, but they'd drawn their side arms, holding them at the ready.

Captain Pangestu turned the care of the men over to his company medic and moved to the control console. The wormhole was still active, which alleviated one of Pangestu's concerns; how to get his men back to Lankmere? He looked at the panel in front of him, the wormhole several feet away was showing on one of the monitors. He could see the building they had entered the wormhole on Lankmere on another. He saw four similar monitors on the console, but they were all deactivated.

"Looks like they might have three separate spots for sending troops to Lankmere, captain." He'd been so focused on the panel in front of him, he hadn't heard Michaels walk up behind him. But he wasn't completely surprised, something in his mind told him the man was there.

"That means if we destroy this facility, the Plordins will have to build a whole new one before they can continue their attacks."

"The who? No, wait, you called them by their name. How do I know they call themselves the Plordins?"

Captain Pangestu stood up and turned to his lieutenant. "It was just there in my head."

"Hey, guys," called Lieutenant Boucher as he was walking down the stairs. "Whatever we're going to do here, we'd better do it soon. The Plordins are getting a cutting torch for that door."

"He called them that also," Pangestu added, surprised. *How did that knowledge just pop into our minds?* Pangestu thought to himself.

"I don't know, captain, but something is going on," answered Michaels.

"Did you just," Pangestu began. *Read my mind*? he finished in his head.

"No. You spoke to me, sir." Michaels responded.

No, I didn't, Pangestu thought. *Private Lester, could you come over here for a moment*?

"Yes, sir," the private responded before walking over to the control console. "What can I do for you, captain, sir?"

"Thank you, private. That will be all."

"You didn't vocalize anything," said Michaels. "Your lips didn't move. Yet I heard you call Private Lester over."

"Or thought you heard. Are we becoming telepathic? Is there something about this planet that allows intelligent life to communicate directly mind-to-mind? It would explain why the Plordins don't speak, while having a coordinated armed force."

"But whatever, we have to get out of here or this information is useless. Michaels, send a squad down to the level below. Find out what's down there."

"Right away, sir." He saluted and turned to grab one of his sergeants.

"Sergeant Chand," he looked around the room to see where the squad leader from Second platoon was. He was turning before he felt the tap on his shoulder.

It was Sergeant Chand saluting him. "I'll get the Specialists going on setting the explosives up here, sir."

This telepathy is going to take some getting used to, the captain thought.

"But if anyone can, it's you, sir." the sergeant replied.

"Sergeant Willow, take your squad up the stairs and make sure the Plordins aren't getting in," he called across the room. The sergeant and his men were near the foot of the stairs heading to the upper floor and closest to the stairs leading down.

"Roger, sir." He and his team pulled their EE-19s in front of them and started up the steps.

A blurry image started to appear in Pangestu's mind. He shook his head to clear it and looked for another egress from this room.

He found a closet with electrical supplies on the far side of the wormhole and a door leading into another corridor on the same wall. The corridor was unlit and stretched further than he could see. As he was turning around to instruct men to seal the entrance, two men were headed his way with a spool of wire.

"We'll have it secured in no time, capt'n," the first one said.

"Well, telepathy does have some advantages," he said under his breath.

One of the men working at the base of the console stood up to address him. "How long do you want us to set the timer for, sir?"

"Two minutes, but wait until I give the word before you activate them."

"Captain," he heard over the company channel. *He's going to need an explosives man down here*, he heard in his head.

"What did you find, Sergeant?" The blurry image he'd gotten before was there again, more foggy this time rather than blurry.

There was the sound of motors in the background as the sergeant called up. "It looks like some rather large generators down here, sir. We were wondering if you wanted to blow them also."

Pangestu looked over to the specialists standing around the control console. "How much of that stuff you got left? Can you take out those generators?"

"We got a few charges left," Specialist Briggs said. *Three generators; yeah, we should have enough*, Pangestu heard in his head. "We'll have to go down there and have a look." *It's going to be one hell of a bang when this place goes.*

"Then get down there. Set the fuses for five minutes then get up here in a hurry. Make sure nothing exists of this stuff after we leave." He watched the four men double-time to the stairs and descend. He called out into the room, "Everyone not involved in setting explosives, immediately assemble by the wormhole. We've done what we came to do, now it's time to leave."

His men stopped searching the room and came over to their gateway back to Lankmere. Even the squad he'd sent to the basement came up the stairs while the explosive specialists were still working.

"Lieutenants, get your platoons together and get them through the wormhole. First platoon leads the way. I'll bring up the rear with the explosives guys."

There was less shouting orders than Pangestu would have expected but the men lined up quickly. Within a minute, First platoon was marching through the wormhole. He was glad he hadn't tried powering it down while they were working, he didn't know if he could start it up again.

Third platoon just finished entering the tunnel when the four specialists he sent to the basement came running up the stairs. "Four minutes left, sir. We'd better get moving."

"Have the charges up here been activated?"

Two of the Specialists dropped to the floor around the console and pressed the activation buttons. Then they got up and headed for the wormhole. "They have now."

Captain Pangestu was right behind his men as they ran into the tunnel.

* * *

He found his company waiting for him on the other side. "Don't just stand around! Back away from here! We don't know how much of a shock wave will be transmitted through the tunnel." Everybody ran until they had at least one house between them and the building.

Some almost didn't make it. The explosion could be heard emerging from the wormhole, but before any debris could be ejected, the connection between the two worlds collapsed, and nothing else got through.

"It looks like it's time to get back to Lenora City," Captain Pangestu said. He stood there for a second, but couldn't hear any mental response from his men.

Lieutenant Fischer spoke up, though. "Yeah, before the Plordins decide to begin their final offensive to kill all intelligent life on this planet."

"Kill all intelligent life," Captain Pangestu looked over to his subordinate. "Where did you hear that?"

"I didn't really hear it, it just came into my mind while I was securing the upper door."

"You guys get back to Lenora City. I have to see General Chi."

Alien Interrogation

"Damn, telepathy," Captain Palmer said as Captain Pangestu walked into the hastily erected Officer's Club. One of the Social Halls had been fitted out with a human bar, next to the dispensary for the Lankmerans. While humans had their alcohol, the Lankmerans had their herbal intoxicants. It was one of the largest buildings by volume in Lenora City, just not one of the tallest. Everyone was welcome to come in, provided they weren't on duty.

"It had to be something with their atmosphere. We only experienced it while on their planet," Latief grabbed a chip out of the communal bowl and plunged it into the dip pot next to it. He'd stuffed it into his mouth and chewed before talking further. "Once we left the planet and were breathing Lankmeran air, the effects were gone."

Palmer gestured to the empty chair at the six-foot round table he and Captain Nilssen had been sitting at. Pangestu swung his leg over the back of the metal chair and sat down. He reached across the table and pulled the bowl of nacho chips closer. "Hey, Mindy, could you pass the dip? They didn't give me a chance to eat up in the station."

"Sure," she pushed the dip pot across the table. "Did you guys really over-hear someone say that the Plondwins want to kill all intelligent life?"

"They call themselves the Plordins, and yeah, Lieutenant Fischer sensed them thinking that. Colonel Vermillan was going to test out both with some of the prisoners they still have on the Nyumbani."

"How?" Palmer asked as he rocked his chair backwards into the wall behind him.

"We still have some of the aliens' space suits intact. From our experience on Plordin, we know their atmosphere is breathable. It just looks like they add minute quantities of some gases into their breathing mix. We haven't identified them yet, but Charlie Company survived the exposure. He's going to test it out and see if they induce telepathy."

* * *

"And you think these suits will give us the answers we need." Mayor L'mere held the red suit up and inspected its look. "We have to wear them to talk to these Plordins?"

"Not so much talk to them," Captain Morrison, Head of Intelligence, said as he tightened up the seam on the front of his suit. "But rather go into a telepathic rapport with them, sense their thoughts. As they will be able to sense yours."

She stripped off her skirt, and sat down on the bench to pull the bottom of the alien suit over her feet. "Well, come on, you guys. I'm not going to be the only one having those aliens crawling around in my mind." She looked over to the other three mayors who'd come to the POW camp for this experiment.

Mayor Z'tor sighed, Mayor D'thon closed her eyes momentarily, and Mayor P'luk shook her head before they all found a garment and a bench and began getting into the suits. Three human officers hovered over the Lankmerans in case they needed assistance.

It wasn't a space-worthy suit. There were enough holes in it to allow the wearer access to the surrounding atmosphere to breath. But with the helmet mounted on top, it kept the extra gas of the Plordins around the wearer's head, so it would have its effect.

The Lankmerans had better luck getting into the suits than General Chi was having. "This damned thing fits like a glove going on the wrong hand," he complained.

Captain Morrison set the helmet he was about to put on, back on the table and went over to his commanding officer. "It looks right, sir. You have to remember you aren't built like a Plordin. The seat of this one piece is too tight for humans, but not its original user, or the Lankmerans, for that matter. And the chest, we do tend to work out more than your average Plordin. But at least they have thicker arms and legs. It makes the suit a lot easier to start getting into."

209

"Well, give me that damned helmet, so I can start breathing their cursed gas."

"Yes, sir." The captain reached over and grabbed the helmet he had been about to put on. All the helmets being the same, he could always find another. He placed the helmet over the General's head, lowered it and turned it until the metal knobs dropped into the holes located in the metal ring around the General's neck. Then with a quick right turn, the helmet was locked into place. Once he did, the dials on the gas reserves came to life, indicating gas was flowing into the glass dome.

L'mere and the other three mayors were waiting for the Captain to finish suiting up. Based on the report from Charlie Company, it was going to take about a half hour before the effects of the gas would kick in. Intelligence had already brought in a POW from the barracks, who needed no encouragement to get dressed in the breathing suit. He was sitting over in the corner with two guards on either side of him.

"Can anyone hear me," said Captain Morrison through the helmet he was wearing.

"Just barely," replied Colonel Vermillan, who was observing the whole experiment. "They appear to be almost soundproof."

Everyone sat down and took deep breaths, waiting for the gas to take effect. The MPs stood at attention next to the prisoner. The clock on the wall ticked away the time. Colonel Vermillan walked out of the door after a couple of minutes and returned five minutes later with a steaming cup of coffee. *Oh, he's going to pay for that*, Morrison thought, *the General loves his coffee and now he can't have any*.

He shifted his gaze away from the General, who he knew would be angry, to the four Lankmerans sitting on the two benches. He could have sworn L'mere smiled for a second.

By the time Vermillan pushed the now empty coffee cup away, Morrison thought he could hear, or rather sense, the General growling.

General, is everything okay? he tried sending out a thought.

Vermillan knows I didn't get my coffee this morning!

General, I think the gas is working, Morrison thought back to him, trying to interrupt the visions of the torture Chi was planning for his subordinate. He placed his arms on the armrests of his chair and pushed himself upright. Walking over to the alien sitting in the corner, he tried to probe its surface thoughts. There wasn't much there. Something about the uncomfortable fit of an enlisted man's uniform. Then an intense hatred poured from its mind as it lifted its eyes to Morrison.

He turned to where the General was sitting. "General, we're ready," he shouted through the helmet.

I know. Not so loud, General Chi responded.

The colonel could see his mouth move as he read his commander's thoughts. *Shouting must have amplified the thought wave?*

You think? No more shouting, Captain, the General responded mentally. *Now get down to business. Find out why they're killing the Lankmerans.*

Morrison turned back to the alien entity still sitting in the chair. *Okay Romactrofund. Wait a minute, how did I know that was its name?*

The same way I know yours is William, Bill, Billy and sometimes Egghead, Morrison heard coming back into his head.

Only my friends call me those names. And Egghead is not one of them.

The alien leaned back in the chair and smiled. *You can't lie with telepathic communications. I can see right through them. You humans, that's what you call yourselves, humans. Well, you humans are not part of God's plan. And like those Lankmerans,* he turned his gaze over to the mayors who had risen and made their way across the room, *you humans will have to be purified to make way for God's triumphant march through the universe. For God to decide where Eden is and bring us to it. His will is for all you sentient non-believers to die.*

Morrison turned to look at Chi. *So this is just a religious crusade,* Chi thought.

Romactrofund jumped out of the chair he'd been sitting in. *This is no simple crusade. We carry out the work of God. We strike all his mistakes out of existence so he may bless his Great Creation. We do not seek to save these people. We seek to pave God's path to create paradise.*

The guards were trying to get the alien to retake his seat. Holding his arms and pushing his shoulders down. Then he suddenly relaxed and went back into the chair. *But now we know about humans and, what is it, oh, Earth. All we have to do is locate it. Thank you, there it is. Now we can go to your world and wipe out the millions, no you have billions of unclean sentients on that planet. God's work be praised, we have located more.*

Chi grabbed the helmet feeding him the gas, turned it and pulled it off his head. "You'll get no more from me."

Oh, yes, I will. Rontogen stays in the system for some time. You know your space platforms can't stop our wormholes, right?

Chi slapped his hip, then turned to one of the guards. "Give me your pistol, Sergeant." When the man complied, he cocked it and pointed it at the alien who was trying to get out of his seat as violently as possible. Chi grabbed the top of the alien's helmet, holding it still as he placed the barrel of the pistol in front of the Plordin's face. He fired two shots before turning the gun back over to the sentry he'd taken it from.

"Earth is safe," he said as he turned away from the dead alien. "Dispose of the body," he told the guards he was walking away from. "Now, Your Honors," he said as the four Lankmerans began removing their helmets. "It seems we have a lot to discuss."

212

Blind Attack

"Well, it's nice to know why we're fighting these people," Lieutenant Mason of Palmer's Headhunters platoon sat down in the fourth chair surrounding the table and set his beer bag in front of him. "Unfortunately, there's no bargaining with religious fanatics."

"Andy, got your men out patrolling the surrounding forest?" Palmer asked just to give his subordinate the chance to show off his competence.

"I've got the squad moving in different directions. Since Listener platoon can keep an eye on the one hundred yards of open land between here and the forest, I'm leaving that for them. We're out in the woods. The squad leaders should have set up blinds for their troops by now and are keeping a watch for enemy movement."

"German or Thai?" Pangestu pointed at the beer bag.

"I found they had a delightful Chinese beer in storage that no one knew about. It's somewhere between a British Ale and an India Pale Ale. Light, refreshing, with just the right amount of that extra hoppy taste brewed into it. If you get a chance, you should try it."

"Maybe I will. Unfortunately we're waiting for a briefing from Colonel Vermillan, and we don't know when that will be."

"You could try one."

"No. I'm too much of a light weight when it comes to alcohol."

* * *

The bushes rustled near the position where Malone had his troops camouflaged. Several of the members of Recon platoon were behind a vine-woven wall of broken branches and leaves. Never more than two of them to one of these shelters but they were spaced evenly through the well-grown forest they were hiding in.

He inched his way out from behind his shelter in the trench they had dug to allow egress when needed. He moved from tree to tree until he was crouching alongside the next bush to rustle in the line a movement had been following. He did a cross-handed pull of the knife in the sheath on the left side of his belt, leaving the one on his right, his dominant side, in case of emergency.

He saw a hand reach out and begin to push through the thick lickoberry bush. As he reached forward to grab the hand, another figure jumped out of the tree above him. One of the new Lankmeran hunters pinned the Earth Force trooper, who'd been skulking in the bush, to the ground and had its paw in the air, with its claws extended.

"Wait," shouted Malone. "He's one of ours."

The Lankmeran turned its head to look at Malone while using the bulk of its mass to hold its prisoner on the ground. A second later, more human troopers appeared from where the first trooper had come from and surrounded the Lankmeran, EE-19s pointed in his direction.

"That goes for you men, also," Malone called at the newcomers. "This is Norn Z'Tor, the Mayor of Onama's son, and part of the Lamkmeran resistance. He's here to prove their worth in combat against the Plordins. So lower your weapons."

He offered Norn his hand to help him off his human captive. "I could have sworn I saw the intruder first. But you beat me to him. Impressive Norn, quite impressive."

"Thank you, Mr. Sergeant. I'm glad to have proven my father's word, that we can be of use to you."

Malone patted him on the back as he got to his feet. "I'm just glad you're on our side." Then he turned and looked at the oncoming patrol. "Second squad, right? Where's Sergeant Nadir?"

"Right here, Malone." He plowed through the bushes to catch up with his men.

"EE-19s, in as dense a foliage as they have around here, don't allow for very responsive movement. My men are ready with their pistols and we have extra clips for them rather than the EE-19s."

"You may be right, but my boys don't have enough pistol training to make them effective."

"Then get behind blinds, set up stands to wait for your prey to come by," said Norn. "When hunting, you do not always have to go to the prey, it will often come to you."

"And that's why I keep the kid around. Good advice. Divide your men up, they can occupy the blinds we have already established. Norn and I can set up more of them."

"But Sargeant Malone, where are your blinds?"

"That's the point of a good blind."

"The prey can't see you," the Lankmeran explained.

"Recon platoon, stand up." As several men began standing over the barriers they had erected, a killing line appeared heading into Lenora City. "Get your men in there."

"You heard the man. Everybody spread out and replace the men in those blinds."

"Pairs."

"What?" Nadir asked.

"There's a pair of them in each blind. You know, the buddy system."

"Yeah," Nadir ran his fingers over the cooling fins of his rifle. "Okay, pair off and replace those men in the blinds."

"I know your squad isn't at platoon level. Just fill what you can." Malone motioned to Norn, and the two of them walked deeper into the forest to scout out more ambush sites.

* * *

After the evening meals were delivered to Malone's new blind, Norn jumped down from the tree he was hiding in directly into the compound that made up Malone's vegetative pillbox. Not the concrete pillbox he would have preferred, but at least it would hide him from the enemy until it was time to rain fire down on their heads.

Pulling a log stool over to his human friend, Norn began, "What'd they bring tonight? It's taken me a while, but I'm finding I like the flavors you humans bake into your foods." He rubbed his hands together as Malone handed him the container.

"Then you'll love tonight's dinner. They fried the chicken." He lifted the spork off the top of the plastic wrap, placed it in one of his vest pockets and removed the plastic covering from his meal. The escaping smells made him want to dig in immediately. It had been a boring day, and when they are, the meals Culinary sends your way really gives you something to look forward to.

Before he could eat, though, he had to wad the plastic wrapper into a ball and rub it in the palm of his hands until it got hot enough to begin decomposition. He dropped it to the ground, and within seconds, it began to dissolve and seap between the leaves covering the soil. In a few more minutes, it would just be the carbon and hydrogen atoms that it had been composed of.

Malone looked over at Norn, who was stuffing the plastic wrapping in his mouth. "Damn good appetizer," the Lankmeran said. "Though it could use some more spices."

Malone thought about correcting him for the dozenth time, but decided it wasn't worth it. *Different species can eat different foods. And something about recyclable plastics trips these guys' taste buds.* He just sat there and tore open his mash potatoes seasoning, sprinkled it on his meal and prepared that bag for disposal. *As long as Norn likes it, why should it bother me?*

Wilford's meal, a cold sandwich, sat waiting for Malone to finish his meal, so Malone could take over the watch while Private Wilford ate. Tomorrow would be Malone's turn to get the cold meal.

* * *

Malone spent each day's waiting by first discussing the prior day's activity with Lieutenant Latifi, recently released from the infirmary on Nyumbani. Then he checked in with the men in each blind, making sure they were doing well. That took him all of an hour, assuming he was trying to stretch it out by walking real slow and admiring the Lankmeran flora.

As he crawled back into his blind on the fourth day, a wind came down the sloped ridge they perched on. Malone got ready for the enemy's incursion, until he decided it was just the wind. As the wind finally began to die down, several of the bushes that had stopped moving, began moving again.

Malone wetted his finger and held it in the air. Yes, the wind was gone. He patted Wilford on the shoulder and pointed at the moving bushes. As he did, enemy soldiers came out from behind them. With the blind designed to look like an impassible object, none of the enemy soldiers ran into it, they just walked around them. There were Plordins on both sides of Malone's location.

Using hand code, he instructed Wilford to cover the opposite side. Then he tapped a text message into his communicator to alert the Lieutenant. A moment later, he could hear the faint clicks of the return messasge, "As soon as the last Plordin passes your location, open fire."

* * *

Captain Palmer, having climbed to the bell tower located in the center of Lenora City, took out his binoculars and lifted them with his right hand to his eyes so he could use his left to contact Surveillance. "Are the satelites picking anything up?"

"We had massive troop movements about ten minutes ago. They entered the woods south of your position and we haven't been able to detect them since. I'm assuming the forest is dense enough to block any heat signatures."

"If you can't see our own men there, then I'd have to say so. Thanks, Surveillance, keep me posted." Palmer raised his left hand to help steady his field glasses as he tried to peer into the trees. "I hope to hell we put our troops in the right place," he said to no one in particular.

"They're not going to get all of them," Captain Nilssen lowered her binoculars enough to talk to him. "But they'll give us the warning we need to stop them at the town's periphery."

"I just wish we had Williams' artillery and Bancroft's tanks backing us up on this one."

"You know the Lankmerans vetoed that suggestion. We have to be mindful of collateral damage."

"I know. But it makes me feel like I'm fighting with one hand tied behind my back. Helpless."

"So this is where you guys have been hiding," said Pangestu as he emerged from the top of the circular stairs rounding to the top of this tower. "That's a lot of steps." He stepped up on the other side of Palmer before setting his coffee cup on the balcony's railing and pulling his binoculars out of his pocket. "Seen anything yet?"

"No," Palmer answered.

"But that's a good thing," Nilssen said. "It means our troops are staying in concealment. If the Plordins had passed their loca-

217

tion, we'd hear gunfire before we ever saw them breaking out of the forest."

They all became quiet. A few minutes later, the predicted gunfire could be heard coming from the forest.

* * *

Malone heard the oncoming enemy soldiers just before he saw them. Spanning across the woods was a line that had to be a half mile long; the enemy troops had spread across the forest away from Malone's position. They were followed, about three yards behind, by another line of soldiers, again stretching a half mile from Malone's stand. He could hear them marching behind him also. Those were for Wilford to keep track of. The important thing was that the density of the blinds had fooled the Plordins.

The enemy troops were trying to walk quietly, but the forest debris made that impossible. As the leader of each line moved up to a branch or bush getting in his way, he'd use a laser knife to slice through the obstacles in their way so the others behind wouldn't be bothered by it. Paths were growing through the woods for the Plordins to follow.

As Malone counted the sixth man passing his position, the sound of the enemy footsteps stopped approaching. "Now," he called out as the sixth Plordin was two yards closer to Lenora City than he was. He took aim at that alien and dropped him. He continued to fire, moving his pistol as fast as he could to take out as many of the troopers as he could.

Wilford hadn't brought his pistol, so Malone could hear the triple round bursts from the man's EE-19 firing behind him. He could almost move his rifle to another position as fast as Malone could.

Above him in the trees, Malone could hear Norn racing along branches to get further down the line of targets, hunting for just the right man to begin his attack.

After he'd dropped his third enemy soldier, and with the rest of that line getting hit from the other human blinds, the enemy broke away from their path, scattering into the woods. They were not as easy a target as when they'd been closer to the blinds. Malone scooted his way under the blind and went tree by tree to get closer to the retreating enemy.

As he was about to bolt around the fourth tree he had sheltered behind, a laser blast took off part of the tree's bark and dropped a leafed twig to the ground. Malone pulled back behind a tree several inches wider than he was.

He lowered himself to a prone position on the ground and looked around the tree. The Plordins had taken up either a seated firing position or a prone one. "Recon platoon, the enemy has taken up firing positions, about forty yards from our original ones. Use extreme care when approaching," he said over the platoon's radio channel.

As long as he was stationary and firing in one direction, Malone decided to switch to his rifle, still slung on his back. As he began reaching for it, things began dropping out of the trees about ten yards ahead of him.

As a struggle ensued in the bushes, he decided to push forward. He stopped reaching for his rifle, pulled his pistol back out of his holster, and stood up. He peered around the tree and saw that the enemy soldiers directly ahead of him were being distracted by something behind them. He ran around the tree, firing in the direction where the enemy knelt.

By the time they'd turned to see what was coming, he had dropped three of them and was on top of their position. He saw Norn clawing the chest of one of the soldiers with another soldier laying on the ground multilated and unmoving. He dashed past Norn and kept firing until he was empty. He slid to a stop behind a tree and changed clips.

As he readied his rifle to continue, he could see Norn spring back into another tree and dissapear into the canopy of the forest. "Okay, Norn, the race is on." He peered around the wooded sanctuary. Picked out new targets, emerged and began his attack before the enemy could bring their rifles back around.

After he stopped to change his clip again, the thought occurred to Malone, *Maybe I should hold up until the others get a chance to catch up.* He slammed the clip home and looked around the tree. A solitary Plordin was sitting on the ground in a firing position pointing his rifle upwards as though he was looking for something in the treetops. Two quick rounds burst his helmet and then his head. The Plordin fell backwards to the ground.

He thought his Lankmeran counterpart might get to the point where he couldn't back him up. "Norn, don't get so far ahead. I'm holding up waiting for the others to catch up."

"Raawwwr," came over the circuit. "It is the hunt, friend Malone. The others are joining me. If you wish to partake, you'd best hurry. We do not hunt in packs, but we will break up this bubble-headed herd. Stretch them out. It shall be great sport. Come, friend Malone, join us before all the prey is gone." Malone heard the branch Norn had landed on creak slightly under his weight. Other similar sounds could only be interpreted as the Lankmeran landing on it.

Malone was on the circuit to the rest of his men. "You guys had better get a move on. I think the Lankmerans are going to need our help."

"Sergent Malone, this is Lieutenant Latifi. What's the situation?"

"Sir, I think the Lankmerans are looking on this as a hunt and the Plordins as prey. They might be getting in over their heads." Malone advanced to the next large tree and looked for enemy soldiers.

"Then your suggestion is?"

"We need to back them up." Malone saw a downed enemy body and moved forward six yards to another secure location. "If we pick up our pace, we can provide cover for their assualt."

He stuck his head around the tree and saw no enemy bodies, alive or dead. The trails the Plordins had cut were empty of people. They'd only stopped the enemy that had come close to the blinds.

"Everyone west of the blinds, pivot southwest. Over." He looked up into the trees and thought he saw something move in them. He called up, "Norn."

"Yeah, I see, friend Malone. We didn't do enough to spook a reaction from our prey." Norn's voice quieted down as he talked on the communicator he'd been given. "Hunters, the prey moves south. We must follow."

Malone moved across ten trails the Plordins had cut. Then looking down the path, he holstered his pistol and pulled his rifle over his shoulder. The area had been cleared enough for him to see at least a hundred yards in front of him.

He went down the trail at a pace slightly faster than he remembered the Plordins traveling at. It wasn't a brisk chase, the fact that the lead Plordin had to cut the trail for the rest had kept them slow, and Malone didn't want to stumble into them before he had time to prepare. The debris on the ground held imprints of steps held closely together, confirming his remembrance of their speed.

It took him ten minutes to catch up with the lagging enemy soldier. In that time, he'd heard sounds of battle to his left. And Norn checking in with him on the radio. But he finally saw the back of the helmeted figures marching determinedly to the south.

He closed on them until he could see three of the marching figures. Then he knelt down, took carefull aim and launched three triple round bursts down the trail. He got the first two before they could react and the third as he was turning to see what was happening. He stood up and moved west to the next trail, figuring the next group of Plordins had been warned of his coming.

On the next path, it took him a minute to catch up with a group of four Plordins that he brought down. Continuing west, he found the body of an enemy soldier clawed up on the ground. *If Norn did this, he did it quietly enough*, he thought before turning to follow the trail.

Norn had not been as quiet as he had hoped. He spotted the two enemy soldiers pointing their weapons up towards the treetops. Raising his rifle, he dropped them to the ground over the body of another soldier who had been laying there.

Just after noon, Malone felt he had to be within a hundred yards of Lenora City. The tree cover here kept him from confirming the distance. Stopping his forward progress, he figured the enemy soldiers should be coming together into battle formation from this point forward. He made his way back east, encountering enough single clawed bodies to tell him his Lankmeran friends were having some luck.

Now it was time for Malone to rally his own platoon and the men of Headhunter's first squad to give Lieutenant Latifi a fighting force that could account for something behind the enemies' lines.

reached over and placed his other hand on Malone's shoulder. "Banook's is the group of hunters working for Lieutenant Mason."

He extended his paw. "Pleased to meet you, Sir Sergeant."

"It's just sergeant or sarge for short." He shook the paw, then dropped his hand. "Is the Lieutenant down this trail?"

"Yes, he is holding the line as we drive the enemy towards him."

"Then maybe we should do some driving of our own. Can you guys scout paths that will allow my boys to run through this woods?"

"Only if they can keep up."

"I've seen you guys move, take it easy on them. We've already done a twenty mile march at least."

Norn responded, "So have we, Friend Malone."

* * *

Lieutenant Mason knelt behind the triple stack of logs, waiting for the return of the Plordin forces. As of the moment, his men had driven them back along the trail. He was hoping his Lankmeran scouts would let him know if they began cutting a new one. Hopefully, he would have enough time for his men to get into position again.

He thought he'd heard gunfire coming from back up that trail after his own men stopped firing, but it had quickly ended and no further fire could be heard. He let it go and focused on the position his men were holding.

He crawled back from his barrier and made his way to where the rest of his men were barricaded up. Most of them had just assumed a prone position, those he encouraged to find local debris that could be used as a form of natural blind they could fire from. Except for one, all the rest had arranged dead brush into a pile they could hide behind. Private Lee could not be found anywhere, until Mason heard something above him in the trees. Looking above him, Mason saw Unsol Lee had managed to work his way up into the tallest of the surrounding trees, was perched fifty feet above the ground.

"Hey, Lee," Mason called up, "see anything from up there?"

"No, sir. The trail is clear."

The Home Guard

Captain Palmer looked over the tree line just north of the city. He knew the Plordins were out there, but couldn't see their approach. Even the squad from his elite Headhunter platoon and Lieutenant Latifi's Recon platoon reported a loss of contact with the enemy. All he could do was stand in the bell tower and visually search for movement. Movement that didn't come.

He turned his head slightly left to relieve the stiffness his neck developed from holding the same position too long. Out of the corner of his eye, he detected movement. A single small tree was moving and there was no breeze to account for the movement. A tree just to the west of the line of troops Palmer had waiting for the Plordins to emerge from the tree line.

"Weber, Becker. Get over here," he called to the two snipers in the bell tower. "Train your scopes on that shorter clump of trees over there." He pointed at the tree he'd seen moving earlier with his left hand, using his right to hold his binoculars in place. His eyes weren't moving off the spot where he'd seen movement. Another movement would confirm what he'd seen.

"I don't see anything, Captain," Weber said after mounting his rifle to the edge of the tower to keep it steady.

"Well, keep watch on it." Then he turned to Captains Nilsson and Pangestu, who were watching from the tower. "I'm going below." Palmer snapped his binoculars closed and placed them in his vest pocket. Then he turned and headed over to the stairs on the far side of the tower.

As he descended to the ground, his mind raced with the possibilities the moving trees suggested. *If the Plordins move around to another point in the city, they could catch us from behind. And if they do, we've gathered all the Lankmerans together for the slaughter.* He increased his pace down the steps.

"Surveillance, I need you to widen your monitoring radius. Cover the grounds all around Lenora City. I need to know if the Plordins are moving around the city." Palmer stopped at the bottom of the steps before going out into the Lankmeran sunlight.

"We'll lose a little detail, captain. But we can do it."

"Let me know if you see any movement anywhere around the city."

"Will do."

Palmer stepped into the sun and thought about contingencies. If the Plordins did go around the Earth defenses, he would need to have troopers there to stop them. The best he had were the Headhunters. He raced over to where Lieutenant Mason had his men dug in.

The Headhunters were anchoring the western edge of the Human defense line. Pulling them out, even though they were missing a squad, was going to weaken the Human position. But Palmer figured it wouldn't weaken it as much as if the Plordins came in behind their line.

He walked into the second-story factory where Lieutenant Mason had set up his headquarters. It was a block from the edge of the city and would give him time to evacuate, should the worst happen. Palmer walked into the foreman's office and found Mason. He was sitting at a desk, feet propped up, and smoking one of his sweet aromatic cigars. He had his body twisted around to keep his field glasses trained out of an office window. At least, until he heard Palmer enter.

"See anything, Mason?" Palmer closed the door behind him and walked over to sit in one of the desk's chairs.

"I thought I saw movement about five minutes ago, but I've seen nothing since." As he twisted around to look at Palmer, he dropped his feet to the floor. But he didn't put out the strong odor generator he had between his lips. "But you could have called me for that. What's up?"

"I need to move your platoon to the other side of town."

Mason leaned forward onto his desk and set his cigar in the makeshift ashtray sitting next to his left elbow. "What? Why?"

"I saw that movement also. It's got me worried that the Plordins may have detected our defenses and are flanking the city to catch us from behind."

Mason thought about that for a moment, picked his cigar back up, inhaled a bit and set it back in the ashtray. "If they are? Well, I know Headhunters are good, but I don't think we're good enough to hold off the entire Plordin army."

"You don't have to. Just slow them down enough, so that if they are coming at us from behind, the rest of our forces will have time to turn and face them."

"Not a suicide mission, then?"

"Hell, no. A delaying action."

Palmer picked his cigar up again and set it back down. "What about the Lankmeran volunteers that didn't go out with my first squad? Can I use them, too?"

"You mean, evacuate that part of the city, draw the Plordins in and make their range weapons useless? That could work. How quickly can you get moving?"

"My guys can be across town in under fifteen minutes."

"I'll have the volunteers meet you in the market district over there. If you make contact with them, sing out. We'll be on our way."

"That's a damned jolly roger, Captain. We'll stop those bastards." He stood up from behind his desk, stubbed out his cigar and walked out of the office.

* * *

Lieutenant Mason stood on the top step of the factory he'd been occupying to give him a good view of the troops he was addressing. He had an unlit cigar in his mouth as he waited for the last of the men to form up. Once he could see the last of his men arriving, he began, "Okay, I'm sending you men to the other side of the city." He stared at his two squads of women soldiers daring them to correct him. Again. "You're to meet up with the Lankmeran volunteers Captain Palmer is sending to the market district. I want you to take up a position far enough into the city to draw the Plordin forces in. Make sure it has been evacuated before you settle in. We suspect the enemy may be doing an end run around Lenora City and we want to be ready for them. Remember, this is not a suicide mission. You were chosen because you're the best. If you make contact, you're to call the captain and the rest of our forces will be here to support you. So stay down and hold. Okay, sergeants, move your squads out. Good luck, everyone."

* * *

The beginning of adulthood was a terrible time for a Lankmeran male to be cooped up in a strange town with absolutely no physical activities happening. Ramin W'tan wasn't about to sit around any longer. He'd seen the space adventure program, "The Next Step", for the fourth time. He ached to hunt down the aliens who were keeping him in this brand new Earth Force temporary barracks.

He got out of his chair and walked over to the television broadcasting in the housing unit's public room. He slapped the off button and turned to his friends sitting around who had been watching their favorite program. "Is this all? Is this all we can expect to do with the rest of our lives?" He began channeling the main star of the show while he leapt into his speech. "Isn't the legacy we have been left that of the hunter? Why are we letting the humans do all the hunting? Why aren't we out there finding and culling the Plordins who want to eradicate us? I say we go looking for them. We know how to hunt, locate our prey and bring them down, even when they're in herds. We need to do the same to these invaders. Who's with me?"

There came a cheer from the bored Lankmerans who'd been sitting around for several days. They rose as they continued to cheer. Ramin walked through the center of the room and urged his friends to follow him.

They marched over to the next barracks assigned to young men and walked in. All the way to the television viewing room, where Ramin gave the same speech, then led the young hunters out into the sun of Lankmere. "Now we must split up," he said to the assembled Lankmerans. "We must rally all who want to engage in this glorious hunt. Go find your friends and new friends and rally back here. For today, we begin the great hunt. Today, we free

226

Lankmere of alien butchers. Now go, find everyone willing to claw back our planet."

Mayor D'thon stepped from the barracks she'd been assigned and confronted the mob Ramin had gathered. "What do you boys think you're doing?" She held her hand in front of Ramin's chest.

"What none of the rest of you are willing to do; take back our hunter's pride."

"We already have a team out there working with the humans to stop the Plordins. A trained team. I don't want to see any of you killed. Go back to your games, and let the soldiers fight this, this, war, I think they call it." Since the youth had stopped moving towards the surrounding forest, she folded her arms across her chest.

Ramin looked over his followers and saw a couple of them begin to turn back.

"No!" he shouted so that everyone around them could hear. "We will not go back. We will not sit placidly by while others protect what is ours. *We* will save you, Mayor D'thon, whether you want us to or not." He raised his arm over his head and motioned to the forest. "Everyone, to the hunt."

The Great Hunt Begins

Norn and his ten friends took a seat on the ground around Sergeant Malone and his fifteen earth troopers. "The Plordins that had been going south to Lenora City have turned. Either we forced them to adjust their plans, or they had no intension of attacking from the north. Norn, here, thinks he's found a single file trail they're following. And it looks like it's going around the city."

"They may be planning on attacking from the other side of the city, from behind our defenses," Norn said.

"Right," Malone continued. "That means we have to catch and stop them from attacking our forces from behind. Now, it's my opinion that Norn's squad should take the lead. They're natural hunters and aren't likely to lose the trail. Everyone else will closely follow, so Norn's people don't get cut down when they catch up with the Plordins. Now, let's get a move on, they're not sitting around."

They followed the trail the Plordins had cut through the forest around the western edge of Lenora City, but never coming any closer than a hundred yards to the roadways surrounding it. Every so often, Norn would scurry up a tree, leaving the human troopers on the path, and cry out some animal signal to the other Lankmerans who had spread out on either side of the trail. After a couple of minutes, he would always return to Malone.

"This is the trail. The others can find no signs of the Plordins straying away from it. You can believe me, we'd know if they had. These people are not very skilled in hiding their tracks. Almost as bad as you humans are." He laughed at the last statement and brought a single claw up to Malone's chin for a couple of strokes.

Malone didn't react. It was not the first time Norn had petted him. "Does anyone have an idea about how far ahead this trail stretches?" He rubbed his chin to spread out the sensation from Norn's claw.

"As long as they stay single file, we can't know how far forward it stretches. But we are of the belief that we are catching up with their marching. The trail grows newer, sap still oozes from the branches they have cut."

"Then we'd best keep moving." The line had kept moving while he'd been talking with Norn, so Malone had to hurry to take up the point position again. As Norn ran ahead of the line to keep the trail in sight. Malone looked up into the trees and saw the shapes of Lankmeran warriors leaping from tree to tree, keeping the ground under their watchful eyes.

* * *

Lieutenant Mason caught up with the remaining Lankmeran fighters as he stood in front of the food market, one of the many stores a mile from the edge of town. He'd already sent the bulk of his forces south to convince any Lankmerans staying in the area to move to the barracks east of that position.

"We need to get everyone situated, in case the enemy does an end run around our main line."

"Rooftop defense?" Banook, the Lankmeran in charge asked.

"Yeah, for you guys. But we'll need the flexibility to move around, since we don't know where they'll hit and we're too small a unit to cover this entire side of the city. My men are trying to get everyone to the barracks so they don't get hurt when the Plordins attack. Could I get your people to help?"

Banook turned and addressed his people, who quickly scattered in different directions. "Once everyone is to safety, we'll take to the rooftops. Every sixth house so we cover more territory. Where will your people set up?"

"We might throw some barricades up in the main streets. That way when we find out where they're coming in, we can meet them with plenty of fire power."

"Good luck, my friend." Banook took off to the private homes that looked like they might still have people in them.

* * *

Ramin crossed the road with almost thirty Lankmeran youths at his back. They all sprang into the trees as they came to the forest's edge and disappeared into the foliage, then climbed high

229

enough not to be seen, yet still had a view of the ground so they could see any signs of their prey. Leaping from tree to tree was a joyful experience for them, like children on a playground. Ramin could feel his muscles thanking him for this release after having been cooped up for over a week.

Within a few minutes, Ramin found what looked like a game trail. He signed for his company to stop while he dropped to ground level to check. The game living in this particular forest did not make trails like the ones he was looking at. The animals were too solitary to track along what appeared to be a herd trail. He studied the indentations in the debris and saw footsteps. Footsteps like nothing on Lankmere would make. He checked the flora surrounding the trail. It had been cleanly cut, not gnawed nor broken. All the signs told him either the Plordins, or the humans, or both, passed this way.

He waved up to his friends watching him from the upper canopy, when he heard something coming down the trail. He dove for cover in the surroundings and blended into the landscape, hidden from anyone using the trail. Human soldiers walked past his hiding place at a faster pace than the signs he read showed. He called to the passing troopers and stepped out of hiding. "Are you going after the same prey we are?" Ramin said as he stepped between two troopers who came to a halt when they saw him.

"Lad," the man with a single bar on his collar walked back to where Ramin was standing. "What are you doing here? You people were supposed to stay in safety until we'd dealt with the Plordins."

"You cannot keep us from the hunt, especially from this hunt. I am Ramin, and my fellow hunters have you under our protection. Just who are you?"

"Lieutenant Latifi, and I know nothing about your volunteer troops. Where did you go for training?"

"This is the trail. Continue the hunt," Ramin called into the trees above him. He returned his attention to Lieutenant Latifi. "We have trained our whole life to hunt, and hunt these invaders, we shall. You can either aid us or stay out of our way. But decide, for I go to join my friends." He stepped closer to a tree with a low hanging branch and leapt into it, climbing faster than the human could follow. Before long, he would not have been able to see the human troopers, even if he'd cared to look back. His enemy was in front of him, not behind.

* * *

"Norn," Malone whispered into his communicator. They suspected the Plordins had trouble hearing outside noises, but Malone wasn't taking any chances. "Get down here, quick."

The tree limbs above Malone moved as a cat-like figure dropped in front of him. "It looks like we might have caught up with the enemy."

"That was my thought also. Some of the greener leaves haven't swung back yet."

"So how do you want to handle it?"

"I'm assuming you can drop, kill, and get back under cover before they have a chance to bring up their lasers?"

"That will not be a problem."

"Then get ahead of us, in the middle of their column, and begin your attack."

He raised his right paw and licked the top of it. "With pleasure." Then he sprang into the tree and all around Malone there were leafy disturbances as the members of Norn's hunting party ran forward.

"Okay, everybody form up on me." He waited for the rest of his dozen troopers crowded close to him on the three-foot-wide trail. "The enemy should be just up ahead. I want everyone off the trail. Spread out into the woods and surround the last six Plordins in their line. Eliminate them and move forward. This is an active fight. We can't give the enemy time to get set up." He looked around at his men. All of them looked ready to end this fight, even the few Malone could see had fear in their eyes. "Okay, let's move out."

They split into groups of six and disappeared behind the trees. Malone joined the group to the south, keeping himself between the Plordins and Lenora City. He let the six men in his party move forward of him as they ran around trees and ducked under branches. They caused a minimal disturbance as they proceeded forward.

231

Within minutes, they were rewarded with the sight of the enemies' line. The Plordins slowly moved forward, Malone assumed it was at the pace of the point person's ability to clear the foliage out of the way. It didn't matter to Recon platoon and friends; they stopped, pointed their rifles at the enemy column, and opened up. Three seconds later, they were on the move again.

There was no getting around the noise made by a discharging EE-19, but the next two batches that Malone's men attacked were still not ready to respond. The fourth group of a half dozen Plordins managed to get a shot off before hitting the ground.

"Anyone hurt?" Malone asked.

When no response came, he continued. "Step away from the path by about a yard and take cover before the next group. Let's keep moving."

At the next spot they came to, a dozen alien soldiers were waiting. As best they could, they had taken positions up off the trail and in the surrounding woodlands. They were prepared to fire back as soon as the humans made their presence known. Malone dropped one of the Plordins and looked up the trail. The rest of the column had not stopped. His men couldn't, either.

He walked deeper into the woodlands and made a run around his men. He told them to keep firing as he did. The enemy troops were down to four, anyway, and it wouldn't be long before his men finished them off and continued their forward advance.

He kept up with the marching line of Plordins, choosing not to engage them by himself. He needed numbers. The sounds of discharging bullets ceased, and he was counting on his men to catch up with him soon.

Then it occurred to him if the enemy would take the time to set up men, maybe he could stop another group of them by attacking from in front. He ran through the trees and passed over twenty of the soldiers in the alien column. He picked a tree for cover and used the rest of his clip firing at the Plordins on full automatic.

A lot of the surrounding foliage was destroyed, but he was able to drop four of the enemy soldiers before they got organized enough to fire back. He slid around the tree, keeping it between him and the Plordins. It was an old growth tree, standing hundreds of feet tall with a thick trunk. The thick trunk was all Malone cared about as he dropped his head back to ground level.

"Sergeant," his communicator bleeped at him. "We heard your fire. We should be at your position in a matter of minutes."

Malone sank down into a sitting position before sticking his head around the tree. "Be careful as you approach. The enemy will be ready for you again, and with four times the firepower."

"Roger that. No one's getting hurt!"

The men on his side of the trail arrived before he expected them. He worried about the men on the north side and was about to key his communicator, just as gunfire came from there. Gunfire that was complimented by the men who had just caught up with him.

It took five minutes to cut down all the Plordin troopers, again without a single human casualty. However, Malone wondered when the Plordins would figure out an efficient response to the whittling Malone was doing to their line.

"Let's move out," he called to his men.

Malone led his men along the trail. Five minutes after their last encounter, they came upon a dozen aliens firing their lasers into the treetops. He motioned to his men to fan out across the trail, and enclose the enemy. They had the dozen alien troops eliminated in their first volley.

Malone walked into the middle of the enemy bodies and counted more of them than his men had taken down. There were thirty alien kills, not the dozen he'd expected. He turned his attention up to the tree tops and called up. "Norn, you up there?"

The young Lankmeran jumped down between several of Malone's men, standing right next to the sergeant himself. "I see what you mean about concentrated fire. Once those Plordins knew where we were, they could keep a rate of fire going that we could not leap through. They had us trapped in our positions when you showed up."

"That's rule number one of combat; stay alive. You can't learn anything if you're killed."

"Sarge, the trail's taking a bend to the south here," said Malone's navigation specialist.

"So you think we're heading for the south side of the city?"

"That'd be my guess."

"Then we'd better get moving and take the rest of these guys out. Norn, you ready to begin hunting again?"

"Friend Malone, you are spoiling me from the half hour hunts I've done in my youth." He sprang up and climbed rapidly out of sight. "Don't be late, cause we won't wait," Malone heard him calling down.

* * *

Lieutenant Mason began to hear rifle fire coming from the east. As it passed his position, the noise began to come from the southeast. Someone was having a firefight in the woods. That had to be the Plordin incursion Captain Palmer had warned him about. But whoever was out there wasn't going to be on his own. If another corps of Earth troopers were attacking the aliens, he wasn't going to sit here and wait for them to come to him.

Mason turned to Banook, "You people want to go on a proper hunt?"

"You mean the gunfire coming from the forest?"

"I think the Recon platoon is chasing the aliens, and they're coming towards us."

"You are the military man, friend Mason. But if you want to know our desires, it is to hunt. To track our prey from the trees surrounding this great city. We would love to turn this into a proper culling."

It took them ten minutes for Mason to rally his men to the edge of the forrest. The gunfire had turned, it was now coming towards their position. It was still about a hundred yards off, but on a course that would bring the fight to them.

The two dozen Lankmerans leapt into the trees and disappeared quickly. Mason wanted to know how far the aliens were planning to travel before attacking the city. As Banook was about to leap into the trees, Mason grabbed him by the arm. "We need to know how far away those troops are. Can you find out and let me know?"

The Lankmeran patted the communicator he had strapped around his shoulder. "I will call you once we know."

234

"Stay safe, my friend." Banook leapt into the trees to catch up with his fellow hunters.

Since Mason didn't know how deep the Plordins were in the forest, it seemed logical to have his men spread out in a line going from the edge of the forest south as far as they could. Each man was within two arms lengths of his comrade as they began their march towards the oncoming gunfire. Passage between the trees was fairly easy since this part of the forest wasn't overgrown. The Lankmerans had kept it fairly clean to allow game to come close to their city. Mason and his troops had no trouble making their way east towards the sounds of fighting.

"Friend Mason," came over his communicator. "The aliens are a hundred yards ahead of you and fifty yards from the forest's edge. They are hacking a trail as they march."

"Banook, thank you. We'll take the first group. Move your hunt further down their line so we don't accidently shoot at you. Over."

Mason stopped his forward movement and looked over the arrangement of his forces. "Everyone hold your positions." He moved to a point approximately fifty yards from the edge of the forest, where he found a five-foot wide tree trunk. Leaning his rifle against the tree, he waved to his men, ordering them to converge on his position. "Make ready to engage the Plordins."

The two ends of Mason's line converged on his position. He instructed his men to bring loose bushes, or anything they could use for cover. They piled the debris up between the trees three feet in front of the one Mason had chosen for his command post. He tied an inspection tag to a lower tree branch five yards in front of his line before returning to his command post.

Mason had condensed his long search-line into a one-hundred foot kill zone waiting for the enemies' approach. He could hear the faint swish of the alien's electro-machetes clearing their way. He, and his men, hunkered down for the coming firefight. "Remember, do not open fire until they reach the tag hanging from the tree. Once they do, pick a target and open up triple-round bursts on them. We have to take these guys quickly."

The blue sheen of an alien's machete punched through the foliage, cutting away branches. Still it had not reached the tag. The machete went low and cut out a bush blocking the alien's advance. But still it had not reached the tag. In the next swing, it took off the branch the tag was tied to.

Human rifle fire erupted on the column of advancing aliens. The first five were dropped before the Plordins thought to disperse and give themselves more area to fire in. Mason's men took down the first line of enemy soldiers trying to form a battle line. The rest of them dropped to the ground and began to crawl forward before opening fire on the humans.

Private Caron cried out and dropped to the ground fifteen yards from Mason's position. Mason moved to check on him, found the wounded man sitting with his back to a tree. "How is it, son?" Mason asked as he looked at the bored hole in the man's left thigh.

Mason watched him take a couple of breaths, trying to relax out of the pain. "I should be okay, sir." He looked at his rifle on the ground, reached down to pick it up, checked it really quick and aimed it at the Plordins. "As long as you hold this line, I can keep fighting."

"Good lad. Whatever happens, we won't leave you behind." Satisfied, he crawled back over to his command post while firing several volleys at the attacking Plordins.

The gunfire approaching their position was getting closer. Mason knew Lankmeran hunters had to be between his men and the approaching gunfire. He swiveled around and sank into a sitting position behind his tree. "We don't have to beat these Plordins," he rationalized. "We only have to hold them here until the Recon platoon meets up with us."

He pushed against the tree with his back until he was again standing. Then he turned to his men. "Slow your rate of fire. Attack with just enough energy to keep their heads down. When Lieutenant Latifi's men get here, we'll have the enemy trapped between us. But save your ammo until they arrive."

"Sir," came an electronic message. "Specialist Shiro and I would like to do a flanking recon maneuver. Maybe get behind the enemy."

"No, we hold this position. No one's getting killed in this little excursion." Mason stepped back from his tree and looked to the south to make sure Black and Shiro didn't move. They'd pulled unauthorized stunts in the past.

* * *

Specialists Takaki and Anderson leaned back on their knees and watched their commander stare off towards the two who had just radioed for permission. Then they slipped into the forest debris and made their way around the enemy line. Forgiveness was always easier to get than permission.

They were guessing the enemy line was shorter than the human line and therefore would be easier to swing around. Crawling north for five yards, they got to their feet, and, stooping over, made their way west around the enemy line. They made their way about twenty yards before turning south.

As they came upon the line of Plordins. It moved at a snail's pace almost as slow as the queue line of an amusement park, waiting for their turn at the firing line.

"We could cut down the feed of fresh troops to the enemy line," Anderson said as he raised his rifle, preparing to fire.

"We could, and then they would simply cut us down. No, we must find a position where we can cut this line in two while offering us enough cover. That way, we can fire and retreat to another position." Takaki pointed back to a spot that had a large amount of dead brush piled up, like someone had been preparing to remove it from the forest.

"What was that course you took on the way from Earth?"

"Historical Military Tactics."

"Well, I just might have to take it when we get back to Earth. Okay, let's move."

They made their way back to the site Takaki had chosen. Once behind it, they thrust their rifles through the brush and cleared enough away for their fixed sights to give them a clear line of fire on the enemy.

237

They opened up with six triple-bursts each. Then waited as the Plordins climbed over their dead, brought their laser rifles up, looked around for where the gunfire had come from. Anderson and Takaki fired another six triple-round bursts into their line. After that, the aliens disappeared further forward and further back from the gap Anderson and Takaki had opened.

"Let's move further up the trail," Anderson said. As they began to move east, the leader of the Lankmeran hunters dropped from the treetops.

"Damn, Banook, you gave me a fright," Takaki said quietly. "What gives?"

"Why did friend Mason send you here? We are almost on top of you."

"We didn't hit any of you guys, did we?" Takaki asked as Anderson led the trio deeper into the forest, away from the Plordin trail.

"No," Banook said. "But we are dealing with the Plordins on this stretch of the trail now."

"Do you guys need any covering fire?" Anderson, having led them three yards from their earlier position, leaned against a tree, and placed the butt of his EE-19 on the ground, using it to lean on.

"No. This is *our* hunt. These men are *our* prey. But thank you for your offer. Now I must go." He leaped up to the lowest branch of the tree he was standing under. "Tell Friend Mason that we will join him shortly. Good bye, my friends." He was into the canopy of the trees before either man could formulate a response.

"Think we can get back before the lieutenant knows we've been gone?" Anderson asked.

* * *

Lieutenant Latifi urged his men into a faster pace. The other Lankmerans who were off hunting the Plordins had been given training in what to expect in combat, and what to expect when the prey is intelligent and fights back. But these children were simply running to their deaths. He had to catch up and defend them.

A half mile up the trail from where he had encountered the Lankmeran hunters, Latifi found the bodies of five Plordin soldiers and ten Lankmeran children. He stopped his column and bent over

238

the bodies. He had to move the body of a dead Lankmeran youth off the dead Plordin. The Lankmeran had been shot in the head and had fallen on his prey. The Plordin had his chest ripped open. Latifi could visualize what had happened. The Lankmeran hunter had dropped on his prey and began striking at its chest but instead of using a single killing stroke, the youth had kept striking its opponent to make sure he'd killed it, giving another Plordin soldier an opportunity to aim his laser rifle to kill the young hunter.

All the young Lankmerans had holes in their heads, all of them had been cut down because they didn't have the training to protect themselves.

Latifi stood up after inspecting the dead and addressed his troops, "We need to move on, or all the Lankmerans on this hunt will be killed. Hansen, get up here and take point. We're beyond double-time here, people. Let's move!"

Hansen took off at a run. Latifi sent him ahead because he was the fastest runner in Recon. He set the pace the lieutenant wanted. But he couldn't check to see if there were any laggards, he didn't have the breathe for it.

Latifi had almost reached the limits of his endurance, when Hansen brought the column to a halt. Yards ahead, the Plordins had been stopped again by the Lankmeran youth, who were again losing the skirmish.

"Take firing positions," Latifi whispered to the men near him. "Pick off the Plordins, not the Lankmerans."

A single shot barked next to his shoulder, followed by several other single shots. Latifi could see the youth Ramin, who had been leading the hunt, reaching back with his claw to rack the Plordin he held on the ground. Behind him was an enemy soldier pointing a rifle at the Lankmeran youth, but looking at the sound of new gunfire. Lieutenant Latifi drew his pistol from its holster and blasted apart his helmet before placing a metal jacketed slug through his head.

Looking further up the trail, Latifi could see the line of enemy troopers kneeling down, taking aim at the attacking party of Lankmerans. "Full auto," Latifi shouted. "Over the kids' heads."

The spray of bullets clipped the foliage just beyond the area the Lankmeran youth were in and dropped the line of Plordins Latifi had seen there. "Now get in there and pull those aliens away from the Lankmerans."

The troopers standing next to Latifi ran to the flattened area where the hand-to-hand fighting was happening. They helped the youths up from the dead bodies. When the Plordin wasn't dead, they placed a foot on its chest and tried to pull away the still-clawing Lankmeran youth. Which wasn't easy, as the youth was highly focused on killing its prey.

Latifi walked up to Ramin and offered the boy his hand. At first the Lieutenant thought the boy was slapping it away until he realized the youth was just cocking his hand for another swipe at the Plordin. A much deeper swipe, one deep enough to pull pieces of the creature's heart out in his claws.

Latifi turned his palm grabbed the boy by his shirt, and pulled him off the now-dead soldier. "Just what the hell were you thinking? You could have got all your friends killed out here."

"He's dead," said the youth standing proudly in front of Latifi. "And we will kill more of his kind."

"You were almost killed yourself. One of the Plordins had a bead on you and a line of them was ready to cut the lot of you down. Is that how you lost your fifteen friends back there?" Latifi whipped his hand around and pointed back up the trail. "Now get out of here, and let us handle this."

"No," Ramin began to turn, looking for a tree to leap into.

Latifi balled his hand into a fist and drove it into the side of the boy's head. The youth dropped to the ground. "I said you're going back." He raised his head and called up to any Lankmeran boys in the area. "If you can hear me, your hunt is over. I will not allow the slaughter of anymore of you boys. Go home." Latifi read a look of defiance on the boy's face. "I mean it. *Go home!*"

He turned to the boys his men had helped up. Twelve of the Lankmeran youth had survived the encounter, some wounded, but most hadn't been, but a single youth had lost his life. *A child lost his future for this foolishness,* Latifi said to himself, then spoke aloud, "Take your dead friend and go home. You all demonstrated your courage today but sometimes courage is not enough. It takes special training to engage prey that can shoot back, and does it in packs. Go home. Be safe. We'll deal with the people who are trying to kill you."

He watched the boys lift the dead Lankmeran boy and carry him into the forest to the south. As the last of them disappeared into the trees, Latifi called local Command. "Captain Palmer, Nilsson or Pangestu, this is Lieutenant Latifi of Recon platoon. Please come in."

"This is Captain Nilsson, Lieutenant. What can I do for you?"

"The enemy is headed east, Captain. I don't have any idea when they are likely to break south to attack the city, but they will not be hitting the positions you've prepared. I suggest you move the troops to the temporary barracks area. I am sending some Lankmeran boys back that way. They were on an ill-advised hunting expedition for enemy soldiers. When you find them, consider us east of that position."

"Thanks for the report, Lieutenant. We will be taking appropriate measures."

He turned back to his troops. "Base has been alerted. It's time we took up the chase again. Everyone, let's move out. Hansen, a slower pace this time."

"Right-o, commander," Hansen said as he started walking at a brisk pace but never breaking into the run he'd used earlier.

Running The Prey To Ground

Malone was stepping over the bodies of his men's last ambush when he heard the sounds of running feet coming toward him. He turned and motioned his men to fan out on either side of the trail and the Lankmerans to get back into the trees. As everyone was still getting set, Plordin soldiers came running in their direction. They stopped when they saw Malone standing in the middle of the trail.

He kicked the enemy leg he was straddling out of the way and brought his right foot forward, landing in a shooting stance. He drew his pistol from its holster on his right hip. He got off two shots before the roar of automatic fire erupted from the woods. After the seven-round volleys decimated the initial ranks of the Plordins, the Lankmeran hunters could be heard dropping out of the trees down the trail fifteen yards away.

Malone waved his left arm above his head and began to walk forward. His men stayed amongst the trees paralleling his advance. He came upon Norn as his hunters were about to take to the trees again. He looked over the corpses of the dozen soldiers they had taken down and nodded his approval to the young man. He watched him jump into the tree on his right and disappear into the canopy above.

Before long, Malone came upon another scene of Plordin bodies. And as he did, Norn jumped down out of the trees. It hadn't been his group that had accomplished the attack. He picked up his pace to see what was happening.

Norn found another group of Lankmerans several yards down the trial. As Malone approached, he had his arm around one of them. The two were facing Malone as he came near. "Friend Malone," Norn began. "I'm not sure if you've met Banook. Banook, this is my Commanding Officer, Sergeant Malone." Norn

"You secure up there?"

"Yes, sir. About five three inch branches are supporting me and I have the trunk to duck behind when needed. A tree is my favorite spot to shoot Dingoes from."

"Well, stay safe, son."

"Roger that, sir." He dropped the volume on his last syllable as he leaned forward to look down the trail. "Sir, it looks like something's coming our way. Yeah, Plordins and they're running."

"Everyone ready your positions. We have incoming." He ran back to his logs and dropped into a prone position, grabbing his rifle in the process. If they were running, Mason figured, they were not ready to shoot his men. He decided to let them get close so they wouldn't be able to flee his men's fire. "Hold your fire until they get two steps into the clearing. Then let them have it."

The Plordins ran into the trampled clearing Mason's men had made setting up their blinds. As the aliens spread out, looking for the direction the path should have gone, Mason's men opened fire.

They dropped every alien soldier that stepped into the clearing, and a few still on the trail. But the ones behind ran to the north into the less dense woods and started burning holes in the barricades the humans had erected. After a couple of minutes, Mason began hearing gunfire from down the trail.

"Full auto fire, men. Pick spots and see how much of the area you can expose. One clip, one clip only," Mason called to his men.

The roar of machine gun fire erupted. Leaves and branches shredded and flew away from a half dozen spots ahead of Mason's line. Mason saw three Plordins drop, he couldn't see if any others did.

When the firing died down, Mason got a call. "Lieutenant Mason, Lieutenant Mason, hold your fire. This is Sergeant Malone of Recon platoon. The Lankmeran hunters want to finish these guys off. Your fire is making it hard for them to drop down on their prey."

"Everyone hold your fire," Mason called to his men before communicating with Malone again. "Sergeant, tell them they have a go. Those men are theirs. Over and good hunting."

The War Drums Cease

Latifi's troops marched along the Plordin trail for about a half hour before Hansen threw a fist up for everyone to stop. Latifi made his way past a couple of men to see what Hansen had. He almost forgot and was about to let go of a branch he'd pushed aside, but caught himself in time to slowly return it soundlessly to where it had been.

Hansen pointed to where he'd seen the back of the Plordin column, they had made a turn to the south and were heading for the city. Latifi motioned for his men to back up some so they could quietly converse.

"They'll break out of the forest in a few minutes. Hopefully, Alpha company will be out there waiting for them. That means we need to take up positions here and keep the Plordins from retreating back into this forest. Let's follow their trail about ten yards east, then spread out to form a firing line in case they do. Any questions?"

No one responded, "Good, now let's go."

They rounded the bend on the fresh trail. The Plordins were far enough ahead that they couldn't see them anymore. But it didn't matter if Captain Nilsson couldn't stop them, they'd be killing everyone in Lenora City soon. If she did, they would be traveling back along this trail. And this was where Latifi planned to stop them.

They cleared an area in front of where they planned their ambush, so everyone would have clean shots at the retreating aliens, then built as many barricades as they could to hide behind. When everyone had finished and were sitting behind their blinds, Latifi worried about the Lankmeran youth he had sent home. Did they all go back to the city or were there some still wanting their chance at glory? War was not glorious, he only hoped they lived long enough to understand that.

He was snatched away from his thoughts when gunfire erupted. Latifi estimated it to be approximately sixty yards away. "I hope Nilssen has enough men there to hold them back," he said to no one. The sound was getting louder, getting closer. When the Plordin troops reached their position, Latifi and his men would be ready.

* * *

Captain Nilsson had her men on the way to the eastern part of town. Not knowing where the enemy was planning to make their way out of the surrounding forest made it impossible to station her men safely. They had to be mobile and spread out to cover any contingency.

She was walking down the road circling the community trying to catch up with the platoon heading to the eastern-most point of the city, when several Plordins emerged from the woods. She ran over to the woodland side of the road, drew her pistol and ducked behind a large tree. She fired a couple of rounds at the closest Plordin, catching him twice in the chest and dropping him, then called her troops. "Alpha company, the enemy has emerged from the woodlands about two miles from where the original city ended and a mile from the furthest edge of what we built. Rendezvous here now." Sword platoon was in her sight, but they were too far to hear if she yelled to them, the communicator was her only option. "Sword platoon. About face. The enemy is to your rear."

She saw a couple of men drop as she spoke and another one fall to his knees. After she finished, the rest of the men formed a line and dropped to the ground in prone firing position. They began raining fire on the incoming invaders as their third row stepped out from the forest.

She maintained her position, watching as most of the aliens were firing into Sword platoon and away from her. She managed to hit about three more before needing to change clips. She saw Switchblade platoon coming towards her position. She waved her loaded pistol in the air so they would know where she was. She went back to firing as they dropped to the pavement and began firing on the far side of the aliens.

246

"No hitting Sword platoon," she called out to her men. In the distance, Remora platoon was running up the road behind Sword to join them. Her entire company was pouring fire into the aliens.

After the fourth rank of Plordin troops exited the woods, no more came out. Those that were already out turned and were running for cover in the trees. Nilsson waved at Sword platoon to close the gap and cover the place where they'd gone back in. Once they had, she waved Switchblade and Remora to follow. It was now time to push the enemy back, surround and finish them off.

* * *

Latifi heard the gunfire cease. "Get ready," he shouted to his men. Either the Plordins had overwhelmed Nilsson's forces, which he hoped to hell not, or the captain was pushing the Plordins back into the woods. Back his way.

He waited. His men were ready and waiting. He heard rustling in the foliage in front of him, not only on the ground, but high in the trees as well. "No, he said, "I told them to go home. They could ruin our efforts to finish this fight." He sat back from the brush covering him and called to his men. "Watch who you're firing at. Make sure it's a Plordin. I think those Lankmeran youths are still around."

A few "Yes, sir," came back in answer and he pulled himself back up into firing position as the first of the enemy soldiers came into view. A quick triple-burst from a soldier on Latifi's right dropped the Plordin. A second later, a Lankmeran dropped on the body that had just fallen.

"Hold your fire," Latifi shouted at his men. More Lankmeran boys started jumping out of the trees on top of the oncoming invaders. Again they were slashing the soldiers several times before abandoning the bodies.

This wasn't going to work. There were too many things in action for his men to hit the Plordins and not the Lankmerans. "Leave your rifles. Pistols and knives," he called to his men. "It's melee time." He looked up and down the ranks of his men, then jumped over his barricade and into the mass of Plordin invaders.

He shot one through its helmet, driving his knife through the chest of one to his right, before aiming his pistol at another invader and firing again. All the time keeping an eye on the Lankmeran boys, protecting those he could. Fortunately, Nilsson had routed the aliens enough they weren't ready for hand-to-hand combat.

As often as he could, Latifi grabbed one of the Lankmeran children and pulled him behind the human barricade. "Stay there!" When he turned to move back to the fray, the boy moved as if he were going to follow. Latifi turned and pointed his knife at the boy, telling him, "I mean it. Don't move." Then he again jumped over the barricade and tried to rescue another Lankmeran youth.

He rescued four boys in all, who sat staring at three others who'd been killed. He could still hear the sounds of battle coming from the south, but it was rapidly fading. Ten minutes later, the fight was over. None of the Plordins surrendered and six Lankmerans had been killed. Two of Latifi's men had taken stab wounds from the enemy, but nothing serious. Many others had scratches that simply needed disinfecting.

Captain Nilsson came marching up the trail after her troops had secured the area and saw her lieutenants huddled around Lieutenant Latifi, with Latifi using Lieutenant Larson's shoulder to keep himself standing.

She looked around at the carnage surrounding her. "Must have been a hell of a fight, lieutenant. I'm glad you're still standing."

"We need to have a talk with those boys' elders." He pointed over to the two dozen boys standing by one of the trees. "We had a hard time keeping them safe. I recommend they be given combat training, so the next time they want to go into battle, they know what to do."

"Duly noted, lieutenant. Duly noted. Now let's get you and your men back to town and some rest. This fight is over."

Now Get Out

The four mayors walked into the Lieutenant of the MPs office and pulled three more chairs around to the back side of his desk, before sitting down. Krisson L'mere, the mayor of Anora, who gave the appearance she was speaking for everyone, leaned forward and addressed the humans.

"You people have done an excellent job removing the invaders, the Plordins, who wanted to kill us off. Though we have a little problem with some of your methods. Mainly the destructive force you used and the devastation it caused our culture."

Mayor Z'tor took up the conversation. "At first your rifles just punched holes into our buildings. Holes can be patched. But your tanks and explosive tubes ..."

"Artillery," Vermillan injected.

Z'tor continued, "Thank you. Your artillery destroyed vast areas of our cities."

Mayor L'mere took over, "You taught us how to adapt our hunts to deal with alien invaders and we will have our guard up for them, should they return."

Mayor D'thon finished for the group, "But now we have to ask that you take your style of war away from Lankmere. Take all your weapons and engines of destruction and leave."

"After all we've done for..." Vermillan began. General Chi placed his hand on the Colonel's chest, holding him in the chair he was starting to rise from.

"We came here to establish peaceful relations between our two peoples, but if our actions hinder that cause, we will leave. Your troops handled themselves superbly in battle. They should be adequate if the Plordins try again. I only ask that you don't cut off all relations between our two peoples."

The Mayors leaned their heads together and talked between themselves for a moment. Then they sat back in their chairs before

L'mere began talking. "If you have any humans with you that do not have guns or bombs, they would be most welcome to stay."

Z'tor took up the statement, "And if you wish to send representatives from your, Earth, did you call it?" The General nodded, so she continued, "If you want to send further unarmed members of your species to Lankmere, they would also be welcomed as valued guests."

"But no guns," D'thon finished.

"If that is what you want," the General said, "we will begin plans to evacuate the planet immediately."

Captain Morrison jumped in before everyone could stand up. "You don't mind if we leave some satellites in orbit, do you? For communication and defense from space only?"

Mayor D'thon looked the human in his eyes. "As long as you give us the means to control them and teach us how."

* * *

Malone walked into the room on the Nyumbani where he'd bunked on the trip to Lankmere. He was about to swing his bag up onto the second level of bunks, the same one he'd had on the trip here.

"Hey, sarge," called out one of the troopers already laying in an upper bunk across the room. "You can't bunk in here. Get your ass over to the NCO section. These here bunks are for people who do actual work for a living."

Malone looked over to the man, a private. He stared at the man angrily before breaking into a laugh. The whole room erupted into laughter. Still chuckling, Malone picked his bag back up and walked out of the enlisted barracks. He stopped the first man he saw in the corridor outside. "Hey, where do us sergeants sleep around here?"

The man pointed down the corridor. Malone swung his bag over his shoulder and started walking into his new life, wondering what Michelle would say about his promotion.

The End

Science Fiction by John Lars Shoberg

The Stone Builders - An accident in the forest uncovers a hidden underground city left by previous colonists. Everything in the city is built of stone. Can the scientists discover what chased these previous colonists away before the same thing happens to them? (273 pages.)

The Waste Gun - Dr Von Scorio has developed a way to permanently dispose of radioactive waste. Others see it as a threat to the Earth. (247 page.)

De-Evolution - Two colony children lost in a violent storm leads to first contact with a sentient native race, and a mystery that must be solved if the colony is to survive.

The Stone Ship - (The Stone Builders #3) The military finds a derelict piece of a spaceship made of stone and reassemble the team that studied the stone artifacts before. Can they figure out what happened before the ship currently bearing down on them gets there? Is it the Stone Builders? Or whatever race cut the stone ship in half? (263 pages.)

Fantasy by Trudy V Myers

The Atlans: The Truth/The Legend - The Atlans claim to be descended from Gods. The legend isn't far from the truth. (E-book only.)

The Woman on the Dock - When an Atlan warrior finds a woman tied to the dock as a direct provocation, she must decide how best to react. (E-book only.)

The Cave - A cave can supply shelter from a coming storm, or danger from creatures that have also sought shelter. This cave, it turns out, offers much more. (E-book only.)

Hero - Herotio grew up hearing tales of the adventures of various heroes of old. He finds out early that being a hero isn't as easy as it sounds. (E-book only.)

Cali - (currently available only in print, from MoonPhaze.com.) Cali has been left for dead—twice—by a gang of men who also killed 2 children left in her care. Sidek tags along as she searches for those men, wondering if there'll be any pieces to pick up if she finds them again. (240 pages.)

Romance by Linda (NMI) Joy

The Secret in Morris Valley - (currently available only in print, from MoonPhaze.com.) Ondrea is sent to Morris Valley to study the wolves, but Barry Morris won't let her out of the house without a heavily armed guard. He has plans for Ondrea. So do the wolves. (60 pages)

The Game - (E-book only.) In the tiny town of Belgrade, 4 cousins have been raised more like brothers, each trying to out-do the others all the way through high school. One night when the eldest is back in town, visiting from college, their relationship is torn apart by revelations made by two of them. (24 pages.)

Hank's Widow - She wanted a quiet place to pursue her writing. He's loved her since he first saw her photo. Will her grief prevent him from claiming her heart? (340 pages.)

Boxed Set - The Game & Hank's Widow - (E-book only.) Get both "The Game" and Hank's Widow in a 'boxed set' for one low price.

Waiting for Glori - (Tentatively scheduled for 2022.) She finally escaped her husband. Now she must grow up and become self-sustaininng. How long will it take her to realize love is still available?

About MoonPhaze:

MoonPhaze started as a very small publishing company. But our authors are into more than writing; they like to cosplay as well as practice various hobbies.

You are invited to visit

www.MoonPhaze.com

where you can purchase copies of our paperback books,

browse our collection of cosplay prosthetics and other items,

visit our author's pages, and

see where we'll be making personal appearances.

Hope to see you there!